FOR SERVICES RENDERED

WILL THOMAS

MINOTAUR BOOKS
NEW YORK

This is a work of fiction. All of the names, characters, organizations, places, and events portrayed in this work are either products of the author's imagination or used fictitiously.

First published in the United States by Minotaur Books, an imprint of St. Martin's Publishing Group

EU Representative: Macmillan Publishers Ireland Ltd, 1st Floor, The Liffey Trust Centre, 117–126 Sheriff Street Upper, Dublin 1, D01 YC43

www.minotaurbooks.com

The Library of Congress Cataloging-in-Publication Data is available upon request.

ISBN 978-1-250-34365-9 (hardcover)
ISBN 978-1-250-34366-6 (ebook)

First Edition: 2026

10 9 8 7 6 5 4 3 2 1

FOR SERVICES RENDERED

PROLOGUE

Devonshire Place!" the omnibus driver muttered just loud enough to be heard by the passengers closest to where a young man was sitting.

Immediately, the passenger pulled the string that clanged the small bell at the front of the vehicle. The horses slowed to a halt, and he hopped down onto the pavement in Oxford Circus. London was still new to him. He'd been here less than a week, and it was a city full of wonders. For example, he'd never seen so many vehicles rushing by. The streets were full of them, and everyone seemed to be late for an appointment. It was enough to make his head swim.

"Devonshire Place," he said to himself, then realized he was standing in Devonshire Street. He looked about at the nearby signs. There was no Devonshire Place. He reasoned it must be close, however, and pressed on with a young man's natural optimism. At the far end of the street, he could glimpse the greenery of Regent's Park Zoological Gardens far to the north. His friend and mentor, Dr. Cantlie, said it was near the zoo. Surely the address must be nearby.

"Are you lost?" a voice asked behind him.

He turned and found himself facing a thin, young Asian man with bad skin and a long queue.

"I am," he admitted. "I'm looking for Devonshire Place."

"Oh, it's this way," the man said. "Easy enough. Come with me."

His new guide put a hand under his arm and pointed to a street nearby. The fellow seemed good-natured enough and apparently knew where he was going.

"Are you Chinese or Japanese?" the guide asked.

"Chinese," the young man replied. "Although I was raised in the Hawaiian Islands."

"It's brave of you to wear a Western haircut, even in London. And a mustache! I've never seen one on so young a man. It's rather dashing!"

"Thank you. I confess it has been difficult to grow."

"Have you heard from home?" the man persisted. "That insurrection in Canton is no longer being discussed. Not a word in any of the newspapers. You'd think it had never happened. Were you there?"

"No," he replied. "I wasn't there."

This fellow was too inquisitive, he thought. One shouldn't have to answer questions from a perfect stranger in a strange land.

"I'm Tang, by the way," the guide said. "Turn here."

"This doesn't say Devonshire Place."

"It's a shortcut. I know the way. I like your Western suit."

"Thank you, it's new."

They were approached at the corner by a second young Chinaman.

"Who's this?" the new fellow asked.

"He's a visitor fresh from Canton!" Tang replied. "He's going to church."

"Actually, I've been in Hawaii," the visitor corrected, hoping to change the impression that the guide was giving.

"Where are you going now?" the second stranger asked.

"Devonshire Place!" Tang answered.

"Really," the young visitor argued. "I can find it on my own."

"It's this way!" the new man insisted.

"Look, I must go to work," Tang said to the second Chinaman. "Can you take him the rest of the way? He's going to church!"

"Are you going to an English church?" inquired the man. "I don't imagine they'll let a Chinaman into a church in this part of town, even with a haircut like yours."

The visitor shook his head. "I never said I was going to church."

"You're dressed like you are going to church."

A third young man suddenly appeared, and Tang seemed to have vanished. This fellow looked older and was sturdily built. Were they thieves, the visitor wondered? A gang of some sort? Or was he worrying for nothing?

"Hello, Wong!" the new guide said. He pointed to the visitor. "He's from Canton."

"No, I'm not," the visitor argued. "I am from Hawaii. What happened to Tang?"

"He went to work," the larger fellow stated. "I hear there's a lot of unrest in Canton."

"I wouldn't know. I've never been there," he lied.

"No?" the man asked. "Then why are you wearing a Western haircut unless you are a revolutionary? Let's stop in here for a smoke."

The young man was about to argue with the third when another stranger bowled into him forcefully. Before he could right himself, the three men held him down.

"I'm just trying to get to my friends!" the young man protested. "They are waiting for me!"

"You will be late, I'm afraid," said a voice behind him.

The young man turned. A heavyset Englishman with gray hair and side-whiskers stood looking down at him. "You are in the Chinese embassy, where you will remain until you are returned to China to face your crimes."

"There must be some mistake!" he cried, pushing himself up. "I'm not who you think I am!"

"Your name is Sun Yat-sen and you are a revolutionary," the Englishman purred. "If you can prove otherwise, you are free to go. Search him!"

They forcibly turned out his pockets. Without provocation, the sturdier one cuffed him in the mouth. He tasted blood. The young man realized he had made a tragic miscalculation: London wasn't far enough away from the events he'd recently experienced in Canton. Perhaps nowhere on Earth was safe enough.

Yat-sen was marched down a hall, while his captors held him by the arms, rending the fabric of his suit. It was a new suit, and he was proud of it. In the scuffle he had lost his new homburg as well.

"This is a mistake," Yat-sen insisted. "My friends are waiting. English friends! Dr. Cantlie is my sponsor. He's a very important man, head of the medical school in Hong Kong. He'll be concerned if I don't arrive when I am expected."

"I'm sorry," the Englishman said, not sounding sorry in the least. "You are going to miss your appointment."

"Where are you taking me?"

There was no answer. The Englishman walked away while Yat-sen's countrymen dragged him up a narrow staircase and stopped in front of an anonymous door. The sturdy man inserted a heavy key in the lock, and the door opened with a squeal of protest. Yat-sen was forced inside, then thrown onto a cot. They locked him in and left him alone in the cell. He looked about and saw there were bars on the window. He was a captive. Dr. Cantlie would have no idea where he'd gone. He would have vanished without a trace. How could he be so stupid?

Sun Yat-sen began to pray, but this cell was the only chapel he'd be seeing that day.

CHAPTER 1

The schedule every morning at Number 3 Lion Street, Newington, is set on a fixed routine as steady as the celestial bodies in the heavens. I often thought it would be easier if one of the planets—Jupiter, for example—stepped out of orbit and went on a brief holiday, than that the schedule created by my partner, Cyrus Barker, would be altered in any way. It was unlikely, if not impossible. The denizens of that hallowed address and its satellites, me included, couldn't imagine a change in the daily morning routine. It ran thusly:

4:45 A.M. The Guv's butler, Jacob Maccabee, awakens, dresses, and steps out into the back half-acre garden with Barker's prized Pekingese. The two of them survey Harm's domain before Mac lights the boiler in the bathhouse.

5:00 A.M. Cyrus Barker awakens. He bathes, shaves, and dresses for the day. Harm is patted, Jacob greeted, and the day begins, though the sun has not yet risen.

5:15 A.M. Fully dressed, Barker emerges from his chambers and goes out into the back garden. His team of gardeners arrive and begin working according to his instructions. Meanwhile, he removes his coat and practices his martial exercises, which had been taught him in far-off Canton by Dr. Wong Fei Hung, a famous teacher.

5:30 A.M. Etienne Dummolard, one of Barker's longtime friends and owner of a celebrated French restaurant in London, arrives and begins tinkering with various new recipes for his establishment, safe from the scrutiny and criticism of his wife.

5:45 A.M., or 6:00, or possibly even 6:15 Barker's partner, Thomas Llewelyn, wanders through the front door, gulps a scalding cup of coffee, and joins Barker in the back garden for lessons under the Guv's critical eye.

6:15 A.M. A light breakfast is served at a table in the kitchen. Matters of importance are discussed.

6:45 A.M. Barker and Llewelyn walk to Newington Causeway to take a hansom cab to Whitehall Street.

7:00 A.M. They arrive at their offices at 7 Craig's Court and are greeted by their clerk, Jeremy Jenkins. Newspapers are brought in and the daily news digested.

7:30 A.M. The door of Number 7 Craig's Court is unlocked, and the agency is open to the public and ready for business.

Need I relate that I am Thomas Llewelyn, the potential broken cog in this carefully planned scheme? I never could keep to a schedule. Life swirls about me like a tempest for all my partner's efforts.

There, I've explained it all, and preambled to my heart's content. I'm sure the reader has anticipated what will happen next. A second and much larger cog bowled in and set our entire schedule at naught. There are wheels, there are wheels within wheels, and sometimes one learns he is merely a small part of other much grander schemes.

Matters were humming along in Barker's little hive as usual that morning in October of 1896. Then suddenly, they were not, because at five thirty that morning, Etienne Dummolard did not arrive in Lion Street as usual. He was not there at five thirty, nor did he appear at five forty-five or six, or even at six fifteen, when I arrived. That may have been of small consequence to the others but was a disaster as far as I was concerned. A Llewelyn must have his morning coffee. He must have his fresh brioche, and an egg or two would not come amiss. Without them we cease to function. We cannot wave our arms in the Chinese garden according to ancient martial texts without a solid breakfast and we most certainly cannot go to work. There are limits, I say. Standards.

"Where is he?" I demanded. "Has he sent word?"

"No," Barker stated over his tea, which Mac had prepared. "He has not."

"What now?" I asked. "Must I make the coffee myself?"

I looked in the larder in case Dummolard left something there for us the afternoon before. I found nothing. Not an egg, not a rasher of bacon, not even a stale crust of bread.

"Where can he be?" I wondered aloud.

Belatedly, I began to worry about my old friend Etienne.

I attempted to make coffee on Dummolard's prized stove, but only succeeded in creating a tarry substance I wouldn't inflict upon a mortal enemy. Hence, after we reached the cabstand in Newington Causeway, we stopped and found a vendor's cart, where I rushed over and purchased a cup of coffee. I drained the steaming tin cup and felt the molten liquid begin to course through my extremities. Alas, breakfast would have to wait.

"It's not like Etienne to disappear without calling," I complained to my partner after we entered our chambers a short while later. "He left no word at all?"

"None," Cyrus Barker replied, taking up his first newspaper. He is parsimonious with his words before noon. I assumed, in fact we both did, that we'd hear from Etienne within an hour or two. There may have been a minor disaster in the kitchen of his restaurant, Le Toison d'Or, or perhaps he'd had an argument with Mrs. Dummolard and was now in hospital with a scalp wound from a frying pan. It's been known to happen. It was useless to speculate beyond that.

It was nearing eleven o'clock when Etienne Dummolard finally burst into our chambers. His appearance was slovenly, but that was normal for him. He was of good French peasant stock. His hair resembled a sheaf of wheat, and he possesses a nose like a potato. However, I noticed our generally phlegmatic cook had a look approaching panic in his eye.

"Good morning, Etienne," the Guv said from his chair. The more panicked a visitor seemed the calmer and more formal he became.

"Mon capitaine!" Etienne burst out. He was once a galley cook on a boat helmed by my partner in the China Seas. They'd known each other for decades. "We must prepare!"

"Prepare for what, Etienne?"

"I 'ave seen a ghost, a dead man!" Dummolard exclaimed. "Sebastian Nightwine was in Le Toison d'Or last night!"

The Guv gave a slight smile of incredulity from under the thick mustache that extended to his chin.

"It was a trick of the light," my partner assured him,

returning to his copy of the *Star.* "You know as well as I do that Sebastian Nightwine is dead. I killed him myself."

"But he was seated in my restaurant, talking with a fat fellow!" Etienne protested. "Someone important-looking. The Prince of Wales, perhaps."

Barker turned and frowned at me, his brow furrowing behind his dark spectacles. Some years previously, the Guv and Nightwine had been in a duel in which Barker was seriously wounded and Nightwine killed. I was my partner's second.

"He was dead when I last saw him," I assured them, standing. "Dead as Dickens's proverbial doornail. You pierced him through with a sword in Hampstead Heath, like a pin in a butterfly. I saw the blade come out his back. His daughter, Sofia, and I were witnesses."

"He's not dead now," Etienne assured us. "That man is like a cockroach. You stomp on him, and he simply crawls away, giving you the . . . how do you say? The malevolent eye!"

"How is this possible?" the Guv demanded of me.

I shook my head. It seemed impossible. He was having us on.

"We must verify if this is true at once," Cyrus Barker stated.

"It's true, *mon capitaine*," Dummolard insisted. "Of that, I assure you. Who calls me a liar?"

Etienne is known for his volcanic temper. He throws things. He rants in his native tongue, then disappears for a few weeks, just long enough to make you wonder if he was ever coming back, back to make the best pain au chocolat in England, if not all Europe.

"If he is in London the man means mischief, and at our expense," my partner replied, ignoring the threat. "What do you intend to do, Etienne?"

"We are leaving London," the Frenchman replied. "My

head chef, Marcel, will run the restaurant for me until I return. That is, if I ever return."

I looked at Etienne. I'd never seen him frightened before. Angry, yes. Contemptuous, certainly. I'd seen him ill-tempered, ill-mannered, and even explosive, but never afraid. I glanced Barker's way, but he wasn't looking at me. I might as well have not been in the room.

"What are your plans?" Barker asked.

"I'm going to Paris, then to the old family *maison* in Dijon," Dummolard said. "I told my wife that I was overtaxed and needed a holiday. Why worry her? What will you do?"

"If it's true, nothing at all," the Guv replied. "He hasn't sent word to me that he is in town. He may have no interest in us whatever."

"You do not have the good sense to be concerned, *Capitaine*. You never did." The Frenchman turned to me and wagged a finger at me, as if to say this was all my fault. "Keep him alive, Thomas. That's an order."

"Keep a wave from crashing on the shore?" I asked, shrugging. "I'll do my best."

"Perhaps we should have taken our punishment in China," Etienne said to the Guv, jamming a misshapen hat on his head. "*Tant pis. Alors*, my wife is waiting for me. Stay safe, gentlemen! Weather this storm and God willing we will share a bottle of '74 Pommery someday. Adieu to you both!"

He hurried from the room, and I turned to the Guv.

"Could it be possible?" I asked. "Surely not! I saw it for myself. The man was definitely dead."

Barker's face was expressionless, as usual. "Etienne wouldn't mistake a stranger for Sebastian Nightwine, no matter how close the resemblance."

Why did Dummolard fear Sebastian Nightwine, I wondered? Granted, Nightwine was a dangerous man, and

Etienne had legitimate concerns like all of us who were dragged along in Barker's wake, but I could not imagine under what circumstances such disparate men could have met. Still, I wasn't going to ask. I promised myself I would not ask.

"How do Nightwine and Etienne know each other?" I asked.

"They clashed aboard the *Osprey*. At the time Sebastian and I were almost like brothers. I thought I could change him, but eventually I had to recognize that his abusive father had damaged him beyond repair. He could be personable at times, and I'd hope he had changed, but I should have known better. When he is moody, or he feels he has been unjustly thwarted, his temper is savage. I've had to stop him from beating Chinese dock workers for minor infractions. It was only a matter of time before the two men quarreled."

My partner had a far-off look in his eyes, or rather, behind the black-lensed spectacles he always wore. Momentarily he was reliving those old times in Canton and the South China Sea. I don't know if a man who has since given himself to the service of a god who gave his son's life for the good of humanity is permitted to hate anyone, but if so, Sebastian Nightwine would be a worthy candidate. I thought the man an out-and-out rotter. He possessed all the mortal sins and none of the beatitudes. However, he looked distinguished with his deep tan, pale hair, and honey-colored eyes, and he had a natural gift for flattery. He wasn't stupid. Oh, but he was a devil. Barker told me he could turn on you at a moment's notice. One was there upon his sufferance, and once angered he made a hard enemy. Under circumstances I still hadn't gotten to the bottom of, Barker had fled to London with the *Osprey*. Having met years later in London, Nightwine had challenged him to a duel. Barker stabbed him through the chest. We believed him dead. His daughter, Sofia Ilyanova took charge of the body, while I took Barker away, for he had been injured as well. I didn't understand until later that the girl could be every bit as dangerous as her father. But that is another story.

My partner sat at his desk, staring out the window at the brick wall on the other side of Craig's Court. I doubt he saw it at all. He was impassive, but then he is generally stony-faced; in fact, his name in Chinese means "Stone Lion." I wondered who had given him the name. Certainly not his missionary parents.

Casually, I went into the outer office, as if to get a file. Once safely there, our clerk Jeremy Jenkins and I began gesturing to each other urgently.

"What was that all about, concerning Etienne?" I demanded, waving my arms in pantomime.

Jenkins glanced at the door to our chambers. "I'm not sure I can tell you with Mr. B. so close by," he gestured.

"I don't care where he is," I responded, slapping a hand into my palm. "Tell me. Now!"

Our clerk pulled me closer and whispered in my ear. "You know how moody Dummolard gets when Nightwine's name is mentioned."

"No," I admitted. "I wasn't even aware that Etienne had issues with Nightwine."

"I've heard he and Mr. B. discuss them once or twice," our clerk said. "Not in favorable terms, you understand. You didn't hear this from me, but I think our Frenchman is afraid of him."

The *Osprey* was a lorcha, a Chinese-made vessel built in the European style. Barker had told me once that he won it in a fan-tan game in Macao. But if so, how did Nightwine become involved? The Guv had never shown any interest in games of chance, but on the other hand I've never known him to lie. Bend the truth perhaps, even twist it into a corkscrew, but never an outright lie.

I sauntered back to my chair and Barker turned to me in an instant. Wondering if he could read my thoughts, I pulled down a dictionary from overhead to find a word, or to seem to. For all his nonchalance my partner was concerned, as well.

After several minutes, we heard Big Ben tolling down the street. It was a catalyst of sorts. Cyrus Barker stood, resting his knuckles on the cool glass atop his desk, staring down as if to predict the future. He must not have been satisfied with the answer, because in one move, he drove a fist into the middle of the desk, sending glass shards flying everywhere. The crystal ashtray atop it bounced off a bookcase and wound up under a small table behind his desk. The contents of a box of cigars he kept for clients flew in every direction, and the telephone set rolled in a semicircle on its cord until it was stopped by my ankle.

Jeremy Jenkins came into the room and we stood in awe, watching as Barker hunched over it. As with the wall across the alley, I doubt he saw the desk before him at all. It was merely an obstacle he felt he must mount. Or a rare bout of pique, I wasn't sure which.

"Thomas, I begin to think it would be best for you and your family to leave London temporarily."

"Why me, sir?" I asked. "I wasn't on the *Osprey*. I've never been to China."

"No, but as you recall, his daughter became obsessed with you later."

"Oh, yes, that," I said. I had a secret or two of my own.

"Also, you have a habit of mocking him to his face. He cannot forgive that."

"Yes, sir," I said. "I'll take it up with my wife."

Then he looked toward the door and took himself off without a word. I noticed a few drops of blood had beaded on the waxed floor.

"Jings," Jenkins said when the Guv was gone. He saved the word for only the most calamitous events.

"Jings, indeed," I replied.

"Look at all this glass!"

I placed the telephone set down on the desk again amongst the thousand shards. It weighed no more than a few ounces. However, Barker's desk suddenly gave a long, shuddering sigh. One leg buckled and the whole thing fell over. His pen and ink set rolled off, and newspapers slid to the floor. Jeremy and I stared at it for a few moments, as if our eyes were deceiving us.

"Best get the broom and pan, then," I said.

"Right," he answered.

Other people have normal days, I told myself. I wondered what that was like.

CHAPTER 2

I could not reach my wife, Rebecca, on the telephone. She is a social creature, often surrounded by her crowd, by which I mean the friends and family from the synagogue she had known since birth. I was the lone Gentile, and only tangentially connected to her world by marriage.

"Blast," I muttered into the telephone, as I watched Jenkins prop Barker's desk with a stack of books. At times a telephone set can be a boon, at others an instrument of torture. I knew Rebecca kept a daily schedule on the calendar in the kitchen, but when I called, the maid didn't answer, either. She sometimes helped my wife with her errands. Surely then, the nanny, Mrs. Skaleski, would answer, but I couldn't remember which day she didn't work.

Barker returned a half hour later with a face like thunder and not two words of explanation as to where he had gone.

Perhaps he took counsel elsewhere or had already made some sort of plan and set it in motion. I decided to go in search of Rebecca and let him sulk on his own for a while. Eventually he would talk to me again, but he had just destroyed his own desk, and I didn't want to deal with his temper. I had enough worries of my own and my nerves were frayed. Sebastian Nightwine has that effect upon people, even when he's not in the room.

I was reaching for the handle of the front door of our chambers when it opened silently before me. I had begun to think that we should put a bell over it, as they do in shops. Anyone could walk in, armed or otherwise. Granted, we are a public agency, open for custom, but a chap likes to know what to expect, at least in enough time to pull a pistol from his desk or hare it out the back door.

The reason our front door had opened so silently was that the hand which opened it was feminine, elegant, and encased in a silk glove. I knew that hand well. It belonged to Lady Philippa Ashleigh, with whom Barker had a long-standing though enigmatic relationship, also going back to his days in China, when he was a sea captain, rather than an enquiry agent.

"Good morning, gentlemen," she said, the last word a trifle sardonic, as if to say we were boys building a fort in a tree, rather than professional men running an enquiry agency that had received a royal warrant. However, one can forgive Her Ladyship anything, and sometimes one must. Having a man like Cyrus Barker at her side is proof enough that she doesn't care a fig what society thinks. That is, if there is another man like Cyrus Barker, which I exceedingly doubt. One is more than sufficient.

Philippa looked a decade younger than she was, with a headful of fiery hair, and eyes the color of the Channel in spring.

She is tall, almost towering over my petite wife. She told us once her height had concerned her mother, who struggled to find suitors both tall enough and wealthy enough to marry her daughter. Barker fit these qualities perfectly, but I'm certain a craggy-faced Scotsman with a questionable past and the look of a pirate would not have been on her mother's list. As I said, he and Philippa had an unusual relationship: neither was in a hurry to wed, and they led separate lives, he in London, and she south on her estate near Seaford, with occasional forays to her London town house for social and court events. Barker kept his boat, the *Osprey*, tethered near her estate, which must have sent a few spinsters' tongues wagging. Philippa informed me once that societal conventions are merely suggestions. One mustn't allow them to dictate one's life.

Even the Guv jumped to his feet when he saw her. We'd have done so even if basic societal manners hadn't expected it of us. She's the kind of woman one stands for.

"What happened here?" she asked, looking at my partner's desk, raising a brow when she saw the books propping it up.

"An unfortunate accident," I answered. "Couldn't be helped."

She shook her head and turned to Barker.

"When I arrived in London just half an hour ago, two messages were awaiting me. One was from you, asking to see me, and the other claimed to be from Sebastian Nightwine." She gave the Guv a long look. "Surely, this must be a prank. If so it's in poor taste. Someone is having us on."

Barker offered her a visitor's chair and took the one next to it. That broke a precedent; I'd never seen the man sit in his own visitor's chair before.

"It appears not," he admitted. "Etienne claims he saw him last evening at Le Toisin d'Or. What did the note say?"

"Sebastian claims that his ardor has not diminished and

that he hopes to renew our acquaintance now that he has returned to London."

"He's quite attentive for a dead man," my partner said. "Do you have the note with you?"

She opened her reticule and removed a folded slip of paper, which she handed to him. My partner read it and then folded it again, although he did not return it to her. Or show it to me, for that matter.

"That's his handwriting," he rumbled. "It has always been distinctive. As I recall, this isn't the first time he's proposed."

She nodded. "As you know very well, he first asked me in my villa on Shameen Island after my husband died."

Barker grunted. "This note is written on fine vellum. Who delivered it?"

"Frost said it was brought to my town house by messenger."

Lady Ashleigh rested on the edge of our visitor's chair like a butterfly, both hands lightly clasping the ball of her parasol.

"What do you intend to do about this?" she asked the Guv.

"We must get you out of London as quickly as possible," he replied. "Obviously, he knows you're in town. Would you be willing to take Mrs. Llewelyn with you, and the child?"

That was a sign of my partner's formality. He'd known my wife for more than a decade, and he was my daughter Rachel's godfather.

Philippa nodded. "I'll go home and pack."

"I suggest you leave immediately. You have clothes at your estate in Sussex."

"Bother," Philippa replied. "What do you suppose he wants, besides tweaking your nose?"

I could see a rare line of worry cross her face. In some ways, I thought her as strong as Cyrus Barker, but Sebastian Nightwine posed a serious threat to us all.

"We don't know yet, but if the last time is any indication, all hell will break loose, as Milton would say," the Guv said, pausing to look at Lady Ashleigh. "Please excuse my language."

"I've heard the word before," she rejoined. "In fact, I believe it was in a sermon. No one doubts the danger, Cyrus. We both know Sebastian. It is astonishing to see how the man has ruined his own life. And several others, as well."

I nodded at the telephone set on his desk. The mouthpiece was now dented. "I haven't been able to reach Rebecca."

The Guv seemed not to have heard me. He turned to Philippa.

"I have much to prepare," he said. "I went to Cox and Co. to make arrangements. If you recall, the last time Sebastian was in London he attempted to drain my bank account, posing as me, so that has been circumvented."

"May I take Rebecca and Rachel to Sussex?" Philippa asked, turning to me. "They will be safer out of London, Thomas."

I had assumed that the three of us would move temporarily into Barker's residence, where we had spent the first few years of our marriage, but Philippa was right. The more distance there was between Sebastian Nightwine and my family, the better.

"That's kind of you," I replied. "I'll find her and tell her the news."

I left them to go directly to Camomile Street to see my wife and daughter, my nerves a jangle. It wouldn't be an easy conversation to have. I had left the house that morning like any other day, and now I would be upending our lives completely, and there might be worse to come. Possibly much worse.

She had been in the house no more than ten minutes when I arrived. Our maid, Lily, was holding Rachel on her hip.

Rebecca looked up at me with a smile, but her face fell when she saw the expression on my face.

"Oh, no. Thomas, what has happened?" she asked, looking at me anxiously.

"Do you recall Sebastian Nightwine? Apparently, he has returned to London," I stated.

"But that's impossible," she replied. Her voice was calm, but she had gone very still. "The man is dead. You told me you saw it yourself."

"I can't explain it," I replied. "According to Etienne, he walked into Le Toison d'Or last night, alive and well."

Rebecca wrinkled her brow. "Surely you must be mistaken. But, even so, why are you home in the middle of the day?"

"To see you and Rachel packed and put on the train to Sussex," I answered. "Philippa is leaving, as well, and wants to take you with her. London is not safe for you at the moment."

"You're staying here, then?"

"For the time being," I replied. "I'll go back to my old room at Barker's temporarily. We'll send Lily and Mrs. Skaleski home for a few days with pay and shut up the house."

"So, that's it?" she asked, arms akimbo. "I'm to be chased out of my own home by a man I've never even met, and you and Mr. Barker will be tracking him until god-knows-when? That's so unfair!"

"All I want is for the two of you to be out of harm's way."

"This is terribly inconvenient, Thomas," she continued a quarter of an hour later as I helped our maid, Lily, wrestle an overladen trunk down the stairs. "I've got events to prepare for at Bevis Marks. There's a bake sale. They're counting on me. I'm no threat to Mr. Nightwine, and after all, he's just one man."

"I'm sorry," I replied. "But I won't change my mind. Your safety takes precedent, and I'm certain there will be other bake sales. The sooner you and Rachel are away from London, the better."

My wife turned to me and touched my arm. "Thomas, you know I'll never forgive you if you get yourself killed."

"Then I won't," I promised.

A little over an hour later we were at Victoria station. We met Barker and Philippa on the platform to see the ladies off to the South Downs. After they were safely seated in a first-class compartment, my partner turned to me and studied my face.

"Will you come to Lion Street and stay in your old rooms?" he asked.

"I was planning to, if that's agreeable to you. I've sent the servants home with pay, and Mrs. Skaleski, our nanny, offered to take Daisy."

"Daisy?" he asked, looking puzzled.

"Our dog, sir," I reminded him. "You remember her from the Dutch Case."

"Ah."

He acted as if the dog were a trial, but she was well-behaved, while his own canine, Harm, is an absolute terror. I've gone around with frayed trouser cuffs for years due to his savagery. Harm is a Pekingese and was originally part of the imperial household in the Forbidden City. A dog with that kind of pedigree will not let you forget it.

Once the ladies were on the express to Sussex, we returned to Camomile Street for a change of clothes or two.

"Will I need an evening kit?" I called down from the top of the stairs.

"I cannot rule it out," he admitted. "But if you need it, I'm sure you can come back for it."

I hurriedly assembled my things and set my luggage by the door.

"You've done well for yourself, lad," the Guv said, surveying the room for a final time. He'd only been in our home once before, as I recalled.

"Well, sir," I said, shrugging. "The house was hers when she was widowed, and whatever I brought to the marriage was due to your generosity."

"Nonsense, Thomas," he replied. "You've earned what I gave you and have the scars to prove it. You've had nearly as many wounds as I, in half the time."

"I certainly have some souvenirs," I said, touching my cheek, where I had once been creased by a bullet.

We hailed a cab in Commercial Road and rode across the river into Lambeth on the Surrey side of London, then south to Newington, the Elephant and Castle District.

"Why do you suppose Nightwine is here?" I asked while we were in the cab. "It's a long journey to London just to settle old scores."

"Aside from revenge I suspect he's drawn a new map of Tibet and hopes to peddle it to Her Majesty's Government," Barker replied. "Perhaps he hopes to receive a knighthood. He's craved one for years, since he and the Prince of Wales were at Christ Church together at Oxford before he got sent down and shipped off to China by his father. He was fiercely jealous of Sir Richard Francis Burton when he was alive. It was Sebastian's ill luck to be an explorer when almost everything has been discovered. Of course, he also wants me dead for personal reasons. I'm willing to meet him at any time he prefers, but I don't intend to make it easy for him. I killed the man once, and I can do it again."

"He came because he wants Lady Ashleigh," I remarked, not realizing how blunt it sounded until I said it.

"Aye, for now," he acknowledged. "But he'd rip through her fortune and cast her aside as he has several women before her, I'm sure. He also desires her because of my relationship with her. He feels the need to triumph over me. The successes he's had are never enough, while mine are magnified in his mind."

"Why such unnatural animosity?"

"It's a long story, Thomas, and the animosity is not all on his side, I must confess."

Alas, his reticence had taken hold of him. No matter. The case had only just begun. Eventually, I would drag it out of him.

Finally, we reached Number 3 Lion Street, where Jacob Maccabee was waiting for us. I climbed the stairs and set my bags upon the bed. It felt strange being in my former room again. Most of my personal items had been removed, and the furniture replaced, or moved about. The ancient wardrobe still stood in its accustomed spot, however, and I hung the clothing from my luggage.

I was thinking of my family. My daughter would have difficulty sleeping in a strange house, and Rebecca would need assurances from Philippa that everything would work out safely. I even thought of Daisy. The dog was elderly, and it had taken a while for her to adjust to the routine of the house, but now she was staying with Mrs. Skaleski, a lovely dumpling of a woman with a Yiddish accent and a maternal manner to all of us. I was in my old rooms, but it was no longer home. My family was unsettled. I was as well, but that was as it should be. I would not take my ease while they had abandoned theirs.

I came down the familiar stairs and greeted our butler, Mac.

"Back again, are you?" he remarked.

We were informal with each other when the Guv wasn't present.

"As you see," I responded.

"Are Rebecca and Rachel safe?"

"Safe as houses," I replied. "Thank you for asking."

"It's Nightwine again, isn't it?"

I sighed and nodded.

"Dinner is at seven," he stated. "Veal cutlets."

"That sounds marvelous."

Mac gave me a sardonic look, as if to discern whether I was sincere or just having him on.

"Mrs. Skaleski is a fine cook," I explained. "But I've been missing some of my favorites."

"I could boil some tripe," he offered.

"Oh, you needn't go to such trouble on my account."

It did feel familiar sitting at the dining table again, with the courses brought in grandly one at a time. Etienne had sent over food from his restaurant and promised to have the restaurant continue to do so while he was in France. Though I hate to admit it due to our long-standing rivalry, Mac is competent in the kitchen, serving according to the Frenchman's high standards.

It was just the lads again after I had lived in a house full of females for a couple of years. Conversations in the Barker household wandered from the latest pistols being manufactured, to recent crimes, and which trials were being covered in the newspapers, while I was more accustomed to the latest fashion advice, and which duchess had said what to whom. Afterward, Barker brought out cigars and walnuts as a treat, along with glasses of sherry. All the same, we were both thinking of Philippa and Rebecca the entire time. I wouldn't have refused some tittle-tattle on the doings of high society at that moment.

Afterward, I said good night and went to bed early. The sherry helped me slide into a deep slumber in my old bed.

In our occupation, one takes sleep where one can get it, and without the customary sounds of staff overhead or Rachel crying in the middle of the night, I had one of the most restful nights of sleep that I could recall in ages. As it happened, I would need it.

CHAPTER 3

Barker was in one of his secretive moods the next morning, if in fact he is ever forthcoming. He gave an errand boy half a crown and sent him winging off to who-knows-where. I set to work clearing my desk and my schedule, knowing that if it were true that Sebastian Nightwine was in London, we would be too busy to take care of more mundane matters. The boy was gone for more than an hour but finally returned like one of Noah's doves with a message. Barker scrutinized it and stuffed it into his pocket.

"We should go," he rumbled, as if I had kept him waiting.

I donned my coat, and we found a cab in Whitehall Street. The cool October breeze ruffled the leaves in the street around our ankles as we got into the vehicle. Barker shouted an address to the driver, leaving me to speculate about which building in St. James's Street we were visiting. I had been inside several of the clubs there due to one enquiry or another, and by process of elimination decided upon the only important address we had not visited.

"White's, is it?" I asked casually, as if I'd known it all along.

To be frank, I was guessing, which isn't the most reliable trick in an enquiry agent's bag but still works from time to time. Even an errant arrow must land somewhere.

My laconic partner grunted as he viewed the scene in front of us from our hansom cab. "I assume he'll be there."

"No doubt," I replied, although we both knew I had no idea of whom we were speaking. I thought it unlikely to be Nightwine himself. Surely it was too early for a confrontation. However, if we were meeting anyone at White's, one could be certain it was someone important.

"Are you a member?" I asked, knowing that one could not simply enter a gentleman's club from the street without the proper credentials. One would find oneself tossed out onto the curb again very quickly.

"Aye," he murmured over the sound of the hansom wheels. He sat back against the leather seat, rubbing his chin, as he tends to do when deep in thought. "White's has fallen on hard times in recent years, and opened its membership to rabble like me, who have more money than pedigree."

"The rise of the common man," I remarked.

"Hear, hear."

White's is *the* club, the first, the oldest. All others in London's clubland sprang from it or in opposition to it. The Junior Carlton, for example, would never have its gravitas, but on the other hand, White's would never have its youthful membership. It was fusty but grand. One couldn't even smoke in the place, though the practice was widely accepted in the other gentlemen's clubs of the West End. White's was a traditional institution, and as everyone knows, there is nothing more British than tradition.

We alighted from the cab in St. James's Street and paid the cabman. White's is a large and grand Georgian building, boasting columns and Palladian windows surrounding its iron doors. I knew that it had long been the unofficial headquarters of the Tory party, dating back to the late eighteenth century. Many of its early members were among the most influential of English society, including Beau Brummell, once the arbiter of British men's fashion. I took in the grand façade for a few moments before following Barker through the front door and into the building.

We crossed the lobby, and the Guv approached the front desk, murmuring to the clerk in a low voice. The porter had taken soberness to a fine art. He responded to my partner in the same discreet manner. I looked about the room, thinking it must have cost a fortune to bring all this Carrara marble from Italy. Then Barker abruptly turned about and pulled me out into the street again.

"For whom are we waiting?" I asked, tugging my coat closer. The wind had picked up and was toying with the branches of the nearby trees like a child blowing at a whirligig.

"Her Majesty's private secretary."

"Henry Ponsonby?" I asked, thinking of a gentleman we had dealt with on a previous case. If I were to create a list of all my favorite men in London, he would not be on it.

"No, Ponsonby has retired from his position," my partner replied. "We're awaiting a fellow named Arthur Bigge. He is expected here soon. The porter claims he is as punctual as the 9:44 from Brighton."

Indeed, he was. He arrived at the curb precisely ten minutes later. Arthur Bigge was a thin, bald fellow standing behind a large mustache. He did not arrive in a hansom cab like any normal private secretary to Her Majesty. He arrived on a penny-farthing, one of those tall bicycles with the impossibly big front wheel. I tried one once and nearly broke a limb attempting to dismount. However, they were all the rage in Pall Mall at the moment, according to the press. White's was still deciding whether it approved of such a newfangled mode of transport. They didn't even trust hansom cabs yet.

"Mr. Bigge!" Barker called from the curb.

I'm certain that after a ride from the Palace, Bigge was hoping for a plush chair and a freshly ironed edition of *The Times*, none of those barbarous modern rags they read at the Junior Carlton. He stepped onto the curb and hefted the ungainly bicycle onto it. Immediately, a porter scurried out of the building and took command of the machine, wheeling it down a discreet alley with an embarrassed air until it was out of sight.

"May I have a word, sir?" the Guv said. "My name is Cyrus Barker."

"Ah, yes," Arthur Bigge said, raising a brow. "Lord Ponsonby has warned me about you. I can bring you in as a guest, but I'm afraid your associate must wait in the lobby."

"There is no need," Barker replied. "I am a member myself."

"Are you?" the man asked, astonished.

My partner nodded. "The porter says you enjoy a game of snooker. Shall we play?"

"Very well," Bigge replied, a trifle annoyed. He'd have refused if he could.

We climbed the impressive staircase to the billiard room. Inside the elegant room, the Queen's secretary chose a cue while Barker corralled the triangle of red balls. It was the first time I'd heard that he could play billiards.

Bigge broke the balls, confidently sinking one and missing another by less than an inch.

Barker attempted a shot but missed. I suspected he really didn't know how to play, after all.

"What can I help you with, Mr. Barker?" Bigge asked, eyeing his next shot. "You seem to have taken some trouble to find me."

"I understand that Sebastian Nightwine is in town."

The secretary looked at him momentarily and then back at the billiards table. "He is indeed. Is he part of an inquiry? Or is it enquiry?"

"Both are acceptable," I answered. "An enquiry involves asking questions, while an inquiry is a more involved affair."

Bigge blinked at me as if he was aware for the first time that I was in the room.

"Thomas Llewelyn," I said, introducing myself. "I am Mr. Barker's partner."

"Oh," he said, dismissively. He potted another ball and looked at the Guv. "What is your interest in Sebastian Nightwine, Mr. Barker?"

"He and I have long been acquainted," the Guv replied. "We fought a duel in Hyde Park a few years ago and I was under the impression that I had killed him. Now I hear he has surfaced in London again unscathed. I assumed he would have an opinion or two about the outcome of our last meeting and I wanted to prepare myself."

"You jest, sir," Bigge said, missing the third ball.

"I rarely jest," Barker assured him, moving closer to the table to take his turn. "Our grievances are many and varied, going back decades."

"Swords or pistols?" he asked, leaning over the table. Another missed pot. "For the duel, I mean."

"Sabers."

"Sabers!" he exclaimed, pausing to stare at Cyrus Barker. "In Hyde Park, you say? How can that be? I'd have heard of it."

"It was a clandestine affair," my partner answered. "We met at dawn and the whole experience lasted only a few minutes."

"I don't believe you," Bigge said.

The Guv shrugged his broad shoulders. "What you believe matters little to me, sir."

"Mr. Barker and I have come to the aid of His Highness," I put in. "We chased away an Irish bomber from him in Pall Mall. I have proof on me. This is the watch he gave us. It has been engraved with the phrase, 'For Services Rendered.'"

I retrieved the repeater from my pocket and the Queen's secretary came around the table to inspect it.

"It is probably a fake," Bigge said after a cursory examination. "One could have one engraved at any jewelers in half an hour."

"Perhaps," I admitted. "But there is also a royal warrant hanging above the door to our chambers. You can't get one of those in a jeweler's shop, I'm certain of it."

Again, Bigge looked at us as if he suspected we were mad. However, he wasn't the first, and he certainly wouldn't be the last.

"What is your purpose in coming here and ruining my lunch?" he asked, clearly growing disenchanted with the conversation.

"I've come to ask if killing Nightwine would inconvenience Her Majesty's Government," Barker replied.

"If it would inconvenience Her Majesty's Government?" the secretary exclaimed. "The man is here on government business, for heaven's sake. I can't believe you admit to planning to kill him. I should have you arrested!"

Barker missed another shot, but didn't seem perturbed. I knew he had little interest in games of any sort.

"I did not declare I would kill him, did I, Mr. Llewelyn?"

"No, sir," I replied. "You merely postulated a sequence of events. You did not claim you yourself would kill him."

"My God," the Queen's secretary barked. "You are as barking mad as Ponsonby claimed you are. Mr. Nightwine is under the protection of the Crown. He is in the process of providing information of a critical nature to this government."

"A transaction, then?" I asked.

"If you like."

"Were I Her Majesty's Government, I would not trust his word," Barker warned. "A more blackguardly fellow you are unlikely to meet."

The Guv took a shot, and it landed in the pocket. He seemed as surprised as I was.

"We don't care if he is an out-and-out bounder," Bigge said. "He has something we want."

"And what is that?" my partner asked.

Bigge stopped and looked at him, frowning. "You cannot possibly expect me to give you information of that sort. It pertains to the government. That is all I can say."

Barker shrugged. "I hope you get to it before I do, sir. The last time he was in town, I burnt his copy of the map of Tibet that he was dangling in front of Ponsonby."

Arthur Bigge placed his cue on the table. "That was you? I didn't believe it when he told me. I suspect that Nightwine isn't the blackguard in this situation."

"Believe as you will, sir, but Nightwine and I are like

magnets. It seems one cannot avoid the other. I think it likely one of us shall be dead within the month."

"But you can't kill the man!" he insisted. "As I said, he is under the government's protection."

"I promise you we don't intend to pursue Mr. Nightwine unless he comes after us first, but he very likely will. Mr. Llewllyn can confirm it."

"Yes, sir," I said, nodding. "Mr. Nightwine very much wants to settle a score."

"Gentlemen," the secretary said, "and I use that word in its most liberal sense, I suggest that you leave."

The Guv put away his cue and turned to Mr. Bigge. "We've said all we came to say. If something happens to damage the government's reputation, it won't be our fault. Thank you for the game. Come, Thomas."

We quit the room and the Queen's secretary, who stood with his mouth open. Once in the street, I turned to my partner.

"You really shouldn't bait government officials like that, sir," I said. "It's liable to come back on us."

"They're welcome to arrest me after Nightwine is dead," he replied, heading down St. James's Street. "Provided they can find me."

"Do you think it wise to have told Bigge about our plans?" I asked, falling into step next to him. "They may try to hinder us."

"Aye, Thomas," he replied. "But it is also possible that government agents will muddy the waters behind us in the process."

"You do enjoy pitting one agency against another," I noted.

"They are slowed by bureaucracy," he reasoned. "We are not. It's why I have kept our agency so small all these years. I shall leave Mr. Pinkerton to fill his offices with dozens of agents and collect enquiries by the droves. The two of us can slip through the nets more easily."

We took a hansom to Pall Mall, and thence past Trafalgar Square into Whitehall again.

"If I may say it, sir, you were very forthright with the Queen's secretary. He shall be in no doubt as to your intentions."

"Not necessarily, lad," he replied as we alighted from the vehicle. "I implied I might kill Sebastian Nightwine, but that doesn't mean I shall."

"Oho!" I said. "So will you or will you not?"

"Who can say?" he remarked, shrugging his shoulders. "I'll decide that at the proper time. One thing is certain, Thomas. Our little tug-of-war will end soon, and with a clear victor. The man has been a mote in my eye for far too long. It ends now."

CHAPTER 4

A half hour later, my restless partner rose from behind his desk and stuffed a pipe and some tobacco into a sealskin pouch. Then he turned to me, and I rose, tapping my pockets for all I needed, including my pistol, which I tucked in my waistband against my right kidney. He often did this, acting as if I weren't in the room and never telling me his thoughts. My duty was to be ready and not be surprised by anything, and I do mean anything. He relied upon my intuitiveness which, I must admit, had been hard-won. I couldn't fathom what he was thinking at any given moment, but I could anticipate his next movement and be ready whenever he rose from his chair, as if I read his thoughts. I understood that I would eventually learn to whom we would speak and over what topic. The trick, then, was to act as if I knew what we were doing. However, Cyrus

Barker is a contrarian and would change his plans to spite me if I too obviously twigged his intentions. He hates being anticipated, working on the assumption that if I can work out what he's doing, someone else can as well.

We left our offices with a nod at our clerk, and I looked about Whitehall Street hoping for an empty cab. However, glancing back at Barker, I found myself alone. The Guv had doubled back and was now progressing east toward the back of Craig's Court and the Embankment. I trotted to catch up with him, but before I could, he darted into an office that had a small metal sign flapping overhead which read HEWITT DETECTIVE AGENCY.

The economy of words on the sign matched the economy of its author, J. M. Hewitt. He was a private detective who eschewed fancy titles like "private enquiry agent." He was once among the rank and file at Scotland Yard until he and a commanding officer had a difference of opinion. He felt the sergeant had too many teeth and knocked out a few for him. The latter objected on personal grounds and there was a scuffle, after which Hewitt was sacked. Not to be outdone, he rented a flat in Craig's Court and hung out his shingle out of spite, much as Barker had years earlier. Hewitt was tall, thin, and not as rakish as he thought he was.

"Good afternoon, gents," our host said, as we entered his chambers.

"And to you as well," the Guv replied. "We've got work for you, Mr. Hewitt."

Hewitt raised a brow. "I'm finishing a case this evening, but I can start tomorrow. What's the work?"

'You'll find it pleasing enough," Cyrus Barker said. "I want you to find where a man is staying, then take a room nearby and watch his movements for a few days."

"I can do that," he agreed. "Why is it pleasing?"

"The man has expensive tastes and will no doubt be staying at a prestigious hotel. Have you an appropriate suit of clothes?" The Guv turned to me. "Thomas, give Mr. Hewitt a retainer. Twenty-five pounds should make a start. The fellow I'm looking for is named Sebastian Nightwine. He is a large-game hunter and explorer by trade, and he has been seen in the company of the Prince of Wales."

"That is some company," Hewitt commented. "Am I merely to watch him, or should I interact with him?" Hewitt asked. He'd pulled a battered notebook from his desk and began writing notes with a pencil.

"Do not approach him and do your best not to be noticed," my partner replied. "Being a professional hunter, the man has a keen eye."

"So, I'll be stalking a hunter," the detective stated. "Is the man that dangerous?"

"Highly dangerous," I said, thinking of the duel.

"And his description?"

Barker grunted. "He is six feet tall, with amber-colored eyes and pale hair. He is deeply tanned from a life spent out of doors, and he sports a mustache. I must warn you the man has no scruples whatever and will kill without remorse."

Hewitt set down the information with no comment whilst I retrieved Cyrus Barker's wallet from my pocket. I placed two twenty-pound notes on his desk for various expenses. Hewitt's eyes opened wide. I doubt he'd seen so much money in one place in recent memory, but tailors are expensive, and so are good hotels. We wouldn't be getting any renumeration for this enquiry when all was said and done, I thought bitterly. My partner was our client. At least he was good for the fee.

Hewitt was wreathed in smiles. If I knew him, he'd start

with a proper meal and a few brandies. Then he'd wink roguishly at the barmaid.

Barker rose from the uncomfortable wooden chair Hewitt provided for visitors and grasped the man's hand with a bone-crushing grip. My partner left, but I couldn't help a bit of banter, from one agent to another.

"I thought you already had a client, J. M.," I said.

"I do," he replied, looking at the retainer on his desk. "Finding a scarpered wife. The man can go hang himself now for all I care."

That was Hewitt, a typical unmarried detective, living one case to the next. The money slipped through his fingers like water, but there was generally another case coming along just in time. His needs were few, and he was his own man. No doubt he was satisfied with his lot in life, but I wouldn't trade positions with him for the world. I enjoyed being a husband, a father, a trusted partner. Some of us are just born that way, I suppose.

"What are you thinking, lad?" Barker murmured in my ear as we approached Whitehall Street.

"How much I prefer my situation to his, sir," I replied.

"Did you ever think your life would right itself again, lad?"

I thought back to the days in my cell in Oxford prison in my university days, the rough cot, the crumbling walls, and my itching woolen uniform with the broad arrows announcing to one and all that I was a convict.

"No, sir," I replied. "I assumed my life was over. I have you to thank for my rehabilitation."

"Perhaps," he admitted. "But you have yourself to thank for not being there again. A good wife and a bairn have made a man of you."

"Thank you, sir," I said, although I did not entirely believe it. An inspector told me "Once a convict always a convict," and I took it to heart. It would be my secret shame for most of my life, though all I did was lift a single coin and consider taking it. It's the Welshman in me. We feel things more intensely than other men and therefore write better poetry.

We returned to our offices. Barker sat behind his desk, which had been hastily repaired while we were gone at double the expense, though the plate of glass ordered for the top had not yet arrived. He stroked his mustache, deep in thought, while I noted the expense of hiring Hewitt in the ledger book. The outer door opened then, and a man entered and looked about. I leaned out to look at him, though the Guv considers such behavior unprofessional. Our visitor was a man of about fifty years, balding and bearded, with gray eyes and a gentle manner. He held out a calling card, and Jenkins went through the ceremony of bringing it to my partner on a silver tray. Barker read it and welcomed our visitor. As he sat, I lifted the card from the desk. His name was James Cantlie.

"You're a Scot," Barker observed.

"I am, sir," Cantlie replied. "From Banffshire."

"I'm from Perth," the Guv stated. "How may our agency help you?"

"A friend of mine has disappeared, Mr. Barker. I've been looking for him for two days. Scotland Yard won't help me, and the Pinkerton agency turned me down. I'm at my wits' end. The poor fellow has barely arrived in London after a very trying ordeal."

"What is his name, sir?"

"Dr. Sun Yat-sen."

I wrote the name in my notebook in shorthand.

"Was he part of the insurrection in Canton last year?" Barker asked.

Dr. Cantlie nodded. "You are very canny, sir. Indeed, he was. After the patriots were overthrown, he escaped by boat to Macao and then Hong Kong, where he conferred with me. He was a former student. I advised him to return to his family home in the Hawaiian Islands. Later he came here to see me in London, where my family and I had moved after I had retired. I was his mentor in China, you see. Like a second father."

"I do," the Guv said, nodding. "Was he staying with you, Doctor?"

"No, he has a room at Gray's Inn in Holborn. He is still recovering from his ordeal. He is a sensitive fellow and spends much of his time at the British Museum or at our home, where he is a great favorite of my wife's."

"I see," Barker murmured. "And he disappeared, you say? Tell me of that."

Dr. Cantlie leaned forward in his seat. "He was to meet us last Sunday morning and go to service with us. Yat-sen was raised a Christian. However, he never arrived. We were all quite mystified."

"Where do you live?" the Guv asked.

"In Devonshire Place," Cantlie replied.

"This was last Sunday, October eleventh? You haven't had word of him since?"

"That is correct, sir."

Barker tapped his lip in thought, but then one side of his mustache curled as if he found something amusing.

"Did you ask at Gray's Inn if they saw him leave that morning?" he asked.

"Of course, Mr. Barker. They claimed he left his lodgings early."

My partner nodded. "Good, good. What does the doctor look like?"

I could tell the Guv was intrigued. He was leaning back in that green cocoon of a desk chair of his.

"Oh, Yat-sen is unmistakable," the doctor replied. "He has shaven his queue and now has a Western haircut. He has grown a mustache as well. Generally, he wears a tweed suit. I've tried to explain to him that such apparel is more appropriate for the countryside, but he considers it properly British. I can't talk him out of it."

"What sort of revolutionary is he?" Barker continued. "Is he a firebrand, protesting for a reformed China?"

"Good heavens, no," Cantlie replied. "He's a serious little fellow. Rather shy and retiring, but an excellent scholar. He has qualified in Western medicine, one of the very first Asian graduates in Canton. However, I suspect he is naïve. He'd protest about what he believes is right without realizing what a danger it could be to his personal safety. Dr. Sun assumed two thousand years of Manchu rule would end if he could just convince them to see reason."

"Not a hardened revolutionary, then," the Guv remarked.

"He was raised in Hawaii and is completely unaware of the struggles that have occurred in modern China," said the doctor. "He holds romantic notions of his ancestral home, and doesn't comprehend how brutal the Manchus can be. He's like a son to me, and I'm very worried about him. He doesn't know London, save for our home and the British Museum."

"Has he been to Limehouse?"

"The Chinese quarter? He's expressed no interest in it. He's rather enjoying seeing the sights of the West End, with my wife and I as guides. He also doesn't have much of a sense of direction. At first I assumed he'd just wandered off and got lost or distracted."

"What sort of trouble is he in from his protests in China?" Barker asked, tenting his fingers on his desk.

"Quite a bit, I'm afraid. He can never return to China. There is a price on his head there, what amounts to a tidy sum, a fortune by Chinese standards. If he were captured by the imperial government, he would be beheaded by sunset."

"I assume anyone who found him would be well rewarded by the Manchu government, since he is one of the few who successfully escaped. Is that correct?"

"I'm certain they would," our visitor admitted.

"How long has he been gone?" the Guv asked.

"This is the third day," Cantlie stated.

"The third day," Barker repeated. "What have you done to find him?"

"It never occurred to me that the police force of London practically shuts its doors on a Sunday. No one was willing to help us. Most of the officials were off at church or enjoying their leisure. It's as if London believes crime does not occur on sabbath days. Your own chambers here were closed as well."

"Our apologies for not being here in your hour of need," my partner replied. "What brought you to my door?"

"We saw your court here and took a chance. You are the only one with a royal warrant affixed to your door."

What was the Guv doing, I wondered? So far, he hadn't mentioned to Cantlie that he was fluent in Cantonese, had lived in the very streets the young Dr. Sun marched in, and was born and raised in nearby Foochow. I also understood that an organization to which he belonged, the Heaven and Earth Society, was strongly anti-Manchu. "Destroy the Qing and restore the Ming" was their motto. Cyrus Barker was also well-known in Limehouse, and his closest friend, Ho, was something of a leader there. However, Barker kept his own counsel for now, and Dr. Cantlie did not appear to notice the miniature penjing tree in a pot by the window, which the Guv had raised himself.

"Where do you suspect he might be?" the Guv asked. "Have you drawn any conclusions about his disappearance?"

"I've spoken to Scotland Yard, The Home and Foreign Office, a few MPs, and the Missionary League. I've tried anyone who would listen and might do some good, but I still have no idea what happened to him," Cantlie said. "I hope you will consider taking on the case to find my young friend."

"I've a mind to," the Guv rumbled. "I'd like to meet your little scholar, brave enough to cut off his queue to spite the Manchu edict."

"Wonderful! Do you require a retainer of some sort?"

"If you have a five-pound note, we can get started."

The money was handed over promptly, a contract written, and the relieved doctor smiled, though I suspected Cantlie would continue knocking on doors the rest of the day. Barker shook his hand and saw him out.

"Well," he said, clapping his hands together when the doctor had gone.

"What about the Nightwine business?" I asked. "You've just taken one enquiry and then accepted another."

Cyrus Barker selected another pipe from his cabinet, as if it were a reward for listening to Dr. Cantlie's tales of woe.

"Thomas, what has convinced you that the cases are unrelated?" he asked.

"No!" I cried, slapping my desk. "Are you serious?"

"It's a theory, mind you. A chance to make a fortune and please the Qing government is just the sort of work Nightwine would appreciate."

"But I thought he was trying to sell his map!"

"Sebastian likes to keep several irons in the fire," my partner said.

"Where do we begin then?" I asked.

"Limehouse, of course," he responded. "The place Cantlie didn't think we should go."

"You believe Sun might be there, after all?"

"Not necessarily, but every other Chinese revolutionary in London is there. Poor Cantlie went everywhere but the one place that should have been his first destination."

CHAPTER 5

Without hurrying, Barker donned his coat and hat. I followed him as he left the building. We hailed a cab and headed east. Barker studied the scene before him, though nothing looked out of place for a normal working day. Traffic was heavy, and leaves blew about, forming a dragon slinking sinuously through the streets. Commerce continued in busy old London town, as it had since Julius Caesar stood on our shores.

Obviously, Barker needed more information about the insurrection and how it was progressing. We were going to visit Barker's closest friend and mentor, Ho, who was his former first mate aboard the *Osprey* and a boon companion since the Taiping Rebellion.

A half hour later, we arrived at a certain narrow and woebegone street near the docks, where I paid the cabman. We stepped over bits of stone and rubble in the shadow of an old church ruin until we came to a dented and weather-beaten door. Going down a set of steps, we found a short tunnel beneath the Thames. At the end, we came to another stairwell, and so to a secret tearoom available only to those of the population who knew of it.

We sat and ordered tea. There was no need to inform Ho we had come. The waiters there are as good at collecting gossip as any professional spy or church auxiliary leader could be. We also knew what the proprietor would feed us that day. Generally, a number of small dishes were fanned in front of us, some of this, some of that, and best not to ask what was in it.

Ho himself came out of the kitchen a few minutes later, frowning. He fell into one of the nautical chairs that circled the room and regarded us. The Chinaman had a shaved head with a long queue, and earlobes weighted down with rings until they met his shoulder.

"We must see Mr. K'ing," the Guv said. "Can you arrange a meeting for us immediately?"

Ho grunted, much in the way Barker did. It was a kind of resigned agreement.

Lunch was placed before us: six small courses. Ho left to speak to Mr. K'ing. Even dockside, telephones were now in use. The world was changing, and thanks to Mr. Bell, we were impatient for it. I was nearly finished with my soy cakes fried in saffron when the Chinaman returned.

"Fifteen minutes," he said. "Will you tell me what is happening now, or must I wait?"

The Guv nodded. "I will, but only because it concerns you. Sebastian Nightwine is in town."

Ho raised a brow and turned to me, giving me a deadly stare. "You said he was dead."

"He was pierced through with a sword," I insisted, feeling the need to defend myself again.

"He shouldn't be alive. I suspect he convalesced in Tibet. I've heard it rumored they have some revivification process there."

It was possible, I supposed. I've heard tales of monks floating about the Himalayas in lotus positions. Revivification might not exist at all, but those Tibetans with their lamas and strange arts, there was no way to know what they could or could not do. Chinese prejudices run deep, especially when it concerns their neighbors. It was a ruse, but for once Ho fell for it. He nodded in acceptance.

"I've heard that, as well," he admitted. He turned to Barker. "Is there more?"

"There is," the Guv said. "But you must come along if you wish to know."

Ho nodded, but with ill grace. He bawled to one of the cooks, and they had a loud but brief conversation in Mandarin. Then he nodded and went for his coat. He muttered to himself the entire length of the tunnel, then burst through the entrance, nearly kicking the old door off its hinges. Above ground, in the daylight, I could see his coat was made of some kind of scraped hide, possibly yak, and the gold rings jangled musically from his ears as he walked. He looked savage, but then that was his intent.

There was more to come. We were heading toward Mr. K'ing's Inn of Double Happiness. In no way did it resemble an inn; it was a combination gambling hall and opium den. K'ing himself was an odd individual. Some claim he is a warlord in exile, the criminal leader of a tong society, the smooth leader of a criminal organization, or simply an Asian businessman with an interest in his country. I thought it most likely he was all of them at once.

Ho kicked open the door to the inn with about the samc force he had exited his own establishment. Young Asian hostesses in silk dresses, and guards in sleeveless tunics moved forward with concern, but when they saw who it was, they relaxed again. Ho was well-known there. He was an associate of K'ing's without his position being fully known to anyone. He might have been an advisor, or an assistant. Nobody is ever one thing in Chinatown, therefore one can never be fully blamed for anything. Whatever happened, it was someone else's responsibility.

Ho growled something to the guards, then climbed a flight of stairs. We followed him up the staircase, past two more burly Asian guards flanking K'ing's office door. The man himself sat behind an ornate teak desk. He had undergone a strange transformation since I had seen him last. He had changed to European dress, and his hair was pulled back into a queue. The only sign of his criminal past was a spiderweb of scar tissue on one side of his face from a burn. I noticed that he had his hand in a drawer where a gun probably lay. He did not trust anyone, even his closest friends and advisors.

"Gentlemen," K'ing said politely in greeting. He is a suave rascal. "To what do I owe this pleasure?"

My partner was about to answer, but Ho beat him to it.

"Nightwine is in town!" he spat.

K'ing frowned and looked to Barker for confirmation. I watched as our host's expressive eyebrows rose, then lowered in concern.

"Tell me what you know," he said to my partner.

The conversation slid into Cantonese and the gist of it was lost to me. My knowledge of the language was rudimentary at best. They spoke for several minutes, before Barker reverted to English.

"There is more," the Guv stated.

"More?" K'ing demanded, like Mr. Bumble in *Oliver Twist*.

"Yes. Are you familiar with Dr. Sun Yat-sen?"

"The name sounds familiar," K'ing acknowledged.

"He is a Chinese nationalist from the Hawaiian Islands," my partner told him. "He may have been involved in the insurrection with the imperial forces in Canton a few weeks ago."

K'ing leaned forward with his hands flat on the desk. "Yes, I might have been introduced to him at one of the meetings. Why do you ask?"

Meetings, I thought. K'ing must have just fled to London from Canton, as well. Being the local leader of the international Heaven and Earth Society, he had been part of the failed crusade. London is a sailor town, and many Chinese mariners came to Limehouse on the Blue Funnel Line. However, wherever they lived, or ever would live, China was their home.

"The young doctor has disappeared," Barker continued. "His mentor, Dr. James Cantlie, has called on me and is very concerned for him."

"Cantlie. Yes, I recall the name. He was at the Hong Kong College of Medicine for Chinese. I think I remember the young man now. Rather moon-faced and innocent-looking. I suspect he looks younger than he is. Now he has disappeared, you say. Where do you think he is?"

"He went missing near Devonshire Place."

K'ing slapped his desk with the palm of his hand. It was a difficult week for desks in London.

"We cannot afford to lose someone like him, an educated young man with fresh ideas and a knowledge of the West."

"At this point, Sun's simply missing," my partner replied. "However, he knows no one in London, and it seems unlikely he traveled to Limehouse. I understand he spends most of his time in the British Museum. I suspect he is an intellectual idealist."

"They make the best leaders," the den owner stated. "Let me make some enquiries and consider what must be done."

Just then, tea was brought by one of the maids. There were few Chinese women in London, but I suspected K'ing imported these himself. All of them at the inn were uncommonly pretty.

"Mr. K'ing," I dared ask. "What sort of trouble is brewing over there in Canton? I know better than to trust the British newspapers."

K'ing put a short cigarette into a long jade holder and lit it.

"England and other Western countries have built towns along the coast and started to develop and populate them," he said, accepting a diminutive cup from one of the maids. "Concessions, they call them. I was in the German encampment a month ago. They are building churches and railways and digging up ancestral burial sites. If you squinted, you'd think you were in Bavaria. They're stealing land piecemeal and challenging the Qing government to stop them. As usual, they think we're powerless, the so-called 'sick men of the East.'"

K'ing looked from me to Barker. "However, men are gathering in the hills by the thousands. Boxers, they call them, training with whatever weapons they can find. They're peasants for the most part. The Chinese are discontent, not only with the Qing government and the emperor, but with the European countries receiving permission to build on the most fertile Chinese land. It will come to a head soon. It just requires a single spark. We'd hoped the march on Canton would be the one, but the government suppressed it. There are always informants."

"What kind of numbers are we speaking of precisely?" the Guv asked.

"They are small bands, but there are hundreds or thousands of them. I predict there will be over a million in a year or so. We support them but we cannot influence these uneducated and militant groups. If and when they organize, they may overrun the embassies and kill the European colonists. They have formed a peasant army calling itself the Righteous and Harmonious Fist, and they're very angry. They'll cover the country like ants, and they won't distinguish between Qing officials and the Westerners who live there. No one can control them."

"There is your revolution," Barker said to the Chinese leader.

"It isn't the revolution we want!" K'ing replied. "We desire an orderly end to the decayed Qing government and a calm transfer of power. We are intellectuals, educated men. The two groups have nothing in common. Your young doctor is a perfect example, educated in a medicine the Chinese people hasn't even heard of and don't trust or understand."

"They'll ruin everything!" Ho cried. "Illiterate peasants don't listen to reason or sign treaties. If matters continue there is liable to be a war between the Chinese and the entirety of Europe, a massive war such as the world has never seen!"

"Meanwhile, Dr. Sun has been snatched off the streets in the West End in broad daylight on a Sunday," Barker added. "If the public learns of this there will be a sensation."

"How can I help you then?" K'ing asked.

The remark sounded casual, but I knew it wasn't. It never is among the so-called celestial people. Words had meaning. Remarks are binding. One must tread lightly, because negotiations are occurring and nothing can be taken back.

However, we had dealt with this Limehouse warlord in the past, and the Guv and I understood this.

Cyrus Barker scratched under his chin in thought. "It's your battle, not mine. I must find Sun Yat-sen."

K'ing wagged a finger at him. "That is not so, unless your allegiances have changed. Your teacher, Wong Fei Hung, convinced us to allow you to join the Heaven and Earth Society. Was he wrong to do so?"

It no longer surprised me that a Scotsman should belong to a Chinese secret organization with political ends. What surprised me was that the Guv belonged to so many organizations, each with their own rules and prohibitions. His arms were studded with tattoos from a dozen different leagues and countries. One would think it impossible to keep all these matters straight, matters that could easily get one killed. It was even more astonishing that he was able to remain his own man, rather than become a lackey to any one of them. It was a delicate undertaking.

"It would be a good thing if a young Chinese doctor with an interest in his people's future would not be cut down in his youth," our host stated delicately.

"Agreed," my partner said. "But he is one of you."

K'ing gave the slightest of shrugs. It was odd to see such a subtle gesture in a Western suit.

"Not to be insensitive, but we have other men," he said. "He is promising, but no individual is more important than the cause."

"I'm certain educated and articulate young men who are fluent in languages and have been trained as doctors in Western medicine arrive on the docks every morning by the peck," Barker countered.

"Nevertheless, he is but one soldier. I would not sacrifice a legion for him. We are known, you see. Don't believe the

Imperial Secret Service is unaware of our presence in the East End. Notes are being taken and carried to Peking. I myself have been whipped in Hong Kong, set in the stocks in Shanghai in the hot sun, imprisoned, starved, and beaten."

I looked from one to the other. It seemed an average Tuesday in jolly old London, but intrigue of the highest order was happening before my eyes in the bowels of Limehouse.

"What would you ask of me in exchange for helping me find Dr. Sun?" Barker continued. "Am I to take up arms, and lead a small army through the docks of Canton? Do you wish me to steal into the Forbidden City and kill the emperor myself?"

"No," K'ing replied. "You are too old."

I felt the sting in that remark. He would relegate Barker to the sidelines in matters that concerned him. My partner's importance to K'ing, his leverage, was decreasing with age. But I knew differently. He was over fifty now, but he still threw younger men about like rag dolls in his antagonistics classes.

"Money, then," Cyrus Barker said. "It all comes to that. You want me to fund your war. I am a man of peace."

K'ing burst out laughing, a grating sound in the quiet of the room. "A man of peace? How many men have you killed in war? How many have you killed in a time of relative peace and prosperity here in Britain?"

Barker ignored the question. "Your people have needs here in Limehouse. Food, clothing, dwellings. I have already given to these local charities. Suppose I double the amount?"

"That would be satisfactory in normal times, but we are burying our dead, some of whom you have met. We must arm new soldiers and forge further alliances."

"At any moment, our countries could be at war," Barker

stated. "To the English, one Chinaman is like another. No one here asks or cares if you are pro-Qing or anti-Qing."

The clandestine leader of Limehouse stared at him soberly. "Still."

"Suppose I were to start a benevolence fund for your sailors, or for widows and orphans."

"Which we can use as we see fit?" K'ing asked.

"No, it must be used as intended," Barker countered. "But it might free other funds being used to support Limehouse itself. What you do with your money is your own concern."

The next few minutes they haggled over how much Barker might give. I didn't pay attention. I was too busy trying to work out why we were giving money away in order to help a young man we didn't know about this very morning. So far, he was only missing. For all we knew he could be having a holiday in Brighton, and here we were ostensibly building a war chest to save him. I longed for an easy enquiry, one that had nothing to do with politics. Other enquiry agents like J. M. Hewitt never had to deal in such matters.

Finally, K'ing nodded. Nothing further was spoken about the agreement. Instead, they discussed Mr. K'ing's wife and daughter. Bok Fu Ying had been Barker's ward when they married. In a way the Guv was his wife's father. Fu Ying was also a close friend of Rebecca's. We were all related in a way, but this wasn't about family. This was about the fate of China, which had the largest population on earth, as well as the fate of a single young man from Hawaii who traveled there because he cared about the country he had never seen until recently.

We all bowed. The men had run out of protocol and ceremonies. We nodded. The meeting was over.

CHAPTER 6

The room where Sun Yat-sen was confined was perhaps twelve feet by ten. It contained a monkish bed with a woolen blanket and a flat pillow. The room may have been a storage closet at one time, but the window had been removed and iron bars installed in the outer wall. It was cold and occasionally windy. Why would an embassy require iron bars, Sun Yat-sen asked himself? Was he the first prisoner to be locked away here? Didn't it attract attention in the street? The young doctor wondered what was on the other side of the wall. The constant stream of vehicles that had so bewildered him on his first day in London continued to flow, but he couldn't discern whether he was on a main street or merely near one.

He was left in the cell for half an hour, his normally buoyant mood sinking every minute. He suspected that was the intent, to isolate him and make him feel alone. However, he had friends in London, friends like Dr. Cantlie, who wouldn't cease searching for him, he was sure of it. But how would they know where to find him? The Chinese embassy was the last place to look, principally because no one would expect him to be so stupid as to walk right by it. It was the height of folly, and Yat-sen felt as if he had just walked through the lobby door and asked to be sent back to China, if it's not too much trouble. What a fool he had been. He was too trusting, too vulnerable and naïve. It was his chief flaw.

Finally, he heard a key being inserted into the lock outside, another sign that this room had a sinister purpose. The Englishman stepped inside, with his white side-whiskers and beetling brow. Sun hoped it was all a mistake, and he would be out on the street again quickly. If the man was caught out, he would claim there had been confusion among minor officials and make a vague apology that only an uninformed European would accept. It was the Chinese way. They were nothing if not clever.

"Sir," the Englishman said, with an air of bumptiousness, "What is your name?"

"Sun, sir," he replied. "Sun Yat-sen."

"Are you also known as Sun Wen?"

"Yes, I am, sir."

Traditionally, Chinese people were known by two separate names; one official, and one more commonly used.

"My name is Sir Halliday Macartney, and I am the British counsel for the Chinese embassy. We received a telegram from the Chinese minister in America, informing us that you were a passenger aboard the SS *Majestic*. He instructed us to arrest you."

"Why did he do that?" Sun asked.

"You sent a petition for reform to the Tsungli yamen in

Peking, asking that it be presented to the emperor. It seems he was not pleased with your insolence. It may have been a very eloquent petition, but it was an exceedingly unwise thing to do. Now the Qing government wants you for trial, and therefore you are to be detained here until we learn what the emperor wishes us to do with you."

"What do you mean, sir?" he asked. "I don't understand. I am on British soil."

"It may be British soil out there in Devonshire Place, but to all intents and purposes you are in China now. The English government cannot help you here. It has no jurisdiction."

"What?" Sun Yat-sen cried, aghast. Had he traveled thousands of miles circumnavigating the globe, merely to step into China again? "Is that possible?"

"It is. I'm sorry, there is nothing we can do for you. Our hands are tied. Treaties, and all that. It's standard practice with embassies."

He apologized, but he didn't mean it. There was a Cheshire Cat grin on his face, and a certain satisfaction in informing him of his predicament. He spoke like a Mandarin. In fact, he spoke like the kind of Mandarin official who readily accepted bribes. Yat-sen was well acquainted with that sort of official, and he despised them. They were an example of the poison that had infected the Chinese imperial government for centuries, but he hadn't expected it could happen here in England, a country known for its common sense.

Sun welled up with emotion, but he steeled himself. "May I at least inform my friends that I've been detained?"

"No," Macartney stated, "but you may write to your lodgings for your luggage to be brought here. We'll see that it's delivered."

Yes, Sun told himself. Delivered and searched thoroughly

for evidence of insurrection. He noticed the councilor said "we" instead of "the embassy." It was a very telling word.

Sun felt as if the ground had fallen out from under him. He'd been standing, but now he sat on the bed, his head giddy. *No, no, no, no,* he repeated to himself. *This can't be happening.* He had escaped the emperor's grasp.

"Steady on, old fellow," Sir Halliday said, sounding like an English aristocrat in a bad play. "Best get some rest. You may be in this cell awhile."

"But this is illegal!" Sun protested. "I'm a guest in your country. I must have some rights!"

"Almost none at all, I'm afraid," the man replied. "We have a treaty with China, most of it due to our lease of Hong Kong, and part of that includes extradition of wanted criminals."

"I'm not a criminal," Sun replied. "I'm a doctor!"

Macartney shook his jowly head. "You should have tended to your patients then and avoided student demonstrations. You fell in with a bad crowd, and now you must pay the piper."

"How long must I stay here?" Yat-sen demanded.

"That I can't tell you. Not long. We're waiting for a ship to transport you back to China."

"May I at least speak to a solicitor? Surely there is some legal recourse. This is England after all, a country of common sense and laws."

"True," Macartney admitted. "Were you born in Britain?"

"I'm from the island of Hawaii."

"Ah, too bad, old fellow. I understand your queen is a favorite of our own, but there is no embassy here in London. You're out of luck. There's really nothing I can do for you."

"May I at least get word to Sir James Cantlie, my sponsor? He'll be concerned for me."

"Mr. Sun, you are a rat that has been caught in a trap due to his own foolishness. I'm not responsible for your safety, nor am I inclined to do you any favors."

"But I didn't enter this building legally. I was thrust inside by a small gang of men who accosted me in the street on English soil."

"They were not a gang," Macartney replied. "They were members of the Imperial Secret Service, who arrest revolutionaries like you."

"But all I did was write one letter to the Qing government suggesting some sensible reforms."

"I see. Are you aware that emperors do not as a rule take advice from citizens? I should think someone would have told you that as a child. The storybooks are full of it. 'Off with his head,' and all that. We all have our duties to perform here. I have been given orders from the British government to counsel the Qing's emissaries. You are like a steaming coal, Dr. Sun, too hot to handle. Be a good fellow, and don't give your jailers any trouble. I assure you that no good shall come of it. Good day."

Sir Halliday Macartney turned and opened the door. He stepped outside and closed it behind him. Dr. Sun threw himself at the door, but it was already locked.

"What's to become of me?" he yelled.

There was no answer.

CHAPTER 7

It has become second nature to Barker and me that we arrive in Whitehall Street cautiously, rather than blundering into our offices heedless of what might be waiting for us. We stay alert even while crossing our threshold. As the Guv has said, it only takes being caught out once.

"Did you notice the fellow by Cox and Co?" he asked after we had entered and put our sticks in the hall stand.

"Nice coat," I remarked. "It was gray with a subtle pattern. Almost tweedy, but more urbane. He looked like an advertisement for a clothier, but I'd have chosen a different tie, myself."

"I know most of the Home Office lads," Barker said. "But I didn't recognize this fellow. Did you?"

"No, sir, but he has the look of an agent recruited out of university. I could be wrong, however. He seems to be about my age."

Barker leaned on the edge of his newly repaired desk. Had I done so, I'd have been reprimanded for indolence.

"Perhaps a year or two younger," he observed. "If he's well trained, he'll wait until we are settled and wander in casually, like a lounger."

A minute later the door opened, and the man stepped in. His brown hair was carefully pomaded, and I could not fault his tailor, or his looks for that matter. His shoes were slightly down-at-heel like any man who works in the city. London is hell on shoe leather.

"Gentlemen?" the man said, after his card was sent in. "Is one of you Cyrus Barker?"

"I am Cyrus Barker," the Guv replied. "This is Mr. Llewelyn. Come in. Are you from the Foreign Office?"

The fellow winced. "Bite your tongue, sir. I'm from the Colonial Office. How did you know?"

"You have the look, doesn't he, Thomas?" my partner asked. "No offense intended. Have a seat, sir. What is your name and how may we help you?"

"My name is Andrew Lorton, and yours came up during an investigation by our office. Are you not the Cyrus Barker who came from China?"

"I came from Canton, yes."

"Do you have an associate named Sebastian Nightwine?"

"I most certainly do not," the Guv replied. "We were partners once, but the man is a scoundrel, and we are no longer associated."

"Are you aware that he is in town?" Lorton asked, leaning forward on his cane.

"Have a seat, Mr. Lorton. By the oddest chance we do. He was seen two nights ago by an associate of mine, Etienne Dummolard, at his restaurant, Le Toison d'Or. I was very surprised, as I was under the impression that I had killed him in a duel a few years ago. I certainly tried my best."

Lorton blinked, then looked at each of us, trying to work out whether we were having him on.

I smiled and nodded in encouragement. He frowned, and cleared his throat, uncertain of how to proceed. I did not approve of the Guv going around telling government officials that he had killed someone, or tried to, but it was his decision to make.

Lorton cleared his throat. "Have you gentlemen been hired to look for a Chinese national named Sun Yat-sen?"

My partner sat back in his chair and tented his fingers. "What is this about, Mr. Lorton?"

"Mr. Sun attempted to start a coup in China last year and fled to London. We understand that several local detectives, some in this very street, have been hired by the Chinese government to find and apprehend him."

"What?" I argued. "It is illegal for an enquiry agent to be in the employ of a foreign government. But you know that."

"Yes, sir," Lorton replied. "However, the Qing government has placed a substantial bounty on Dr. Sun's head. Obviously, they plan to make an example of him. The Chinese embassy intends to find him, so he can be tried for an attempted insurrection."

"I can assure you that this agency will not help the Qing government," Barker growled.

"Yes, I'm sure," the government agent replied.

"Mr. Lorton, let me be perfectly clear. I am not helping Mr. Nightwine, whatever his plans may be, and I am always at the disposal of the British government. Do you need an interpreter? I speak fluent Mandarin and Cantonese."

"I will pass your offer along," Lorton said. "Tell me, are you familiar with a revolutionary named K'ing?"

"Of course," the Guv stated. "He is married to my former ward."

"And an organization called the Heaven and Earth Society?"

Barker stood and removed his jacket. He rolled his sleeve and presented a heavily tattooed forearm. He pointed to a triangular tattoo, with several Chinese characters written on it.

"I am a member, as you can see," the Guv said. "Please note that I am being transparent, Mr. Lorton. I have nothing to hide. I am also a thirty-third degree Mason, as you can see by this devise here, and a member of the Knights Templar. Here is their sword and crown. Have we established my bona fides?"

Lorton was taking notes while watching Barker warily. His eyes went to the bloodthirsty broadswords on the back wall of our chambers and guessed that we were armed, or if he didn't, he was a fool. Poor fellow. He'd come along hoping to intimidate a suspect and was being intimidated himself instead.

"Did you provide funds to the failed revolution in China last year?" he asked.

"I did," my partner replied. "I've seen firsthand what the Manchus have done, severed heads stacked like cannonballs. It has to end. However, I haven't participated in any insurrections myself. I'll leave that to the native Chinese combatting oppression. It is their war. I only contribute to it as I can, out of respect for an old boxing master."

"Have you met Dr. Sun before?" Lorton asked.

"I have not. However, I fought alongside General Charles Gordon with the Ever Victorious Army during the Taiping Rebellion, so you can see where my sympathies lie. What of Mr. Nightwine?"

"His name came up during our investigation," Lorton said over his notebook.

"I assume you mean because he's become close to the Prince of Wales, and you're trying to investigate his past?"

The Colonial Office man's shoulders sagged. The Guv had proven he knew far more than anticipated. Now Lorton's superiors would become interested in us. Barker's candor has put us in a cell more than once. It isn't that he has no guile; he has plenty, but he knows how to use it to his advantage. Innocence becomes a commodity. In his eyes it was merely another weapon to deploy.

As for me, I had little connection with China save for that I ate at a Chinese tearoom once a week and studied a form of boxing Barker had learned in Foochow. However, my innocence concerning any particular matter has never stopped anyone from wanting to do me mischief.

"Tell me, Mr. Barker. What do you suppose Mr. Nightwine is in London to do?"

"An excellent question," the Guv conceded. "First of all, Sebastian is always in need of money. I've heard him bemoaning the fact that he hasn't set anything aside for his later years. Also, he's had a desire for fame. There were talks a few years ago about a knighthood, but the man has no patriotic or altruistic side. He prefers power and glory. And money, of course. Lots of it. Tell me, has the Qing government placed a bounty on Dr. Sun's head?"

"Yes. A substantial one."

"There's your answer, then. Nightwine is trying to earn the money and to ingratiate himself with the Qing court. You must understand. Nightwine was born in Darfur. His father was an explorer and linguist, and a devout Darwinist taken to the extreme. My former friend holds no allegiance to any one country. China, England, Tibet, it makes no difference to him. He'd call himself a citizen of the world."

"And that is the prince's new favorite!" Lorton said, pinching the bridge of his nose.

"Sebastian is a rascal, and possibly a traitor, but I have no evidence of any current plans at hand."

"He has a daughter as well," I remarked. "Her name is Sofia Ilyanova. Generally, she's involved in his affairs. She participated in the shooting here a couple of years ago when the tsarevitch of Russia was in town."

"Involved how, sir?" Lorton demanded.

"I assumed the Foreign Office would have informed you. She was the attempted assassin. They call her La Sylphide."

Lorton frowned and put down his notebook momentarily. "You're having me on."

"I wish we were," I admitted. "She nearly shot me, as well."

Agent Lorton shook his head and scribbled in his notebook again, then tucked it back in his pocket.

"My superiors may want to speak to you soon," he said after a moment. "Please do not involve yourselves further in this matter."

Too late, a little voice sang in my ear.

Barker came around the desk and clapped a hand on his shoulder. "Would'na think of it, man. I'm always pleased to meet a member of the intelligence community. Mr. Llewelyn, show this gentleman to the door."

I did so under Jeremy Jenkins's approving gaze, and thrust him out into Whitehall Street, where it had begun to rain.

"There's that sorted," I said.

We had lunch at the St. James in Picadilly. Scotsmen must have their haunch of mutton now and again. I dawdled over my sole à la Dugléré and thought of our recent interview.

"The Colonial Office is not very far along," I stated. "Do you suppose the Foreign Office is investigating Nightwine, as well?"

"I think it likely, lad, but there is no reason to suspect they are any more informed than their brethren. We find ourselves in a fortunate position and should take advantage of it."

"Should we aid them?" I asked. "Our lives are in danger, after all."

Barker wiped his mustache with a serviette, but didn't answer. I hoped that at least he was considering it.

"It concerns me, sir," I continued, "that you have referred to Nightwine as 'Sebastian' as if you are still chums."

"Chums?" he asked, perplexed by the word.

"Friends, then," I clarified. "How well did the two of you know each other? When did you first meet?"

He put down his fork and sipped from his glass of water. The Guv would allow beer during lunch, but not wine. He considers it decadent before dinner, and a danger to one's morals. However, I'm no great winebibber myself, so I've never felt the need to defend it.

"First of all, he was my commanding officer during the Taiping Rebellion," he said after a moment. "We ran into one another again a few years later at a dockside tavern in Macao. He was searching for a new captain for his ship. I had experience aboard boats, and I spoke English. Of course, at the time he had no idea I was Scottish and not Chinese. I wore these spectacles and had grown a queue. I'd been living among the Chinese since I was a youth, posing as one of them. I found work chiefly as an itinerant boxer, accepting challengers."

"Wait," I interrupted. "Are you saying the *Osprey* was Nightwine's? You've always claimed it was yours. You said you won it in a fan-tan game!"

"Do I strike you as the kind of man who plays fan-tan? No, I bought it from him outright later, but he never gave me the deed. You see how the man works? To say his honesty in business dealings is suspect is an understatement."

"I'm not surprised. So, were you actual friends?"

He considered the question before he answered.

"Yes, after a fashion," he said. "If a delivery outside of China required his presence, we would talk on the journey. Certainly, I knew him better than most people. A good deal of the work involved questionable practices, running guns to Singapore for example, but many small crafts working in the China Seas do that to make a living. It is dangerous work, and the *Osprey* was not as pretty then as she is now. The sails were patched and much of the wood worm-eaten. She was quick to the helm and seaworthy, though, and that was all Nightwine asked of her. It was my duty to keep her afloat and stop the crew from mutinizing.

"Then one day he took me to Shameen Island, the British quarter of Canton, where he introduced me as his servant to a charming couple, Lord and Lady Ashleigh. Not long after, Lord Ashleigh met with an accident, falling off a stone stairway at the docks, or so it was claimed. Sebastian felt the need to comfort the grieving widow and see her through the bureaucracy of a death on Chinese soil, which can be quite complicated."

"That's how you met Lady Ashleigh," I said.

"Aye, what a beauty she was to behold!" he replied. "But I didn't speak to her until I met her in Canton by chance months later and warned her not to trust my partner. I was forced to explain my brogue to her and how I came to be in China."

"You believe Nightwine killed her husband," I prompted, pushing away my plate. I'd overeaten.

"Let us say the method was typical for him. How easy

would it be to hire someone to push an Englishman off a steep stone staircase with no handrails?"

"The two of you had a falling-out, I assume," I said, waving the waiter for a coffee.

The Guv nodded. "It had to come eventually. His friendships have a purpose and do not last. By then we'd changed our trade to diving for wrecks in nearby Bias Bay. There were rumors of a pirate queen's treasure sunk somewhere nearby in shallow waters, so we rigged an old church bell into a diving bell with a winch. It was our hardest work yet. I had to pierce my own eardrums like the Bajau people to withstand the pressure of diving so deep. We found Zheng Yi Sao's wreck eventually, however, and made quite a find. All of us have lived on it ever since, except Sebastian, of course. He went through what should have been a lifetime's share in a matter of months."

"I assume he wanted it all," I added. It seemed logical.

"Aye, although he wasn't even on board the day we found it. We gave him the largest portion, a double share, worth a fortune, which was standard practice for sailors. Then we split the jewels and left the ship in port along the Pearl River. When Sebastian found out, he was furious. First, he demanded my share, having convinced himself he'd earned it, without doing any of the work. What do you suppose I did with it?"

I slapped the table. "You gave it to Lady Ashleigh!"

"Very good, lad," he said with a cold smile. "I did, for safe keeping. He didn't think of her. He was furious that the crew had absconded with over half his treasure. He claimed I had robbed him and tried to have me arrested, but neither the English nor the Qing government would help him. So, then he showed the truest sign of his knavery."

By then I was hanging on his every word. I'd waited over ten years to hear this tale.

"What was that?" I asked.

"There was a rumor at the time that the Empress Dowager was being poisoned and was in a bad way. A call went out for an investigator. Nightwine suggested my name and invented all kinds of exploits."

"But you weren't an investigator then," I said.

"Precisely," he said, nodding. "The Forbidden Palace in Peking is full of intrigue. The chances of returning successfully are few. It was a neat little way for Nightwine to rid himself of me, so he could search for my portion of the treasure. In his eyes I had betrayed him, his only friend."

"That must have been your first enquiry!" I said. "I presume you went to Peking."

"Aye, Thomas, it was, and I went, though unwillingly. I had no choice. Unfortunately, it is an indelicate matter. I'm afraid I cannot reveal it."

I threw a roll at him. He ducked it, of course. So many contradictions, the Guv. Through all the enquiries of my career, some of them bizarre and most of them dangerous, Cyrus Barker has been the greatest enigma, and the most maddening.

CHAPTER 8

That afternoon we went to Gray's Inn to inspect Dr. Sun's personal belongings. It seemed unlikely that anything would come of doing so, but it wouldn't be wise to leave this particular stone unturned. We made our way to Gray's Inn Place, in the shadow of one of the famous Inns of Court, first built in 1370. I wondered what they would have thought of the little Chinese doctor with his Western haircut and herringbone suit. If Dr. Cantlie had booked the rooms under his own name. I'm certain Sun's arrival was a shock to the owners.

The present owners were taken aback that week as well. A group of Chinamen claiming to be relatives of Dr. Sun had come for his luggage. The proprietors had refused, even though they had a note from the Chinese embassy, requesting Sun's personal belongings.

We made our way to the young doctor's room, then when Barker and I came to his door, he stood guard while I picked the lock. We were in within a minute or two, but I'll admit it was luck. Once inside we went through his possessions, which were packed into a small valise and a battered leather suitcase. A Malacca stick lay on his bed, and there was a copy of *The Lancet* on a side table, along with a copy of *Oliver Twist* with an old but beautiful binding, printed when the author was alive.

I lifted the book and opened it gently. I owned a copy much like it. I fished among the pages for a note or photograph, but there was only a receipt written a few days earlier from a bookseller in Charing Cross Road I'd been to many times. There were quaint illustrations in the old volume and a florid portrait of Mr. Dickens. I wondered if it was purchased because the novel was set in London, or as a souvenir to take back with him.

"He was near our offices a few days ago," I remarked, holding up the book. On some maps, Craig's Court is considered part of the Charing Cross District. "If only we'd found him then."

I wondered where Sun would go if and when we found him. Certainly, it was impossible for him to return to China with a price on his head, but would he settle in London or return to his native home in the Pacific? Thanks to Barker's training I'd learned how to make deductions about a person's thoughts or beliefs based on his possessions, but a young revolutionary physician born on the island of Hawaii was rather beyond my scope.

I looked inside Sun's medical journal, grasping at straws, but there were no notations, and nothing tucked inside. I found no watch or wallet, but then he would have had those with him. On a table there was a printed church bulletin dated from the week before his disappearance. Nothing in the room was out of the ordinary or would have placed him in any kind of trouble.

Barker was more energetic than I. He searched under the bed, in the water closet, and even knocked on the floorboards. Finally, he sat on the bed and examined the Malacca stick.

"Ah," he said, putting pressure on the handle to unscrew it. The ball came away in his hand. He peered down into the hollow stick and then upended it. Nothing came out at first, but under the Guv's vigorous shaking, scrolled papers began to fall and unfurl on the bed. They were about the size of a grown man's hand, easy to pass from one person to another, and were written in Chinese pictograms.

"Printed or handwritten?" I asked.

"These are handwritten," Barker replied, glancing over one. "No one with a printing press would dare print them under penalty of death. The Manchu government doesn't even allow newspapers. Wars have broken out in parts of China that the general population has never even heard about."

He began to read aloud:

"'My brothers, the time has come for the citizens of China to finally throw off the yoke of tyranny inflicted upon us by the Manchu government. Are we to remain a subjugated people forever? Will your children and grandchildren endure the same poverty and humiliation you have suffered all your lives? Today your sons bow and grovel in the mud when a Manchu official is carried by in a grand palanquin. Shall your daughters become concubines and slaves to their lusts tomorrow?

'Our coasts are being overrun by Western devils, and precious land good for farming is being stolen by them to build foreign cities on our own soil. Meanwhile, money continues to flow into Manchu coffers, while our children are forced to live on millet and rotten vegetables. It is time to stand and defend ourselves and our country. Join the Young People's Resistance!'"

"Stirring, I must admit," I remarked. "Do you think Sun Yat-sen wrote this?"

"Most likely," the Guv rumbled. "Do you?"

"Yes," I replied. "Have they a chance?"

"Not yet, but soon, perhaps. This generation is less rural than in the past and there are more people aware of the West and Western freedom. Hong Kong and Canton send workers around the world, who settle and learn more about Western civilization."

"Then their sons, young men like Sun Yat-sen, return to their homeland with skills and funding," I said.

"Precisely, Thomas. It's a tall mountain to climb, and many die trying to do so, but the Qing government can't last forever."

"'Destroy the Qing and restore the Ming!'" I muttered, quoting the Heaven and Earth Society's battle cry.

I dared try on one of Sun's jackets and it fit me. I reasoned he was near my size. Considering what Cantlie had said about him, he must have visited his ancestral home and fell in with the wrong crowd as far as his safety was concerned. However, he did carry revolutionary flyers inside his cane, which could easily have earned him time in prison.

"He's a zealot," I stated. "He might not be as innocent as Dr. Cantlie thinks he is. And perhaps he's paying the price for it. We should have the embassy watched."

"That's a good idea," Barker replied. "I'll speak to Ho as well. He's aware of what ships carry Chinese goods. Have you become sympathetic to the doctor's plight, or was he a damned fool?"

"I haven't studied it enough to form a reasoned opinion," I said. "Why didn't he just stay in Hawaii where it was safe?"

"I understand there has been trouble between the Chinese citizens and the government there, as well, which is heavily influenced by the United States," Barker answered. "His parents may have thought they were sending him to China where it was safe. 'Out of the frying pan, fair into the fire,' as Thomas More said."

"Uneducated men in Canton may have looked up to him for leadership," I said. "In his case being foreign-born may have worked in his favor. Some may have listened to a doctor and an educated man from the West."

"He had no idea what would happen once he reached London," the Guv said.

"No?" I asked. "Perhaps he did. Perhaps he even hoped to create an international incident. It would strengthen interest in his cause among the English."

"You believe he is that clever? Dr. Cantlie did not."

"I'm merely speculating," I admitted. "It would be a dangerous game. He would have been risking being imprisoned or beheaded. It's barbaric."

Barker shrugged his burly shoulders. "One means of killing a person is much like another, I suspect, Thomas. The embassy would try anything to send him back to China again."

"Is it unusual for a foot soldier to receive such attention?"

"No, the Qing government lays down blanket condemnations. It would be in your best interests to read Jeremy's newspaper clippings on recent Chinese events."

There it was, I thought. The obligatory rap across the knuckles. Well deserved, no doubt. I'd dig into our clerk's files when I had a few moments. It wasn't my fault I hadn't been raised in the exotic Orient. I'm certain I'd have preferred it to the miserable mining town in Wales where I was born.

"Are there any leads?" I asked.

"Dr. Cantlie mentioned there is another doctor friend working in London, by the name of Patrick Manson. He helped train Yat-sen when he was studying medicine in Hong Kong and came here with Cantlie when Hong Kong had become politically unsafe. I'd like to hear his thoughts on recent events. Perhaps he knows something about Sun Yat-sen that has not been revealed to his host. Come."

We took a hackney cab to St. Bartholomew's Hospital in the City, not far from my home. It was a teaching hospital, the oldest in London, having been founded in 1123. We had not made an appointment, but Barker would be satisfied with a brief conversation with Dr. Manson in between his lectures. At the front desk, we asked which classroom he was teaching in, then cooled our heels for half an hour on a bench across from the door. After the bell sounded, one fellow came out looking rather green, and it seemed as if the rest of the students were fleeing.

"Ah," Barker rumbled. "Anatomy class."

We stepped inside and approached Dr. Manson. He was of sturdy build, with a gray mustache and small spectacles perched on his nose. He wore no coat, and his sleeves were rolled to the elbows. There was a body that had been almost completely eviscerated on a table, and the room reeked of formaldehyde.

"A word, sir!" my partner called.

"Who the devil are you?" the man asked, frowning.

"We are enquiry agents," my partner said. "My name is Cyrus Barker and this is Thomas Llewelyn. We've been hired by Mr. Cantlie to find Dr. Sun."

"I assume he's been snatched by the Chinese embassy," Manson stated. "The question is where they've taken him."

Unlike Cantlie, Manson was a peppery fellow, the kind who didn't suffer fools, and perhaps not enquiry agents, either.

The Guv nodded. "We'll see what can be done. Do you have another class now?"

"Within the quarter hour. You can stay if you don't mind my cleaning up."

So saying, he packed a liver and two kidneys into the open body cavity as if it were a Gladstone bag. I'd have turned green myself if I hadn't spent years visiting the Scotland Yard Body Room to observe the coroner there, Dr. Edward Vandeleur. I was acquainted with the stench of death and decay, having viewed many autopsies, but I had little patience for the rank, cloying, and pungent odor of formaldehyde. I'm certain it is an excellent preservative, but I had no wish to become better acquainted with it.

"Can you give me your impressions of Sun Yat-sen as a student, Dr. Manson?" my partner asked.

"Two years ago, I would have called him the best Asian student to graduate with a degree in Western medicine in our program, but since then he has become distracted with politics. I've asked him several times what he intends to do with himself but never received a satisfactory answer."

"Is that so, Doctor?" my partner asked.

"Yes," Dr. Manson replied. "He has changed mistresses, if I may say it. He's giddy with love for China itself. He'd never seen it before he came to Hong Kong but had built fantasies around it. He was born in Asia but was taken to Hawaii as an infant. Once he returned to China as an adult, he was appalled by the poverty, the living conditions, and the indifference of the Manchus. He sought out local youths who supplied him with literature about the widespread corruption in the Qing government. In short, he became a radical of the worst sort: the intellectual kind. He nearly gave up his studies in medicine, and after he finally graduated, I saw little of him. When I was transferred here, having heard of his arrival, I spoke to him, trying to encourage him, but he was more fervent than ever, I'm afraid. His interest in medicine had waned, though he had been in the top tier of his class."

"Dr. Cantlie said nothing of this," Barker stated.

"They were like father and son, by which I mean James had little idea what Sun was doing. Also, James is an administrator, not a teacher who sees him every day. Sun couldn't hide his opinions or his lack of interest from me. Hold this for me, will you?"

Manson placed a small object in my hands, redolent of formaldehyde.

"What is it?" I asked.

"A gallbladder," he said. "Human, obviously. Let me move these organs into place. Nearly forgot the little fellow last time, being so small!"

It was a ghastly greenish, thumb-like thing, thoroughly revolting, but I couldn't display the slightest sign of disgust, or I would risk disappointing the Guv. It was a medical teacher's trick, I think, hoping to make a student faint or become ill. I held it while he moved the organs about inside the corpse's abdomen. Poor fellow, I thought, looking down at its withered features. He donated his body to science and now someone was mucking about inside him for instruction.

Manson took the gallbladder again and slipped it among the pile of organs, just under the liver. I suspected I was turning green myself.

"I saw Sun last week in the Reading Room of the British Museum," he said, resuming the conversation. "There was a stack of books at his elbow. I glanced at what he was reading. It was Karl Marx and Montesquieu. I've seen it before, when a student becomes disenchanted with his subject, or finds a new love. I thought he'd get himself in trouble and now he has. Politics!"

The latter he said with as much loathing as I felt about the gallbladder he'd given me. I looked down at my soiled hands, looking for something to wipe them on, but there was nothing in sight. Barker was watching me of course and enjoying himself. No one would dare give him a gallbladder as a prank. He'd grass them with one blow.

"It was a loss to science, Mr. Barker," Manson continued. "He could have made something of himself. We were hoping to find a Chinese student ready to go toe-to-toe with these Chinese charlatans and their folk remedies. I would have dearly enjoyed witnessing that argument."

"Do you suspect the young doctor has been taken?" Barker asked.

"I'm no fool, sir," the doctor replied. "I lived in Hong Kong for years. I can recognize a Chinese government agent when I see one. They're about, I tell you. I suspect they even know who I am. Now, if you'll excuse me, I've got to get this fellow back to the storage closet before the next class."

"Thank you for speaking to us, Dr. Manson," the Guv said, bowing his head.

The man gave a sharp nod and wheeled the corpse out of the room.

"This is why one should always interview more than one witness," my partner instructed me.

"You'd think they were talking about two different people entirely," I complained. "Which was he? The academic or the radical?"

"Both, I should think," my partner replied. "A man can be two things at once. Take yourself as an example. You're an enquiry agent and also an anatomy class assistant."

As we walked down the hall of St. Barts, I held my hands outstretched until I found a water closet and washed them. However, the odor permeated my clothes and encircled my head for the rest of the day.

Outside, we found a cab. The driver didn't seem to notice the smell, but the cab horse turned and glared at me as if offended.

"Dr. Manson is able to recognize an Imperial Secret Service agent," Barker rumbled. "I wonder that Dr. Sun could not. Just because a student decides to become a patriot does not prove that he is skilled at it."

"I suppose one must start somewhere," I remarked.

The cab took us to good old Craig's Court. There I washed my hands several times without making the slightest difference. When I came out of the back rooms, I could hear men speaking.

Going down the hall to our chambers, I found the Guv talking to J. M. Hewitt. Barker had a satisfied look on his face.

"What now?" I asked.

"Sebastian Nightwine went into the Chinese embassy this morning," the private detective answered.

"No!" I said.

"And there's more," Hewitt added. "Last week, I was hired by the embassy to track Sun Yat-sen from his liner at the docks to his rooms in Gray's Inn. I didn't know he was the man you gents were looking to find until now."

"Who hired you?" I asked.

"The British liaison, Sir Halliday Macartney," Hewitt answered. "Shall I keep watching Nightwine, Cyrus?"

"If you'd be so kind."

"It's your shilling," he said, shrugging. "I should sprint. I left him in a restaurant in Soho."

"That's a nice suit," I remarked. "Where'd you buy it?"

"Ede and Ravenscroft," he remarked, turning about to show it off.

"Smart," I remarked.

Hewitt and his suit left to follow Nightwine. I wondered why I didn't get assignments like that. It seems I always find myself holding the gallbladder.

Just then, the telephone set on the Guv's desk jangled. Barker frowned and put the receiver to his ear. I don't consider myself sensitive in any psychic way, though some of my race are. Nevertheless, I had a sudden sense of foreboding.

"Barker and Llewelyn Enquiry Agency," Barker said. "Good morning. Yes. Ah. Stay there and lock the doors. We'll be along directly."

He hung the receiver and stood, a grim look on his face. I was already standing. As I said before, I was learning to become intuitive. I smothered my latent need to ask what had happened and let the bad news wash over me.

"That was Lady Ashleigh. Paul Beauchamp was guarding her estate in Sussex last night," Barker said. "Now he is missing."

A wave of shock went through me.

"What of Rebecca and Philippa?" I asked.

"So far, they are safe, although everyone is upset, of course. Beauchamp's wife has been crying in the kitchen."

I recalled that Mrs. Beauchamp was Lady Ashleigh's cook.

"What shall we do, sir?" I asked. "I assume we'll be moving Philippa and Rebecca to a safer location."

"Aye," the Guv agreed. "We must take the women to Paris, but it won't be aboard the *Osprey*, lad. She's been stolen."

CHAPTER 9

It was a grim journey to the South Coast. Barker was impatient to arrive and paced the corridor of the train the way a lion paces a cage, while I sat in a railway compartment in first class on the very edge of my seat, my heel bouncing on the floor as steady as a metronome. My unfettered mind invented dire scenarios: Rachel crying in her mother's arms. Rebecca reduced to tears on Philippa Ashleigh's shoulder, or for that matter, Philippa crying on hers, for Paul Beauchamp was a friend to her. He was always nearby, mending something. He filled the role of caretaker far more than the man Lady Ashleigh had hired for the position.

I confess I didn't know Beauchamp well. He was a man of few words and I too many. Most of our conversations, brief and hesitant as they were, ended in failure. It wasn't that we disliked each other, we simply had different interests and temperaments. I'm not happy if I'm not spitting words like a Gatling gun, while he could go an entire day in silence.

On the other hand, Beauchamp was my partner's mate, his second mate, in fact, aboard the *Osprey*. Barker must have hired him in Asia, when Paul had been temporarily between voyages. I'd have liked to sail on one of those excursions, but then I was at school at the time. Those were the days before my partner became the pious man he is now. I imagine a good deal of hijinks occurred on that vessel among the Guv and his young crew. After all, diving for treasure is not the task of sober gentlemen.

Barker opened the compartment door, nodded at me, and closed it again. I rose, looked out the window at the passing farms and woods, before stepping into the corridor. It was just as well. I had been fraying the passengers' nerves with my fidgeting.

"Did Lady Ashleigh mention Rebecca when you spoke?" I asked my partner.

"Only that your wife regretted the need to go to Paris," he said, looking slightly puzzled. "I was of the impression that women longed to go there."

"Yes, Rebecca loves Paris," I admitted. "But I'm sure she's worried about Rachel's safety, if not her own. I know I am. How will we get to Paris without the *Osprey*?"

"We'll take Philippa's carriage to Newhaven to board the ferry to Dieppe, then travel by rail to the Gare Saint-Lazare in Paris. She has already booked a few rooms for them in a hotel nearby. You and I will see them settled and then return to London. When Nightwine has been dealt with, and the ladies are safe, I intend to hire a vessel and hunt for Beauchamp and the *Osprey*."

"Do you believe Nightwine is behind Paul's disappearance?" I asked.

"I can think of no other explanation, Thomas," Barker said. "Paul was widely admired in Sussex, having been a fixture there for a number of years now. He ran the local fishing fleet, and helped in local events with his wife. No one who knew him would wish him ill."

"If Nightwine is indeed responsible, do you suppose he is still aboard the ship?"

"I cannot say," he answered. "I presume Mr. Hewitt is still following him. First, we must take the women to a secure location and then we will get to the bottom of Sebastian's plans."

Within the half hour, I began to see gulls and fulmars wheeling overhead from the carriage window and knew we were nearing the coast. I'd never wanted to see Rebecca's face more in my entire life. I needed to make certain my family was safe. Human life meant nothing to Sebastian Nightwine. He'd kill for the most trivial trinket or gut you for an imagined slight. His father had harbored extreme theories concerning Darwinism: survival of the fittest with no regard to the cost of human life. We were but another species of animal, and not a very skilled one at that. It was his fault that his son was the very devil, let loose upon an innocent and unsuspecting world.

Although the women were under Frost's protection, Her Ladyship's capable butler, we hurried when we reached the station to hire a trap. When we reached Tulsemore, the two of us alighted and went inside. Rebecca met me at the door, seizing my arm and refusing to let go. She murmured a greeting to Barker, then dragged me into a side room where Rachel was playing with a small pup that I suspected was sired by Harm. On any other day I'd have enjoyed watching them chase each other, but there were questions to be answered and decisions to make.

"Isn't it awful?" Rebecca exclaimed. "The poor man dined with us late yesterday evening and then he was gone this morning!"

I nodded as she gestured toward the window.

"We were so upset we didn't realize the ship had been stolen for hours," she continued. "Philippa wondered if the whole thing was a ruse to allow Mr. Nightwine to escape with the boat. I understand there was some kind of warrant against him in China, but Mr. Nightwine wanted Mr. Barker's boat. He would find a way to get it in the end."

"Perhaps he did," I added.

"Paris, you say," she went on as if she hadn't heard where we were going, her head was so full of concerns. "I love Paris, but not this way. I'm sure we shall be barricaded in a hotel the entire visit. What's wrong with that terrible man? He ought to be locked in a cell forever, like the Count of Monte Cristo. He is not worthy to call himself a human being. Poor Ginny!"

"Ginny?" I asked, nonplussed.

"Ginny Beauchamp," Rebecca said. "She's gone home with her sons. An inspector was here from Brighton asking the most frightful questions. It was horrible, Thomas. I'm so glad you're here."

She hugged me fiercely then, as if she would never let me go.

"I'm sorry I wasn't here when it happened," I said.

Being alone, I lifted her off her feet in an embrace. A moment later someone gave a short clearing of the throat. It was Philippa's butler, a sturdy, broad fellow with stony features.

"Sir, Mr. Barker is looking for you."

"Thank you, Frost."

I put down my wife, a trifle shamefaced.

"I wish we were a thousand miles away from all this," I said. "Perhaps we need a holiday when this is over. How is Rachel?"

"As you can see, Philippa's new puppy was the perfect distraction," she replied. "The little thing was a present from Mr. Barker. I must admit I have a difficult time thinking of him as an attentive swain who brings gifts."

"I'd better be along but stay as close as you can," I instructed. "I don't want you out of my sight for long."

"Likewise," she replied. "If you go missing like Mr. Beauchamp, I'll never speak to you again."

With that twisted bit of logic, we returned to the sitting room where Philippa sat beside a tea tray, Barker in a chair beside her. He often came to see her on Saturday afternoons when he wasn't working. Rebecca was right. Seeing him seated there I had the oddest impression: he looked comfortable. It was as if he lived there as well, which in a way he did a few days each month. I thought it likely that the Chesterfield in which he sat had been purchased for him. I could not imagine Her Ladyship sitting in it. Married or not, they were a pair. This was a matter I hadn't considered often before; he might retire someday. There was no certainty of it, but it seemed likely, even logical. They would and should get married at some time in their relationship. She had remained unwed for many years because of him, despite numerous offers, including Nightwine's, of course.

I watched the tableau, where she drank tea while he lounged in the chair that suspiciously met his dimensions. Then I glanced at Rebecca, who was observing me as I watched them. She had a dimple in her cheek, the sign of a suppressed smile.

"So," I remarked. "Paris, then?"

"Is it safe enough?" Rebecca asked all of us. "Is anywhere safe enough? Mr. Nightwine may not be far away."

"He has other concerns, I'm certain," the Guv replied. "And with you safely away, we can hunt the man down."

It was a short carriage journey to the Newhaven docks and the Channel ferry. We were up and about early the next morning packing. I suggested to Rebecca that she might buy a new dress or two while in France, aware that she hadn't packed enough for an extended trip, but there was no way for us to know how long we would be in danger. Barker was down to monosyllabic replies. I noticed Philippa stayed at his side, often close enough that they were nearly touching. Both were frowning, despite the puppy frisking about. They had each faced Sebastian Nightwine before and understood the risks.

The Guv insisted that we accompany the ladies to Paris. I suspected he wanted to satisfy himself that we were not being followed. Here we were, a party of five fleeing the country, while Nightwine was probably back in London enjoying a late breakfast. I hoped that J. M. Hewitt had tracked him to his lair. At least something would have been accomplished.

"You're very quiet," Rebecca noted. We were on the deck of the ferry, showing Rachel her first glimpse of the Channel. My wife reads my every thought. I'm like a book to her, an old favorite, I hoped. "You're upset."

"Well, of course I'm upset," I replied. "We're being chased out of England, and nobody chases the Guv out of England."

"He's merely evading him, dear, and he's protecting us all," she reminded me. "You know better than to suspect the disappearance of a close friend will go unavenged."

"Now you've become the expert on Cyrus Barker," I said.

We stood at the railing of the ferry. She linked her free arm in mine, attempting to improve my mood.

"Of course, I am," she said. "My view is unbiased. Also, you're incapable of considering Mr. Barker silently. You need someone to complain to, therefore I know most of what occurs in those chambers of yours. Do you complain to him about me?"

"I might if you ever did something to complain about," I said.

"A proper answer," she replied. "Let's go inside. The wind is getting cold, and I'm afraid Rachel will catch a chill. Do you suppose they have tea?"

We went inside and were soon drinking some rather dreadful tea. The ladies were talking, and Rachel had fallen asleep. I had my first chance to speak alone to the Guv since we were on the train the day before. If anything, he seemed to be in a worse mood than I.

"I wonder where the *Osprey* is now," he grumbled.

"He's unlikely to sink her, so we're bound to find her eventually, sir," I said.

"I'll have Jeremy place advertisements in the newspapers offering a reward," he replied. "What's put you in such a good mood?"

"It's my naturally cheerful optimism, sir. Do you believe it is still best if we return to London immediately? I'd like a glimpse of Paris unless we must return by this evening."

"I'd prefer to sleep in my own bed tonight, Thomas. You may stay in Lion Street or return home. The choice is yours."

"I'll stay with you then, sir, if you don't mind," I stated.

"You're always welcome, lad. You know that."

I was a bit mollified. At least we weren't being chased away by Nightwine. We'd just stepped out for a breather and would be home by evening. I should have known better than to doubt my partner.

Paris is a beautiful city, but the area leading into it is

completely devoid of interest. Every building seems to face in the opposite direction from the tracks, as if Parisians had no interest in *les touristes.* Even the Eiffel Tower is centered within the city, its citizens showing little desire to share their steel marvel with the outside world. Paris is Paris, however, and must be forgiven for her insularism and self-satisfaction. Alas, we cannot all be Parisians.

A short while later, a fiacre deposited five weary travelers in front of a private hotel in the third arrondissement, away from the more familiar travel accommodations. We did not change our clothes but had a quiet early dinner in a small but serviceable brasserie that was part of the hotel. The ladies would have to forego their caviar and champagne. We were incognito, after all, and Paris is a city of intrigue.

Too soon, we were saying goodbye. Rachel was crying, and everyone was tired and out of sorts. The evening was chilly, and as the Guv and I stood on the platform a half hour later, consulting our timepieces and waiting impatiently for the next train to Normandy, I felt like a gladiator preparing for battle. It's a shame Barker was born in our modern century. He'd have looked proper in a suit of armor.

We crossed the Channel, and by nightfall we reached London again. Even a railway enthusiast like myself had been jostled and shaken enough for one day. I was looking forward to a book by a cozy fire in my old room. However, a message had been left for us on Barker's doorstep. It was there when we reached Lion Street; a single word in yellow painted on Barker's red front door: COWARD. When my partner called Mac to the front entrance, he was appalled, not to mention ashamed that he had not caught the fellow in the act and given him a load of buckshot for daring to step on the property. It was a slight on Jacob Maccabee's honor. Honor and slights were being passed around rather freely that day. Rebecca would call it silly, but how many young men die in battle every year because of Honor and Duty? How many wives and mothers cry by the hearth? How many children will have no memories of their fathers, save tales of his bloody Honor and Duty? Rachel wouldn't, I swore to myself.

"You're reserved tonight, lad," Barker remarked.

"I promised myself I would remain calm," I answered. "It's only a word, and that cursed Nightwine is trying to bait us."

"I'll purchase red paint to cover this . . . this desecration, sir," Mac murmured, his voice uneven with emotion.

"That won't be necessary," Barker replied. He has a low voice, but this time it was as low as I've ever heard it. It seemed to come from deep within the earth, from some fiery pit of Hell perhaps, or from the voice of a tortured soul. "This door will stay as it is, to remind me, and when I have deserved to do so I will paint it myself. Take our luggage, Mac. We are famished. Bring us whatever is in the larder."

"Yes, sir," Mac said, vanishing into the kitchen. I knew him. He would remember this humiliation for months, if not forever. He'd castigate himself far more than Barker or I ever could. I thought of saying something, but no. *Best leave the fellow to his own misery*, I thought.

I was exhausted. After a cold supper I went upstairs to my former room to forage for a book. I began to read some H. Rider Haggard, but even Allan Quatermain could not keep me awake after traveling six hundred miles in a single day. When I woke the next morning, the book was lying on the floor beside my bed.

CHAPTER 10

It was cold the next morning, and I could feel winter coming on. Maybe not yet, but there was no way to avoid it, short of moving to a balmier clime. In the back garden the plants were bedded down for the winter under a blanket of mulch, with only a few cold-loving plants in bloom. The gardeners were hard at work, preparing the half acre for the coming months. And where was I? In a patch of dry grass, wearing trousers, a singlet, and boxing gloves. There were no gentle, flowing movements today. It was combat against a larger and better trained opponent, the Guv himself, who assured me it was for my own good. Personally, I had my doubts. A man could catch pneumonia, while being punched in the nose.

I shuffled about in a semicircle looking for a weakness, and finding none, of course. My next option was to look for targets I might possibly strike, places where nerves crossed or an organ might be near the skin, such as a kidney. The first attempt resulted in a smack to the nose for being so obvious. At the second attempt he jammed my stomach into my spine with a kick, and I feared I wouldn't be able to eat breakfast afterward. However, I managed to tap the goggles he wore, which might have temporarily blinded a genuine opponent, giving me time for an assault.

"It's frigid out here," I said, looking for an opening in his guard which never came.

"Keep your left guard low, or I'll rattle your rib cage."

Training is a lesson in humiliation, a ceaseless litany of the mistakes you just made with an occasional acknowledgment that if you practiced fiercely enough for the rest of your life you might be able to take on a grammar school bully. Might, mind you. However, I'd heard all the remarks before, and thought he needed a few new helpful insults. I shot out an arm, hoping to tap his ear, but he evaded it easily and circled the patch of dried grass, intent on doing me mischief. I got a good kick into his lower ribs, but in turn he caught me under the chin and knocked me down momentarily. Of course, I quickly jumped to my feet, or he'd have kicked me like a football, over the gate and into the alley behind his house.

Blast, it was cold. Even the gloves didn't sufficiently warm my hands. One would think they were quilted like thick pillows, but no. They were hard, unforgiving leather.

Finally, he snagged one of my heels with the toe of his boot, and I fell on my back with the grace of an aging camel. I felt a fool, but that is not a new experience. As he approached to help me up, I wondered what horrors he had seen during his own days of training. I suspected we were just playing hopscotch compared to what he had endured in China under Dr. Wong.

We went inside. I dressed quickly and went into the kitchen where Mac had boiled eggs and made coffee. I missed Etienne's pain au chocolat, but hoped he and his family were safe in Dijon. I had downed most of my first cup of coffee when Barker appeared, ready for work and not in the least winded. He bit the boiled egg in two with his square teeth and washed it down with the scalding tea. Perhaps the kick to my stomach had jarred something, but I decided to screw my courage to the sticking place and pummel him with more questions whether he wanted to answer them or not.

"Sir, you said the Qing government lays down broad condemnations against what it considers its enemies," I remarked.

"Aye, they do," he said over his cup of tea.

"Did you ever receive one?" I asked. "I mean, is there a poster somewhere with your likeness and a reward?"

"There is."

"Do you know how much it is?"

"The reward?" he asked, raising a brow. "I've never seen it. I was never curious, since I have no intention of being caught."

I was treading lightly and promised myself I wouldn't be disappointed when Barker shut down the conversation. However, I had got him talking at the restaurant, so precedents can be broken.

"Was the reward as substantial as Dr. Sun's might be?" I pursued. I wasn't going to ask what he had done to earn it.

"It might be," he conceded. "The Imperial Navy chased us along most of the coast of China, from Peking to Macao. She was, I mean, they were exceedingly wroth."

She was? Did he mean the Empress Dowager who was being poisoned, or some other woman? I hadn't thought a woman was involved. Barker inhabits a very masculine world of enquiry work, boxing schools, and danger. I knew he had been married briefly while in Japan, when a war was going on, and I wondered if I would have a new story with which to enthrall my wife before the end of these matters. She's as curious about the man as I am.

"Were the rest of your crew also wanted men?" I continued.

"They were."

I could hear the first hint of annoyance in his voice.

"Then if there were a reward for Sun which Nightwine traveled all the way from China to earn, and there was one for you as well, might he not stop to collect it?" I asked.

"He might."

"Especially if it gets you out of the country when he's trying to propose to Lady Ashleigh, and you are his only rival?" I pressed.

The Guv nodded. "Aye."

"Was there a reward on Paul Beauchamp's head?"

"There was."

"And for Ho, and Etienne? What about for Lady Ashleigh herself?"

"They wouldn't dare," he replied. "She is a titled Englishwoman, not dockside riffraff like us. From what I was able to learn later, Nightwine convinced the Qing government we had kidnapped her. It was another charge against us."

"I see," I said. "These posters must be very old by now and buried in dusty files. Do they expire?"

"Not to my knowledge, Thomas."

"So," I continued. "With some bit of effort, Nightwine could collect the rewards on all of you. Would he have to bring you back alive?"

"That would be best," the Guv acknowledged. "If the person is dead, the reward is generally halved, but I suppose it would require proof, such as a photograph of the body or some form of personal identification. I can't gauge what would be acceptable evidence to the Imperial Clan Court system. Obviously, Nightwine could not shoot me here and deliver my rotting corpse to China within the month. I'd be unrecognizable."

Barker poured himself more tea from a cast-iron teapot. I noticed his cup was blue-and-white Canton ware and held not much more than a thimbleful. Everything pointed to Canton.

"Well, sir, as you have said before, he has not saved anything for his old age."

"I suppose the man didn't expect to live this long," he rumbled. "It wasn't for lack of trying on my part. But here we are prattling on when we need to be at work. Look at the time! I'll go upstairs to comb my hair and straighten my tie. Then we'll find a cab."

Recently I complained that I hadn't helped enough in our enquiries, that he was taking the lion's share and leaving the scraps for me. I didn't have his acumen, but I had a friendly manner and could question people without terrifying them. I had a working brain and had spent a little time at university, and I was now one of the best fighters in London despite my size, thanks to his tutelage.

Eleven years of training had taught me a few tricks of my own. I could have opened an agency myself; I was better trained and qualified than Hewitt. Also, I understood that Barker, having been raised in the East, didn't give compliments. I was always lacking. According to the Cantonese tradition, I was raised in the coddled West and had no stamina, no finesse, little ability. My headmaster in Wales had said the same thing when I was younger, but I was trying now. I understood my own strengths and weaknesses and no longer complained when I did our exercises in the garden in the extremes of heat or cold. When we practiced in the rain, I understood that he had done so during monsoons. I tried not to complain, though my friends will tell you I have a certain talent for it. It made the few compliments he gave especially encouraging.

"We aren't doing much," I said, as we walked to the cab queue in Newington Causeway. "People come to us and give a litany of problems. Then we go somewhere and ask people things. Government officials warn us off, and we argue or ignore them. It's dull stuff."

"You would rather be shot?"

"Shot at, but not necessarily shot," I remarked. "I've tried it. Can't say I cared for it."

"You'll get your wish, I'm certain of it," he said. "The Imperial Secret Service lads are known for their fighting abilities."

"Good," I replied. "I've been waiting to try my skills against a real Chinese boxer."

"What made you think you would fight just one?" Cyrus Barker asked. "They specialize in what you might call dirty tricks."

"Sir, according to the Marquess of Queensbury rules, our school is nothing but dirty tricks," I said.

The Guv paused, but he could not disagree. The day flew by with no results, and no clues as to where Nightwine or the *Osprey* might be. We locked our doors promptly at five thirty. I remembered as a child that merchants in my town of Gwent would keep their doors open long into the night. They still might do so, but here in London we expect our dinners at a timely hour. Mac came through with dinner for us. Our meal that night was catered by the nearby Elephant and Castle Public House. We enjoyed a fine sampling of traditional British fare: steak and kidney pie, mushy peas, and a Bakewell tart for dessert. He also pulled a few bottles of ale from the cellar, which Mac makes and bottles himself, since the water in South London is villainous.

After the meal we all went our separate ways, Barker to his kimono, his tea, and his books, an odd combination of Puritan classics from the age of Cromwell, and Asian classics in their original languages from a musty little shop near the docks. I had once been proud of my own bookcase, but since moving to the City I had been inspired by my friend Israel Zangwill into springing for a true library like his. I now possess several hundred volumes in my new study in Camomile Street. However, the books in my old room in Barker's house had been hard won in my earlier days and were like old friends. I settled in with an ancient copy of *The Faerie Queene* by Spenser.

It was a novel experience, being in my old room. My house can be raucous at times, with the baby crying and long conversations with Rebecca. The maid, Lily, and our nanny, Mrs. Skaleski were on hand as well, so it was not often that I could retreat to my study, and it was not proof against the bustle of activity outside my sanctuary door. Here the silence was profound. Barker rarely makes a sound overhead; he lives a monastic life in the evenings. I'm equally quiet. Once I purchased a gramophone. It caused such an uproar to Barker's tranquility that he made me return it the next morning, during working hours, or risk expulsion.

When I had read a couple of chapters, Jacob Maccabee shimmered in and stopped at my elbow. I looked up at him.

"A . . . person to see you, Thomas."

"Person?" I asked. "What sort of person?"

"Female. Stout. Broken English. Around sixty years of age."

"Mrs. Skaleski, our cook! I wonder what she could want."

I went downstairs to find the resident dragon had awakened. Harm, Barker's Pekingese, was circling the lobby door and caterwauling. I nudged him back with the toe of my slipper and squeezed through the doorway. There stood the quaint and homey figure of our nanny.

"Mrs. Skaleski," I said. "Has something happened?"

Before she could answer I was knocked off my feet. I fell into the grass near one of the urns that flanked the front door, and something began to attack my face.

"Daisy!" I cried. My face was lashed by her insistent tongue. She stood on my chest and wagged her tail enough to cause a breeze.

"She has been pining for you since you shut down the house, sir," she said in her faulty English. "She barks; she howls. She stands by the front door. She misses you all. She is, what is the word? Inconsolable!"

Just then there was a growl behind me. Mac had put Harm out the back door, but somehow he had escaped captivity. Daisy began running about the lawn, and Harm followed after her, baying his bark of alarm, which could be heard for a quarter mile. Daisy leapt into my arms until she was almost clamped around my head, while Harm circled my knees, snapping at her tail. Neither dog was especially young.

"Lad?" Barker said in my ear. Perhaps he, too, had climbed over the back gate.

"She's been frantic, sir. She misses us."

"That is to her credit," he answered. "What do you intend to do with her?"

"Do?" I asked around a mouthful of fur.

"She can't stay here. Harm won't allow it."

"Mrs. Skaleski," I said, sighing. "I'll take you back to your residence. It appears I'll be sleeping in my own bed tonight."

I slowly peeled the dog from my head and gave her to the good woman Then I turned to the Guv.

"I hope this doesn't inconvenience you," I said.

"You may come and go as you like, lad, you know that. Come, Harm."

He scooped up the frothing little dragon in his burly arms and carried him inside. I shrugged an apology to Mac, who burst out laughing.

"Such a little dog to cause such trouble," the nanny said, as I helped her into the cab a few minutes later, then climbed aboard with Daisy. I lifted the dog around to face me.

"You see what trouble you have caused?" I asked.

She licked my nose as we rode off into the night, bound for the city.

I realized then that Burns said it best. "The best-laid schemes o' mice and men gang aft agley." *The Faerie Queene* would have to wait.

CHAPTER 11

Sun Yat-sen was kept in the cell for four days without explanation. He was fed regularly by a brutish guard who never spoke, and when he tried to initiate a conversation, he was rudely shoved back onto his cot. Yat-sen wondered if the man was unable to speak.

Finally, the cell door was unlocked the morning of the fifth day and a man stepped inside. It was Tang, the fellow who had kidnapped him. He was a thin man in his late twenties with a queue, a round cap, and a gleaming gold tooth. It was clear that the man was grinning at his misfortune.

"Greetings, brother," he began.

"You are no brother of mine, I assure you," Sun replied.

Tang shrugged. "That is best for me, then. I wouldn't want to share your fate. Cigarette?"

"Thank you, no. I don't smoke."

The Chinese agent opened a small box and removed a cigarette, fat and poorly rolled.

The light of the match revealed Tang had poor skin and a scar above one eyebrow. After a puff, Tang took a chair and sat on it, crossing his legs.

"I demand to be released," Dr. Sun said.

"Grow wings and fly, then," Tang answered. "It's your only option."

"I demand to speak with someone from the British government!"

Tang looked about him at the miserable cell. "I don't see anyone here. If he should appear I'll tell him you are asking for him."

"I am being held here against my will! This is illegal! I need to speak with the Chinese ambassador."

"He's a busy fellow, I'm afraid."

"I must speak with someone!"

"Speak with me, then," Tang said. "How long have you been a revolutionary? Are there many of your kind in Hawaii? Yes, Doctor, we know all about you."

"You know nothing," Sun replied. "I'm merely a doctor who is trying to bring medicine to China."

"Nobody needs your tainted Western medicine, Dr. Sun. Or your traitorous ideas. You should have remained in Honolulu. I understand it is beautiful there, but alas, you will never see it again."

"What's to become of me, then?" the young doctor asked. He tried to appear calm, but his heart was racing. The question wasn't academic to him.

Tang shrugged. "When I saw you last, it was part of my official duties. Now I appeal to you as a friend. Confess that you attempted to take over Canton with your revolutionary ideas."

"Are you mad?" Sun cried. "We lodged a small student protest. A peaceful demonstration!"

"You are well-known in China. The emperor and the authorities are acquainted with your history. Perhaps it will be worth dying to have your name on everyone's lips."

Sun shook his head. "Don't be ridiculous. No one knows my name. I am a nobody."

"Not so, Dr. Sun Yat-sen. I predict your name will become well-known in just a few days."

Tang blew a mouthful of smoke in his face. The tobacco was cheap and rank. The doctor waved the smoke away.

"What will you do with me?" he demanded.

"We will wait a few days and smuggle you onto a ship. The emperor wants to meet you."

"He wants to meet me?"

"Yes, the noble emperor of China, Guangxu, wants to meet you in person so he can see you beheaded. I've heard he likes to watch the expressions of regret on a revolutionary's face change the second he meets his fate."

"This is England, not China," Dr. Sun argued. "If you wish to extradite me, you must let my imprisonment be made known to the British government. I don't believe Her Majesty will give me up so easily."

"She'll never know," Tang taunted him. "Everything is ready. The steamer is engaged, and you are to be bound and gagged and placed on board with no disturbance. There will be a Chinese gunboat waiting for us in Hong Kong Harbor in a week. You will be transferred on board and taken to the yamen in Canton for trial and execution. You should be impressed that His Excellency has gone to such trouble for a worthless little worm like you. You are to be an example to other nations not to come to China and try to influence us. We want no foreign revolutionaries there."

"Perhaps some of the crew will be sympathetic to my plight," Sun suggested.

"No, they are friends of Sir Halliday Macartney and will do what they are told." Tang shrugged his narrow shoulders and then stepped on the last of the cigarette. "He's the one that ordered the ship."

It took Yat-sen a few moments to master himself. Everything seemed hopeless.

"When are we leaving?" he asked.

"Sometime next week," Tang replied. "You'll be hidden among some cargo, which must be loaded."

"You are very cavalier about my death," Sun said.

"Not cavalier," Tang argued. "I look forward to it. I hope to be promoted to a high position for arresting you and securing your fate. When you stepped off that bus, it was one of the best things that has ever happened to me. Thank you very much. I'll even see you buried. Then I will drink some plum wine in your honor. You see? I am not such a bad fellow."

The secret service agent stood and turned to leave.

"Don't drink it just yet," Sun said between gritted teeth.

"There is nothing you can do," Tang said, opening the door. "No one is coming to rescue you. Your death is inevitable. You will die but your name will be remembered. Somewhere, I'm sure, Doctor."

The door swung shut behind him. Yat-sen moaned and buried his face in his pillow. Tang was right. No one was coming to rescue him. No one cared if he should live or die, save for the bloodthirsty emperor who wanted to watch him being beheaded.

Sun spent the rest of the day vacillating between prayer

and bouts of despair. Surely Tang was wrong, and someone was working for his release. He could only hope help would arrive before he was bundled onto a ship bound for China. However, he was a realist. Once the vessel left British shores, he was as good as dead.

CHAPTER 12

Barker was at the window again. To be precise, he was standing in the bow window, looking through the pane that faced Whitehall Street, as if mesmerized by the traffic rolling by. However, I doubt he saw anything there at all. He was stroking a spot under his lower lip in thought with a thick thumb. These scratchings often led to some kind of action on our part, so I let him think.

"Would you say we have a confrontational profession, Mr. Llewelyn?" he finally rumbled.

"Decidedly, sir," I said to his back. "One of the most confrontational occupations, I'd say."

"So far no one has bearded the lion."

"No doubt. Of which lion do we speak?"

"Sir Halliday Macartney," the Guv replied. "Mr. K'ing suspects the man is in the pocket of the Chinese ambassador,

Luo Fenglu. Macartney is a true Orientalist, but perhaps he has carried his interests in Asian arts and literature too far. He wants to be one of them, a self-styled scholar and minister within the Imperial Clan Court, the first Caucasian to do so. For whom would he truly be working? If given the opportunity he might betray his native country."

"Not unlike Sebastian Nightwine," I remarked.

Barker turned and regarded me from the brightest spot in the room. The man gleamed from his cuff links and tiepin to his brass-framed spectacles. His watch chain and his glossy boots completed the scene. He was Apollo in a morning coat.

"Precisely!" he cried, pointing at me as if I were his pupil and had won so many house points. "You won't find two such different men on the same continent, yet Nightwine has slipped into the embassy to consult him. What are those two men about? What subject attracts them both? Whatever it is, it cannot be wholesome for Dr. Sun, I suspect. If they collude, there is no telling what mischief they can cause."

Barker went over to his ornate smoking cabinet and stuffed a pipe with tobacco. He lit a match with a flourish and kindled it.

"How do we ask the Chinese embassy if they happened to have come across a spare revolutionary?" he continued. "I don't believe even Dr. Cantlie has had the courage to ask them. What is the worst that can happen?"

"I don't think I want to know the answer to that question, sir," I replied. "But I suppose we are going to find out. Enquiry agents rush in where angels fear to tread."

"Let us use that in our next advertisement in *The Times*," Barker suggested. "Come."

It was a cold day for autumn, and Whitehall Street was a long bar of frigid iron. The horses' shoes and the metal shod wheels of passing hansoms shot sparks across the cobblestones.

"What do you know about Macartney?" I asked, flagging a cab.

"Only that he is likely related to George Macartney, who founded the first British diplomatic embassy in China a century ago," Barker said, as we stepped up into our seats.

"Another Scotsman," I complained, climbing in after him. "London is lousy with them this year."

"Cheek," he responded. "Someone needs to take matters in hand. Why shouldn't it be us?"

Our cab horse trotted across the City until we reached the Chinese embassy, as English a building as one can find in London, a square, brown and white mansion of seven stories in Portland Place. There was no obvious flag flying outside the entrance, and I would have passed by without noticing what the establishment was, and very possibly had. I paid the driver while Barker descended from the cab and made his way into the building. When I entered, he was already speaking to a secretary, who looked no more Chinese than the building in which we stood. I anticipated a lengthy wait, but I had come prepared. I had a small pocket copy of George Gissing's *New Grub Street*. I read as we waited, while the Guv's hands rested on the ball of his stout cane. He sat without movement or conversation for a solid hour, like an automaton that had run to a standstill.

At last, a party of anonymous men came down the hall and departed the building. The secretary turned to us.

"Sir Halliday will see you, gentlemen," he said.

We rose and followed. Like the building, Macartney's office was an unorthodox mixture of oriental and occidental. There was a jade paperweight on his desk, and a penjing tree not too dissimilar from Barker's own. I hazarded a guess that had they not been on opposing sides the two Scots would have found plenty to discuss.

Macartney was a sturdily built fellow with graying hair and swags of side-whiskers like jib sails connecting his ears and lips. He wore an almost military suit to show his status as an envoy and ambassador. I couldn't imagine his work was easy, given the disparate importance of each country, and the current state of things in the East. Europe appeared to think that China was done, and ready to be stripped of its flesh, but many enemies had made that mistake before over the centuries.

Macartney was standing by a large globe near his desk. He held my partner's card in his hand and was studying it.

"Private enquiry agent," he read aloud as we were ushered into the room. "Is that some sort of detective?"

"Some sort," I admitted.

"I don't have any need for a detective, gentlemen," he stated, tossing the card into a small bin by his desk.

"Perhaps not," the Guv said. "But you might need the services of a solicitor."

Macartney frowned and puffed up his chest like a bantam.

"I don't know what you mean," he said.

"A young visitor here in London has unaccountably disappeared, Sir Halliday. It happened only a few days ago in this vicinity. He is wanted by the Qing government for his involvement in the demonstration in Canton last month."

"Did he participate in the demonstration?" the counselor asked.

"He did not," the Guv replied. "However, he wrote a letter to the emperor about the need for political reform."

Macartney pulled out his chair and settled behind his desk. It was of a reddish hue, and now that I was close to it saw that it was of a subtle Asian style, like K'ing's. I could picture it wrapped and lashed in the hold of a ship from Hong Kong. It had already traveled farther than all the men who built her, counted together.

"That was unwise," Macartney commented. "I haven't heard of such a fellow, but it appears he's in a good deal of trouble. Has he fled directly from Canton?"

I shook my head. "He crossed the Pacific to his native town in the Hawaiian Islands, then continued on through the Americas and then here."

"Who are you?" he asked.

"I'm the Llewelyn on the card you just pitched into the waste bin," I replied. "*Cartes de visite* are rather dear, you know. You could have just returned it."

Macartney blustered, but so far Barker had been sweetness and light. I'd seen men tossed in midair by this time. Of course, they weren't generally peers of the realm.

"We've been hired by the young man's English friends in London to find him," my partner explained. "He was supposed to attend services last Sunday at a nearby church, but he never arrived."

"We've seen no sign of him here," Macartney said brusquely. "I'm sure he would have given this place a wide berth."

"We thought perhaps he had blundered in here by accident," my partner continued. "Perhaps there was a misunderstanding, and he was detained or diverted. Mistakes occur from time to time and can't be helped. Perhaps the ambassador's servants apprehended the rascal by mistake, assuming him Chinese-born, and then were uncertain what to do with him."

I knew what Barker was doing. He was fabricating an excuse that would allow the embassy to retain its dignity and save face. It would be the easiest way for them to give up

Dr. Sun if indeed they had him in custody. It was a diplomatic way of escape.

"I'm sorry," Macartney said. "I know nothing of the matter. We are keeping no one here. We're still sorting out the events of the insurrection in Canton. It's all so distressing. I understand most of the participants were no more than lads. One could call it a student's march, really, but the emperor takes these kinds of demonstrations very seriously."

"Perhaps the ambassador is under the mistaken belief that the doctor is Chinese, while he is actually from the Hawaiian Islands," Cyrus Barker said.

"Was he born there?" the councilor asked.

"He moved there as a child, I understand."

"Then in the eyes of the Qing government, he still belongs to the emperor," Macartney replied. "If you require more help in this matter, I suggest you visit the Hawaiian embassy."

The Guv chuckled. "Sir Halliday, a gentleman as astute as yourself would be aware that there is no Hawaiian embassy here in Britain."

"Yes. A pity, isn't it?"

"A great pity indeed, sir. It would expedite matters."

"I'm afraid I cannot help you," the man said, shrugging. "I wish I knew where your young man is. What is his name?"

"Sun Yat-sen," Barker replied. "He is a practitioner of Western medicine, trained in Hong Kong. The very first Asian doctor of Western medicine, in fact. He is exceptional. And while his name is unknown at the moment, it may be very well-known in a few days."

Macartney lifted his bulk from the chair and offered a flipperlike hand. "Apparently, not exceptional enough to keep from getting lost in London. I hope you find your revolutionary, Mr. Barker."

The Guv nodded. "I will, sir. Of that I have no doubt. I shall put all my energy and resources into it. Tell me, have you received a notice from the Forbidden City offering a reward for him?"

"Not that I'm aware, but then I am just here to advise," Halliday blustered. "I don't generally notice such things."

"Is the ambassador in the building?" my partner asked. "Perhaps."

"Luo Fenglu is out of town. Also, he speaks English very poorly."

I knew it was a lie. The emperor would not send a man with poor English skills to England. He might sign a document he didn't understand. I wondered what his story was. I imagined the Colonial Office kept a file on him that would make interesting reading. Macartney acted the pompous windbag, but I didn't think him stupid. Working daily around the subtleties of the Chinese embassy would have been an education in itself.

"No matter," Barker stated. "I'm fluent in both Mandarin and Cantonese. I'll ask for an appointment."

The councilor's brows rose. It was as if he was noticing Barker for the first time.

"Tell me, is Sebastian Nightwine staying at the Savoy?" the Guv asked. "I saw him getting into a cab here the other day and need to have a word with him. We're old acquaintances."

"I-uh," Macartney began. "Who?"

"No matter. I'll find him myself. You might want to dig my card out of the bin. Luo Fenglu will want to see it. If not today, then certainly later this week. Come, Thomas."

I rose and bowed.

"Gào bié," I said to Macartney, before following after the

Guv. It was one of perhaps six words I knew in Mandarin. *Goodbye.* I was proud of myself for remembering it.

A minute later we stood on the pavement again. Hansoms and delivery vans rolled by. It seemed a typical day in London Town. Barker put his hands behind his back and began sauntering down the street. When he reached the corner of the building he turned. He was casually reconnoitering.

It was difficult to get a view of the upper stories so close to the embassy. Behind the front façade the building was a jumble of floors, wings, and alleyways. There was a loading bay in the back, and a ceremonial entrance in gold and red, like an imperial fantasy, which I assumed was for announcements to the press.

Barker continued to circle the property. He idled about in a narrow alley, leaning against the wall with a foot up against the brick. Cyrus Barker does a lot of things, but he does not idle. It's not in his nature.

He raised his head and looked behind him. I followed his gaze. A window sat high up on the wall, or rather, a window frame. It held no glass, only bars. What use would an embassy have for a room with barred windows? Not a respectable one, I thought.

The Guv next studied the alley's cobblestones. I didn't understand what he was looking for. He walked to one end of the alley, then to the other, which took us to the front entrance again. Then he returned to where we stood before, studying the ground as he walked.

"What's that?" he asked, pointing to something fluttering near the ground.

"It appears to be part of a celluloid collar," I said, reaching down and pulling it from a tangle of dead grass. I handed it to the Guv, noting marks upon it. They looked like pencil scribblings.

"'Help!'" Barker read. "'I am imprisoned inside the Chinese embassy. You are my only hope!'"

"Well, that seems simple enough," I said. "Let's do as he says. Or if you prefer, we can take this to Dr. Cantlie."

"It's not as simple as that, lad," the Guv said.

I looked over his shoulder. Two Chinamen in blue tunics and trousers entered from Portland Place. I looked in the other direction and saw two more coming at us from behind. One of them was heavily built, likely part of the Imperial Secret Service that Barker had warned me about. Of course they would come. Without doubt Sir Halliday Macartney had summoned them. We were a problem that needed to be dealt with quickly.

They were young and fit. Also, they were smiling. I imagined their jobs were boring for the most part. This was something to do, a bit of excitement in an otherwise dull day. We were two foreign devils putting our exceedingly long noses where they didn't belong. They had permission to knock us about a little, anything short of killing us. Macartney would come up with a story to tell whatever government services arrived to sweep up what was left of us.

I shucked my coat, wishing I had brought my pistol. It was safe and snug in a corner of my desk in Craig's Court. I only wished I were as safe.

CHAPTER 13

I raised my fists and settled into a crouch. I am five foot four, and most men I fight are taller than I. However, I am an instructor in antagonistics, which means I am an above average fighter, particularly because there are no rules in Asian boxing. I prefer not to be beaten, and Rebecca agrees with me. Therefore, I'll do whatever is necessary to finish a fight successfully.

Three of the four men in the alleyway were approximately my size. The fourth, a burly fellow with knuckles like steel bearings and bad teeth, would be taken on by the Guv, I hoped, along with one of mine. However, I had never fought an Asian before, let alone two, and the fact that they were Imperial Secret Service agents probably meant they could box. Well, box, kick, throw, eye gouge, and all the rest of it. I had been trained in how to fight two men before but had never had the opportunity to try it on government agents trained in China. How fortunate I was, I thought. Now I wouldn't have to search for a pair.

The trick was not merely to survive, though there was something in that. As I said, Rebecca would not approve of me brawling, especially if I arrived at the synagogue with a mouse under one eye. Her friends already thought me a liability, and it would embarrass her publicly. But it wasn't only my wife I was worried about. I didn't want to disappoint Cyrus Barker. I couldn't disgrace myself, for in doing so I would disgrace my teacher, which is about the worst thing one could do, especially if one is a junior instructor. The choices for the Guv would be to either drive me out of the school and retire in disgrace, or he'd have to start my training all over again. This would mean intense antagonistics classes with him every day for months, requiring many hours of the day and night that I'd rather spend with my wife and daughter. Rachel's father would become a mythical being she would only hear about in stories, like Father Christmas. I'd be out late at night and early in the morning, and that, considering I am constitutionally lazy, would be torture.

"Northern, lad!" Barker called.

Northern? I thought. What did that mean? He could be deucedly cryptic at times. Then it came to me. Barker had taught me a Southern Chinese form of boxing from Foochow, a suburb of Canton. This meant low stances and mostly hand techniques. The northern boxers up in the mountains beyond Peking were known for their high kicks, a more acrobatic style. I ducked just in time to avoid a boot that sailed over my head. Then I delivered a stout kick of my own, low and straight, to the inside of the fellow's knee. I didn't hear the crack, but he fell to the alley cobbles bellowing. It was music to my ears.

Matters didn't work out in my favor after that, but then they rarely do. I've grown accustomed to that by now. The big fellow decided to beat on me for practice before attempting to take on the Guv, not that I blamed him. He battered me a while with his ham-sized fists and clouted my ear so hard that I couldn't hear out of it for an hour. However, large fellows are slow on their feet. I managed to avoid being kicked.

I danced out of reach, avoiding his hands, glancing over his shoulder. Barker was smacking a fellow repeatedly against a brick wall. The other was unconscious on the ground a dozen feet away. One could almost hear the Guv humming to himself. He enjoys his work.

The giant—well, he was a giant to me—seized my lapels and pulled me off my feet. I objected by scraping his face with my nails, and poking my thumbs in his eyes. Then I jammed a knuckle into the flesh just below his Adam's apple. He gave a harsh cough and pushed me away. I landed on my feet. This little Welshman has claws, and don't you bloody well forget it.

I only had a few seconds to respond before he rallied. As soon as my foot came into contact with the ground I leapt forward and kicked him hard in the cobbles. He seized the tender organ, and I clapped both his ears with my open palms, bursting his eardrums and throwing off his balance. The man could not hear and barely focus. Unfortunately for him, Cyrus Barker was now behind him. Perhaps the Guv was waiting for me to finish and had come to hurry me along. The bully turned and Cyrus Barker laid him out with a single punch. It was worth the price of admission for his little demonstration on this big bully. The shame of losing the fight was now on the Chinaman.

"Thank you," I said.

"I apologize, Thomas, for stealing your opponent," the Guv said. "He turned my way. I didn't want him to escape."

"Not at all, sir. He is a large fellow and I appreciated the help. I hope the others didn't cause you any trouble."

"No, no," he answered, shaking his head. "In fact, I'm rather disappointed. I was hoping for a scrap, but it was over too quickly. Obviously, they assumed we didn't know what we were about."

"They were overconfident," I agreed. "But they had no way of knowing we were more than just a pair of average blokes. What shall we do with them?"

"Just leave them, Thomas. I don't think they can hide their defeat from Sir Halliday Macartney for long."

That was all. There was no "Good work, lad," or "You defeated him handily." No, in Barker's eyes I had defeated him because I was at a certain level of my training. He was right, I supposed, but still, one likes to be appreciated. They are spare with their praise, these boxing masters, I must say. Ah, well. I decided to be philosophical about the matter. At least I wouldn't be going to service with a black eye. For the record, I had been lucky, but I don't use that word around Barker. He doesn't believe in luck.

"So, Dr. Sun is behind those bars, is he?"

"Most likely, Thomas," he replied. "As you said, there is no logical reason for an embassy to have barred windows. The fact that they installed them when they built the structure is suspicious in itself."

"We should have brought our pistols, sir," I remarked.

"Aye, but what's the fun in that?"

There is a certain bloodthirstiness in my partner, I've noticed. For example, from time to time he enjoys smacking some poor devil against a building as a kind of sport or exercise. I was glad he was on the side of good, or he'd have been a terror as a gang leader on the docks.

"Shall we go?" I asked.

"Aye," my partner replied. "Let Sir Halliday sort them out. He'll understand the message we sent."

Sent? I asked myself. Perhaps my partner hadn't stepped into the alley innocently.

"Are ye well, lad? You took a few punches to the head."

"My neck is sore, sir, but then you're always calling us a stiff-necked generation."

Barker threw back his head and laughed. I give him my best bon mots daily, which seem to sail over his head, and then he laughs at this.

Back in Portland Place we passed along the street like upright citizens, doffing our hats at ladies and nodding at men, as if we hadn't just trounced four men in an alleyway. Still, I couldn't hear in one ear. I hoped it wouldn't swell like one of those professional boxers. Rebecca would hate that. She'd ban me from being seen in public until it stopped swelling.

"What shall we do next?" I asked or possibly shouted. I couldn't be certain how loud I was.

"If this collar is what I think it is, we may have found Sun Yat-sen," he said. "I'd like to talk to Dr. Cantlie and see what he's been doing over the past few days. Would that we all had a friend like him."

It was a short walk to the doctor's house, and the weather had somewhat improved. I could understand how a visitor might become lost in the honeycomb of streets nearby, where the mansions were all uniform and anonymous. Even the shop signs were discreet, as if they apologized for bothering potential patrons with hoardings.

We reached the doctor's door, where we straightened our

ties and adjusted our clothing to conceal the fact that we had just been brawling on a Tuesday morning in a respectable part of town. The butler showed us into a snug study where we inspected the titles of the books from our chairs. They consisted mostly of medical texts. *What a waste of prime shelf space*, I thought, but then I prefer fiction. There are fewer chromolithographic diagrams of vivisected bodies.

Cantlie appeared five minutes later, full of apologies.

"Have you found Yat-sen?" he asked.

"We believe we have," the Guv replied. "It appears your pupil has been locked in a cell deep within the Chinese embassy these last few days. The councilor to the Chinese ambassador, Sir Halliday Macartney, is a rascal. He's got Dr. Sun jugged like a hare, but denies any knowledge of his existence. We found this in an alleyway."

He extracted the strip of celluloid collar from the pocket of his coat and held it out to Dr. Cantlie.

"I believe that is his handwriting, yes, sir. In fact I'm sure of it."

The Guv nodded. "I find it doubtful that Ambassador Fenglu would be hiding a second revolutionary illegally in this city. How is your work coming along?"

"I convinced *The Times* to print a small article about Sun's disappearance. I also spoke to the Queen's private secretary, a fellow name Bigge, but was unable to get word to Her Majesty herself, not that I expected him to."

"We've met the gentleman in question," my partner replied. "I can't say I was impressed with him. Who else have you spoken to?"

"Everyone I could think of," Cantlie said. "I saw the Lord Mayor, Scotland Yard, the Foreign Office, nearly thirty people in all."

"Try the socialist publisher, William T. Stead," my partner

suggested. "This is just the sort of matter he likes to champion. Injustice is his forte."

"Thank you, I shall."

"You look tired, Doctor, if I may say it."

"I haven't been sleeping well, worrying about Sun. I'm very concerned that they will smuggle him aboard a cargo ship in the middle of the night."

"I've got several Chinese friends who are watching the docks for us. They are a close-knit group, and any white men marching an Asian to a pier will be noted. I suspect Dr. Sun found his way to Limehouse at least once. He would be curious."

"Did he, by Jove?" Cantlie asked. "That little scamp."

"For all his innocence, I suspect Yat-sen has some natural abilities for organizing protests or he would not have a price on his head," Barker observed. "Tell me, are you familiar with a fellow named Sebastian Nightwine?"

"The famous Darwinist?" Cantlie asked.

"No, his son. He visited the Chinese embassy and has been involved in several illegal activities over the years. I suspect his arrival has to do with Sun Yat-sen. It's possible he left Southern China shortly after the reward was offered, following Sun to Hawaii and then here. He would have been angry when Sun more or less strolled into the embassy of his own accord, but it's likely he and Macartney have an arrangement. Nightwine will take Sun back to China to be executed and they will split the reward."

"Why, Mr. Barker?" Cantlie asked. "What are Macartney's motivations for splitting the reward?"

"A sound question," the Guv remarked. "There are several other men in London who escaped from Chinese justice, as well. Only the opportunity to profit from these rewards would draw Nightwine back to London. A single arrest won't provide enough money for him for very long. He is continually in need of funds."

Dr. Cantlie puzzled over this information. It sounded suspect even to me, and I had been involved for a decade in Barker's feud with Sebastian Nightwine.

"How did you come by this information?" Dr. Cantlie asked.

"Because I myself am one of the men wanted by the Qing government."

It was one step beyond what the doctor could accept. He turned to me, and I nodded.

"What did you do to draw the ire of the Chinese government?" he asked.

"I entered the Empress Dowager's bedchamber in the palace in Peking, which is forbidden. I prefer not to discuss the matter further. It is unsavory."

Again, Cantlie turned to me for confirmation. This time I just shrugged my shoulders. An idea came to me, then. I should be asking Ho and Etienne about Barker's past. Perhaps even Lady Ashleigh.

"I'll have to believe you," Cantlie finally said. "No one would make up such a tale."

"There you are, then," Barker said, as if that settled the matter.

"What's to be done?" the doctor pressed. "Sun can't be smuggled to China and executed."

"Let me consider the matter. At some point, Macartney's going to attempt to smuggle Sun Yat-sen out of the embassy. We could overpower the guards or stop the cab when it reaches the docks. We have choices, which is always a good thing."

"What about this Nightwine person?"

Barker looked at him gravely. "A final reckoning between us is long overdue. Leave that matter to me."

"I feel sad about this, gentlemen," Dr. Cantlie said. "Sun is a sensitive soul. His being sent to China to be executed would be on my conscience for the rest of my life. I'm sure Dr. Manson feels the same. Find some way to release him, I beg you."

"I have several options to explore, Doctor," Barker said. "I need to decide which one has the best chance of working."

"I cannot believe the Yard wouldn't help in any way," he complained.

Barker gave him a cold smile. "The laws have been set up by government officials to tie our hands in matters of international significance. If you are frustrated, imagine how Scotland Yard feels. Was there any group to whom you spoke which seemed likely to help? We can't do this alone."

"The dockworkers, Mr. Barker," Cantlie responded.

"God bless them," Barker murmured. "They won't let a Chinaman be forced onto a boat illegally. Even if they consider the Chinese to be taking their jobs, they have a strong belief in right and wrong."

"Is there anyone else you can recommend I speak to that I haven't?"

"Just one more, if you're brave enough," my partner said. "He runs a gambling and opium den in Limehouse. His name is K'ing. He supports the revolution. You could consider him the leader in London. He represents the Heaven and Earth Society here."

"Triads! How will I find the place?" the doctor asked.

"You speak fluent Mandarin, Dr. Cantlie," Barker said. "It shouldn't be difficult."

My partner stood. He had a habit of ending a conversation

on his terms. He shook our client's hand and left. I raised my bowler and raced after him.

"Don't ask about my time in Peking," the Guv warned me when I jumped into the cab.

"It would be indelicate, sir," I acknowledged. I tried to imitate his accent, but my voice is not low enough. His drags the floor.

"Where shall we go next?" I asked.

"I'm hungry. Let's go to Ho's."

"Mmm," I said. "Pork dumplings in soy sauce. A little fried rice on the side."

"Precisely."

We hailed a cab and crossed into the Strand, which led to the Commercial Road. Soon we reached Limehouse and turned south toward the docks. We found a familiar narrow road and skirted the Reach until we saw our destination.

"Oh, my word!" I cried when I saw it. The old door to the tunnel had been blown off its hinges. The water over the tunnel that led to Ho's restaurant was brown and muddy.

"Ho!" Barker cried, as he leapt from the carriage.

CHAPTER 14

We ran to the bank of the bend near Limekiln Dock and found the water gurgling and murky over the area where Ho's tearoom lay. The establishment is reached by an underground tunnel, and people entered through the tunnel door in semidarkness, descended the staircase, crossed the long, echoing passageway, and finally ascended into the tearoom. At this time of day there were patrons in the restaurant. I only hoped people were not in the tunnel when it collapsed.

"It might have been a bomb," I reasoned. "But the tunnel was old. One loose brick and all that stinking water would pour in. Still, the tunnel is empty most of the time."

I was trying to convince myself as well as Barker. Ho and I didn't have the most cordial of relationships, but I hoped he was safe. I couldn't picture London without him.

"It's too much of a coincidence that Nightwine should arrive in London and a second of his enemies is mysteriously attacked," Cyrus Barker stated. I could see this upset him, though he tried not to show it. The closest thing he had to a mentor might lie under a pile of rubble in the river below us.

We heard a voice calling in Mandarin and looked about for the source. There were a handful of Chinamen on the roof of Ho's building on the other side of Limekiln Hill. The restaurant was on the ground floor. After the explosion, finding the tunnel blocked, they must have climbed to the roof, and were now trapped there.

"Thomas, get a rope," Barker ordered.

Anywhere else in London I would have been hard-pressed to find such a thing, but this was Dockland, and I, a dockwalloper, a student of such exotic places, where two cultures met and mingled, or sometimes didn't. It was a kind of test. Did I have the ingenuity to find a place that sold rope at a moment's notice? In fact, I did. A chandlery was nearby that sold stout sailing rope by the yard. I rushed in and bought almost more than I could carry. On the way back to Ho's entrance, it writhed like a live python, and I was perspiring freely when I returned, but it was worth it to see Barker silent nod of satisfaction. He threw the rope up to the men waiting on the roof as easy as you please. Ho was not among the patrons, waiters, and cooks that I could see. He should have been there.

After the rope was securely tied to a ventilation pipe, the men began to descend. The cooks, clad in trousers and singlets, ran to Barker, all shouting at him at once in Mandarin or Cantonese. A few moments later, the Guv stepped out of the crowd and seized my arm.

"He's missing, lad," he said. "He was standing in front of the door when the tunnel exploded. Like most of them, he was covered in cuts and bruises, but he was able to direct them onto the roof. When the last man reached back to help him up as well, he was gone. We must look inside the tea-room."

The Guv motioned me forward, perhaps to see my technique in ascending a rope. It turned out to be better than either of us expected. After several years of antagonistics training, I was in the best shape of my life. I swarmed up the rope, then helped my partner over the parapet. Once on the roof, we flew down the stairwell.

It was dark inside, and the dining room, while intact, was full of rubble. Barker and I dug through it to see if anyone was trapped inside and if there was any idea which way Ho had gone. We made our way back to the roof and looked for the fellow who seemed to be in charge. He was the headwaiter, whom we knew well from our many trips to the tearoom.

"Was Sebastian Nightwine here?" the Guv demanded.

"Who?" the Chinaman asked.

"A white-haired Englishman," my partner said. "He's large and imposing. You would have noticed him."

"No one was here who matches that description," the fellow replied. "One of the other waiters told me he saw a woman at the entrance. Moments later, we heard an explosion. When we couldn't reach the tunnel, we decided to go up to the roof."

"Are any of the other men badly injured?"

"Two of them are hurt worse than the others."

We milled about among the staff, all of whom were disoriented and distressed, asking if anyone had seen which way Ho might have gone, but in their panic to escape, no one had noticed. We sent one of the younger men to get a doctor to see to the two who were badly injured. He returned with a traditional bone-setter in tow within minutes. The Chinese would not trust an English physician.

"I had intended to turn Sebastian over to the authorities," Barker said. "Now I am seriously considering killing him with my own hands."

"Sir, you already did kill him, if you recall."

Barker flashed a wicked smile. On the rare occasions when one successfully draws a smile out of him, one wishes one didn't. His canines are sharp.

"So I did," he said. "He's a hard man to kill, but I refuse to be stripped of all my friends without seeking some kind of reprisal. He has brought this to my door, and he must pay the consequences."

I considered arguing with him but stopped myself. I had been forced to move my wife and child south, and had sent the servants away for who only knew how long. If Barker was seeking someone to help him bring Nightwine to book for his many crimes, I was his man.

I wasn't one of the crew of the *Osprey*, although I helped him from time to time, I wasn't aboard when the warrant for the crew had been proclaimed by the emperor in far-off Peking. Still, I was fairly certain Nightwine would try to kill me as well if I gave him the chance. He'd make no money from it but would have the satisfaction of watching me die. I'd done all I could to badger and heckle him, because that's what I do to people I despise. Why make it easy on men like him, I say.

Crossing through the restaurant to the tunnel entrance, I watched the muddy water flow below my feet. I must have walked through that tunnel hundreds of times. Barker dined here at least once a week. I'd grown accustomed to the exotic fare enough that I craved it. Fried pork in sweet and sour sauce, braised chicken legs, fried vegetable rolls, and pan-fried prawns. Would Ho's ever open its doors again? Would we ever find the Guv's closest confidant and friend? I vowed that we would.

I considered Ho a fixture in London, like the Tower of London. He and I had an adversarial relationship, which we hadn't yet resolved. He always said a Westerner could not be trained in Eastern arts, considering us like a pampered breed of dogs who won't obey commands. In his opinion, we did not have the temperament for hard work and sacrifice. He talked of China as if he thought it the most wonderful place on earth, but it sounded barbaric to me. He was exiled here because he, like my partner, had made himself an enemy of the Qing emperor. There is often a cost for being an associate of Cyrus Barker. Death follows him about like a lapdog. It's a troubling thought when one is his partner.

I shut the door and turned away, trying to forget the possibility that I would die in the Guv's service, as my predecessor had. His name was Quong, and he had been found floating in the Thames nearby as a warning. I would prefer to die in my own bed, surrounded by generations of Llewelyns after a long life, if you don't mind. I tried not to think about the danger. After all, I'd survived close to a dozen years in the enquiry trade so far. That in itself was a kind of miracle, although Rebecca claims it wasn't for lack of trying. Barker dives headlong into danger and I feel the need to get him out of it. He's done the same for me on countless occasions, albeit at the last minute.

The Guv and I made our way back to the street, where the bone-setter was treating his patients. Barker was still on edge. I could see his blood was up. I steered him into a coffee shop, where I ordered two hot cocoas, hoping to calm him. He didn't care for sweets but would take a cup of chocolate now and again. It arrived in Russian-looking glass cups with pewter handles. They appeared to be as fragile as gossamer, and I thought Barker would break one with his rough hands, but he calmed himself and was careful with the cup. I felt I must ask him questions without raising his ire again.

"Is it possible that Ho and Paul Beauchamp are dead?" I asked.

"It is," he admitted. "We were near Beachy Head, the tallest point along the south coast. Paul might have been dashed to the rocks below. However . . ."

"However, Nightwine might use him as a bargaining chip. A hostage to be traded."

"It's possible," my partner agreed, wiping his thick mustache on a serviette. "There is a reward for his head, quite literally."

"Can the Qing government put out a reward for an Englishman?" I asked. "I would think our own government would have something to say about that."

"I have no idea, lad," my partner admitted. "However, the Manchus are more inclined to overreach than to be timorous. That's what comes of owning a fifth of the earth's landmass. For all England's power, we are a flea on China's hide. I learned that to my detriment during the Taiping Rebellion."

Barker took another sip of his cocoa and strained his mustache again. It is thick, black as pitch, and extends to his chin in the Chinese manner. With the stylized brass dragon holding his spectacles together, he made a most oriental Scotsman.

"I wish young Dr. Sun good fortune," he said. "But an incredible number of hurdles would need to be surmounted for China to be wrested from the grip of the Manchus. It might take decades. The country would have to be shaken to rubble and rebuilt."

He sipped again, and I felt that his words were more for his own benefit than mine.

"K'ing's words worry me," he continued. "These Boxers. It's a peasant uprising. Few are trained to fight, they're armed with farm implements, and there are few provisions. It is a ragtag army, against a government with a navy, artillery, and allies it can call on if needed."

"Including Britain?" I asked.

"Let us hope not, Thomas. As K'ing said, there are several British outposts in China now. My sympathies are with the Boxers, but if the European compounds are sacked and citizens slaughtered, we might see a war larger than any in history."

He gave a sigh and finished his cocoa.

"Thank you, Thomas," he said. "I needed the drink."

Barker stood, and I left some coins on the table.

"Where would Sun Yat-sen find himself if such a situation occurred?" I asked as we left the shop.

"I doubt an army of angry Boxers shall care much about an intellectual student from an island they've never heard of. Yat-sen's chances of accomplishing his objectives are practically naught. If we rescue him, perhaps we can talk sense to him, but otherwise his odds of survival are negligible at best. If he's wise, he'll cut his losses and return to his island, but I suspect his time in Hong Kong and Canton has made him a zealot."

"Shall we return and look for Ho?" I asked.

"No, Thomas. If he is to be found, his employees will find him. He owes them pay. I'm more concerned about what Nightwine is doing."

CHAPTER 15

I must confess that when I first saw our clerk, Jeremy Jenkins, on that fateful day in 1884 when applying for the position of Cyrus Barker's assistant, I was not impressed with him. I wasn't so sure that I wanted to be an enquiry agent's assistant, but I believed I could very well be a clerk for one. Most certainly I could do better than this casual fellow at the front desk, smoking a B&H cigarette and reading a copy of the *Illustrated Police News* right in front of the applicants. When I came to the front desk, I could smell the odor of fermented hops emanating from him. He didn't care tuppence that he was surrounded by people more qualified than he, or at least that was my impression. I didn't know then that he was the son of an infamous forger with whom my would-be employer was impressed, and that a few of the paintings in the offices which one would take for a Turner or a Millais had been tossed off by his clerk merely to give the place a touch of gentility. His skills, aside from general clerking, included creating copies of any bits of identification required, making hoardings of all sorts, and scribing false business or trade cards.

Lastly, he was the Cerberus at the gates of No. 7, Craig's Court. When a visitor appeared, Jenkins took a card and delivered it via a silver salver to Barker's hand. I thought it an affectation, an eccentricity that Barker accepted. It took me years to work out that it allowed us time to decide whether or not to reach for our revolvers. In turn, Jenkins let in fellows such as our friend Detective Inspector Terence Poole of Scotland Yard or J. M. Hewitt, without a second glance. He wasn't merely a clerk and would defend his office and its occupants with his antiquated Beaumont-Adams revolver, and his life, if necessary.

All in all, he was an eccentric choice for a clerk, but there isn't a better one in all London, in my opinion. Or perhaps I should say he is the perfect clerk for an enquiry agent's offices. We are lucky to have him.

A man appeared at our door that afternoon, a tall, thin, elegant fellow in a Savile Row suit that would have cost Jenkins a month's wages if not two. Our clerk ushered the visitor into our inner office without a moment's hesitation. The fellow entered and sat in our visitor's chair, removing a gray top hat that matched his suit. Then he ran a hand through his light-colored hair.

"Greetings, gentlemen," he said.

"Hesketh," Barker acknowledged with a nod.

Our visitor was Hesketh Pierce of the Foreign Office. The man exuded governmental intrigue and professionalism.

"Whenever your name comes up, I am assigned to come

see you," the fellow remarked. "And for the record, your name comes up frequently. Why is that?"

"You never visit otherwise," I answered. "No cards, no flowers."

"Cheek!" he replied. "You spoke to a Chinese government counselor."

"We did," the Guv admitted.

"The man was displeased," Pierce said. "As a matter of fact, he complained about you."

"I'd have been insulted if he hadn't," Barker rumbled.

"He claimed you believe a foreign visitor is being held at the Chinese embassy."

My partner leaned back in his chair and folded his hands over his stomach.

"I'm sorry to inform you," I said, "but the Colonial Office has been here already. You're an also-ran."

"The Colonial Office couldn't find its left ear with a diagram," Pierce quipped. "Would you care to tell me what you gentlemen have been doing to arouse the Chinese embassy's ire?"

Barker cleared his throat. "We believe the Chinese embassy has taken a young man by force and is keeping him prisoner pending a return to Canton to be summarily tried and executed."

"I see," Hesketh said. "Sir Halliday Macartney is most unhappy with your interference."

"I invite Sir Halliday Macartney to jump up his own nose," I replied, making Pierce smile.

"He isn't the most pleasant of fellows, is he?" the Foreign Office man admitted.

"Indeed not," my partner agreed.

"I'm not a dentist, Barker. Must I pull teeth?"

The Guv frowned. "Very well. There is a young man

newly arrived from Canton named Dr. Sun Yat-sen. He was taken to the Hawaiian Islands as a child, and was raised there, but later went to Hong Kong and studied Western medicine. While there, he fell in with a crowd of student protesters. He took part in a protest and later fled to his home after the government suppressed the demonstration. Unfortunately, he wrote a damning letter while in China which found its way into the Chinese emperor's hands. He was not pleased."

"The man is Chinese born, but raised as a Hawaiian?" Pierce asked.

"He is," the Guv agreed, nodding.

"As you probably know, as far as the imperial government is concerned, as a Chinese, one is subject to the emperor forever. Was this young man aware that he was putting himself in such extreme danger?"

Barker went to his smoking cabinet and chose a pipe from his arsenal. He stuffed it and returned to his chair. Then he struck a vesta on a small ceramic striker on his desk, and lit it with deep breaths, seemingly in no hurry whatsoever to answer. Pierce looked on, bemused.

"We don't know," the Guv replied. "From what I've been told, Dr. Sun seems a very callow young man. Intelligence is not necessarily accompanied by wisdom."

"Did Macartney acknowledge they had the young man?" Pierce asked.

"He did not."

"May I ask for whom you are working?"

"He was hired by Dr. Sun's former tutor, Dr. James Cantlie, who recently returned from Hong Kong," I replied, desiring to be included in the conversation.

Hesketh nodded, deep in thought. "How did Dr. Sun happen to disappear?"

"He was to meet Dr. Cantlie and his wife at a local church on Sunday morning," Barker explained. "However, he didn't know the city well. It's possible he walked by the embassy without realizing it was nearby. We met a few members of the Imperial Secret Service. Have you encountered them before?"

"Once or twice," Pierce admitted. "They are contemptuous of our rules, believing the counselor can get them out of any scrape. I suspect they are changed often to retain anonymity. Is there a reward on Dr. Sun's head?"

"There is," Barker acknowledged.

"That complicates matters."

"No, this complicates matters," the Guv replied. "Someone else visited the embassy yesterday. A man named Sebastian Nightwine."

Pierce didn't take notes. He was one of those individuals who remembers everything. He was probably also captain of the cricket club at university and the youngest son of an earl, may he choke on his silver spoon.

"Nightwine," he repeated. "Isn't that one of the Prince of Wales's cronies?"

"You're well-informed."

"I have to be," Pierce replied. "You believe this Sun fellow is being held in the embassy? To what end?"

"They'll smuggle the lad onto a boat, sail him to Canton or Peking, and behead him."

Hesketh nodded. "I see. And how is Nightwine involved?"

"I suspect he is seeking to claim at least part of the reward for himself with Macartney's aid. He came back to London from China and has been seen going into the embassy."

Pierce had been sitting with one leg crossed over the other. He uncrossed it now and leaned forward. "How much is the reward?"

"A few hundred pounds I should imagine," Barker said between puffs.

"Worth the effort, then," Pierce said, one corner of his mouth raising.

"Mr. Nightwine and I have a history," the Guv told him. "We were once partners. I captained a ship for him in China."

"I can imagine you as a ship's captain," Pierce said. "Is your intent to rescue this fellow Sun, or to avenge yourself against Nightwine?"

"The first, since we have a client," Barker replied. "The second is merely old business."

"There's another matter," I said. "It is unproven but highly likely that Nightwine's daughter, Sofia Ilyanova, may be here in London, as well. If you recall, she was the one who winged the tsarevich last time she was here. I have no proof, but she often follows her father about."

"You gentlemen should have led the conversation with that piece of information," Pierce said, looking irritated. "Can her presence be verified? I would think a professional assassin a work of fiction, but most of your warnings over the years have proved true. The two of you do get yourselves in scrapes. Do you know where Nightwine is staying?"

"He's at the Savoy, of course," my partner answered. "He has expensive tastes. I have an associate watching him."

"Really?" Pierce asked. "Who?"

"J. M. Hewitt. A private detective. His office is near the end of this court."

"Heard of him, but we haven't met."

"He's competent enough," Barker rumbled. "I've used him before. Our agency is small, as you can see."

"Very small," the Foreign Office man said. "Most agencies have at least five operatives."

"Aye, well, I've had an assistant die on my watch," the Guv replied. "I can barely keep this one fellow safe. I'd be hamstrung trying to keep five among the living."

Pierce nodded. "I've been promoted. I understand what it means to hold other men's lives in your hands."

"Congratulations," Barker stated, but it was said with no inflection.

There was a momentary pause. Hesketh Pierce cleared his throat and shifted in his chair.

"You know why I'm here, then," he said.

Cyrus Barker nodded. "Aye, I do. Have you brought anyone with you?"

"Just one constable. Do you intend to cut up rough like last time?"

"No, I don't believe so. Bram Cusp is my solicitor. He'll get us released soon enough."

"You're arresting us?" I asked incredulously.

"Of course. I could have had Scotland Yard do it, but I thought you deserved better treatment."

"Of what am I charged?" I demanded.

"Causing an affray," Pierce said. "Macartney is just trying to get you out of the way."

"While he's bundling a young fellow into the hold of a cargo shipbound for China," Barker rumbled.

"Perhaps," Pierce agreed. "He's flexing his muscles. He's got a reputation at the Foreign Office for being a complete toady to the Qing government. I suspect he will eventually retire to China after his time here is finished, and make himself useful to the Qing government over there."

"Sebastian Nightwine might wish the same," the Guv said. "By chance, do you know if he has presented the Queen with a map of Tibet? He was trying to peddle it to our government the last time he was here. It's only a possible lead."

"No, but it might be of interest to find out. There's a reception tomorrow night, which I plan to attend."

"Will we go to 'A' Division, then?" I asked. "They're still unhappy about our breaking out of one of their cells last year."

"We'll find out, I'm afraid," he said. "It has been rather quiet lately."

"I could punch you if it would help," I offered. "That could liven matters a bit."

He raised a brow. "You could try."

"May I have time to warn my solicitor that I'm about to be arrested?" Barker asked.

Pierce pulled an expensive watch from his pocket and consulted it.

"Go ahead. I'm in no especial hurry."

We waited while my partner arranged for our release. At this stage in my career an afternoon in "A" Division was only a minor irritation. At least Rebecca was not in town to hear of it.

"Bracelets?" I asked, lifting my arms.

"I don't carry any, and the constable has only one pair," Pierce said. "I think I can trust you gentlemen."

Blast, I thought. Now if the opportunity presented itself, we couldn't escape. It was a matter of honor. Barker and Pierce were ahead of me, while I walked beside the constable, who was doing his best to look intimidating. He was rail-thin, and looked as if a stiff wind could carry him away. I don't know who hires them these days. I had to admit it was the most casual arrest I had ever endured. The day was cool, and leaves blew in every direction in Whitehall Street. It was almost pleasant, by enquiry agent standards, not that there is ever a good day to be arrested.

"Mr. Barker and Mr. Llewelyn!" the desk sergeant at "A" Division bawled to us as we passed. "Welcome home!"

"Good afternoon, Sergeant Kirkwood," Barker replied.

"Are you visiting or will you be staying for a while?"

"That remains to be seen."

"Sergeant, I'm with the Foreign Office," Pierce said with authority. "These gentlemen must be incarcerated immediately, but I expect that their solicitor will be along soon. Will I need to speak to one of your inspectors?"

"Yes, sir," Kirkwood replied. "But we'll relieve you of your burden and you can wait for the next available inspector."

I looked about. The few officers I could see from the lobby entrance seemed available enough, chatting over their desks to their comrades, or shuffling papers with an air of boredom.

Kirkwood's suggestion was merely for show. The various intelligence agencies considered themselves in competition with one another. They'd rather help a bear out of a trap unarmed than be seen aiding the elite intelligence services, those university educated scions of wealthy families. Pierce was all right, I suppose, but my sympathies were with the men in blue.

We sat on an ancient bench by the front door, while Pierce went in search of a fellow who didn't look deliberately lazy or thick. We were within ten feet of the entrance to Scotland Yard and had escaped through the front door the last time we were here, which meant the turnkey would start foaming at the mouth when he saw our faces. I wanted to avoid him if possible, and we didn't particularly owe the Foreign Office any favors. I gave my partner a questioning look, but he shook his head. Blast.

It had been fun escaping from the cells at Scotland Yard the first time. I believe we were the first to have done so in these hallowed halls, which made us a legend of sorts. Some of the prisoners had held the turnkey through the bars, further darkening his reputation. However, Pierce had been a gentleman about letting us follow him unfettered and had even given us the opportunity to call our solicitor. We'd been treated as gentlemen, even though we actually weren't, and never could be. However, we had given our word, which was our bond. Of course, we hadn't exactly promised. We hadn't actually spoken those precise words. The toe of my shoe began to rock with the impulse to bolt out the door.

"Thomas," Barker chided, his voice at its lowest register, somewhere in the basement. I crossed my arms and sulked.

An officer came presently to deliver us to the cells, looking a little surprised that we were without chains while standing so near the door. He led us back to the cells, which are generally reserved for the worst prisoners in London. Anyone from among the other districts who looks as if he's capable of causing extreme chaos is brought into the caring bosom of "A" Division. We should have felt flattered, I suppose.

I did the wrong thing when we met the turnkey again in his own personal kingdom. I grinned. It wasn't intentional, rather like when one is caught by the headmaster defacing a locker with one's penknife at school. I didn't mean to do it, it just happened. I'm certain behind his black-lensed spectacles, Barker closed his eyes in disappointment.

The turnkey, a rascally looking old fellow with the lower half of his face covered in downy gray whiskers, glared at us in triumph. His name was Proudfoot, if I recall. I wondered what indignities we would be subjected to. First of all, we were forced to turn out our pockets. It had been a little pearl-handled penknife I kept in my waistcoat pocket that allowed us to make our escape on the previous visit. I must point out here that the escape almost a year ago was all the Guv's doing, and I was appalled at the time. If it weren't for the outgoing commissioner of police being a friend of his, we might have been sent to a real prison. Unless we were shot, of course. It isn't often that the yard breaks out the artillery.

The turnkey thrust us rudely into a cell. Not all of them are uniform; some are for more sophisticated prisoners, former MPs, or men of business defrauding their constituents. Then, they descended in a gradient scale to the worst of humanity, the near mad murderers, the violent and insane. We were placed in the final, of course, mainly out of spite. The cell was revolting.

"Here!" a voice came. It was the officer who had escorted us to our cell.

"What is it?" the wizened jailer demanded.

"His solicitor has just posted bail. They're free to go."

"What?" the man demanded. "No! I refuse! They are mine! I'll release them tomorrow. Give me the one night at least!"

"You know the rules, Charlie."

My grin broke out again, but it was with relief. The constable led us back to the front desk, where we met Bram Cusp, our solicitor, the best in London in my opinion. He was talking to Hesketh Pierce as if they were old acquaintances.

"You're fortunate I was between court appearances," Cusp said, a short but canny barrister. "Another five minutes and the two of you would have been out of luck."

"Tell me, Hesketh," Barker asked. "Will you require any more information?"

"No, I believe I have enough for now," Pierce replied. "I'll investigate Nightwine's background. There's not much we can do about Macartney or the embassy. I hope you will keep me informed about Dr. Sun. If you need me, I have the authority to stop any boat in Limehouse."

"Thank you," the Guv said. "And thank you, Bram, for coming so quickly. Come, Thomas. We mustn't dawdle. We've work to do."

I wasn't dawdling any more than he was, but when has that ever stopped my partner?

CHAPTER 16

Sun Yat-sen lay on the cot in his cell, his knees pulled up to his chest. One of the guards—the big one—had punched him in the stomach for no particular reason. He hadn't been punched by a bully since grade school in Honolulu, but it still hurt the same. Some things never change.

He was dispirited as well. What if China never changed? Had they been wrong to rebel against the tyranny from the north? Surely the Manchus couldn't rule forever. It was unthinkable.

He'd brought this on himself. No one cared about a Chinaman raised in Hawaii. He had put his own neck on the chopping block by getting involved with the students hoping for change. He hadn't sought it out. He'd gone to Hong Kong to learn Western medicine in order to return and help his people. Qualified doctors were in short supply on the islands.

Yat-sen had never wondered who ruled China before he went there, nor had he concerned himself in any sort of political causes. He swore he would never do so again. This is what happens when you lose your head and write something that can never be taken back. You find yourself in a cell, and a guard displays his authority over you with a blow to the stomach. The impotence of his position beat within him. Did they really intend to execute him just because of one brief, ill-conceived letter? Why should they care what he thought? He was no professional rabble-rouser, and this was not Napoleonic France. He imagined his head rolling off the chopping block. There wouldn't be the surety of a guillotine. It would be the axe, like Charles I. What if they didn't cut it cleanly?

The situation made him miss his mother. She'd dice a mango for him, and he'd sit on her porch with his bowl and listen to her prattle about nothing while he ate. Local things, unimportant matters, nothing like failed coup attempts in China. And there's nothing like the possibility of imminent death to make one miss one's mother.

He was going to die, he realized. What an idiot he was! He hadn't even married. There would be no children to carry on his line. It would die with him, perhaps rightly so.

Get hold of yourself, he thought. *Be a man. Think of Sydney Carton in* A Tale of Two Cities. *'It's a far, far better thing I do now, than I have ever done.' No, don't think of him. He was beheaded.*

The door slowly opened with a prolonged squeal, as a man stepped inside. He was a homely figure who might have been created by Dickens himself. What was his name? Cole. He was a caretaker of sorts, a servant doing menial work. He had come to empty the slops bucket.

"Hello," Sun said, glad to speak to someone in English,

someone who wouldn't hit him or kick him in the stomach. He'd been sick in the bucket, and he felt ashamed.

"Afternoon," the man answered, nodding his head.

"Could you possibly get a message to a friend of mine?" Sun asked. "My family will be wondering where I am, you see."

"I'm not 'lowed to do that, sir."

"No. I understand," Sun said, sighing. "I'm sorry. It's just that they say they're going to send me to China to be executed. To be beheaded like Anne Boleyn. I just want my mother to know where I am and where I'm going. She'll always wonder, otherwise. I don't want her to wonder the rest of her life, hoping I'd turn up again. Best let her grieve."

"Sorry, sir," the man answered, a regretful look on his face. "I can't do it."

"I have friends here, as well," Sun continued. "Dr. Cantlie, my mentor. It was him I came to London to see. I didn't expect to be executed. Do you know what I did? I wrote a letter explaining to the emperor of China what I thought he should do for his people. It was a polite letter. I was simply trying to help him understand. I wasn't even raised in China. I live on an island in the Pacific Ocean!"

Cole nodded. He probably had no idea where the Pacific Ocean was, and perhaps not even China. He didn't look too bright, but obviously smart enough not to want to get into trouble and risk his meager salary.

"Look," Sun said. "I'm not asking you to release me or to help me to escape. I just want my friends and family to know what happened to me. You can do that for me, can't you? No one would need to know. Certainly, I wouldn't tell anyone."

"Well, I don't know," Cole said.

"Keeping me here is illegal, you know," Sun insisted. "Sir Halliday is breaking the rules of international law. If the prime minister heard of this, he'd be very angry. People need to know I'm being kept here against my will."

"I wouldn't want to get in trouble."

"Nor would you. I won't tell anyone your name, and you don't have to do anything else for me. This is just a scrap of paper I've written on. Give it to Dr. Cantlie in Devonshire Place. Hand it to his manservant and go. You don't have to speak to anyone or guide them here."

Cole considered it for a moment while emptying the slops.

"I reckon I could deliver a message," he said. "Not speak to someone, just hand it over and be on my way."

"That's all I ask of you, sir. Take that scrap of paper to the doctor and that's all."

"I'd have to think about it," Cole said, backing out the door.

Sun wanted to stop him, to convince him as he walked away.

"I'm sure Dr. Cantlie would give you some kind of reward for your troubles!" he called.

Cole left, leaving Sun with no idea what he would do. Sir Halliday Macartney and his agents arrived a half hour later. The counselor looked angry and held something in his hand. It was an appeal for help. It wasn't the one he'd given to Cole. He'd written it the day before and tossed it out the window. The notes had been written on the last few strips of his celluloid collar.

"I was asking for aid," Sun stated. "I'm being held here against my will. I demand to be released. This confinement is illegal."

Macartney slapped him across the face. Sun recoiled, as much in surprise as pain.

"Search him," said the counselor.

The secret service men did, thoroughly. He received a

pummeling from them as they searched through his pockets. However, they found nothing but the stub of a pencil, which they confiscated immediately.

Had Cole turned him in? No, no, the message was obviously not the one he had just given the caretaker. There was a chance, a small one, that Macartney had no knowledge of his request of Cole.

After Macartney and his men left, Sun Yat-sen rolled off his cot, knelt on the floor, and prayed as he had when he was a little boy. *Pray without ceasing,* he told himself. Surely God would not forsake him now.

CHAPTER 17

The next morning, we were at loose ends. There was no obvious next step for the Barker and Llewelyn Agency, save going to visit Nightwine himself in his hotel and haranguing him. We both knew he'd have an explanation for everything. He's not a stupid man. It would be much simpler if he were.

An hour after we'd arrived in Craig's Court, a man entered our chambers and presented his card. I was typing our movements over the past few days and looked up in time to see Jenkins and his blasted salver, which he set carefully on the Guv's desk, as if he were Etienne Dummolard presenting his latest culinary masterpiece. Barker lifted the card and studied it for a moment.

I was growing cross. Why couldn't they let a fellow alone to get on with the enquiry? They were like flies entering our chamber every time someone opened the door. Etienne, Cantlie, Pierce, the Colonial Office, it was too much. And now this new pestilence. Let's jam them all in at once and have done with it, I say. At least I'd have time to type my notes.

"Show the fellow in, Mr. Jenkins."

I glanced up from my report. He doesn't call Jenkins "mister" very often. Barker was standing as well, so I jumped to my feet. A moment later a gentleman entered the room. It was Arthur Bigge, the Queen's secretary. The word that flitted through my mind as he crossed the room was "taut." Every muscle of his body was stiff. It was not an auspicious beginning.

"Mr. Barker."

"Mr. Bigge," the Guv said, nodding. "Won't you have a seat?"

The secretary was looking about our offices. I supposed he had expected a grubby little den like J. M. Hewitt's, with a table stained with pint rings and placards of criminals on the wall. Our offices more closely resembled prosperous barrister's chambers. Barker extended his hand, but Bigge rudely sat without taking it. I knew I didn't like the fellow.

My partner sat down behind his desk and laced his fingers together on his green baize blotter.

"How may Mr. Llewelyn and I help you this afternoon?"

"You can't, I'm afraid," Bigge said. "I have some unpleasant news for you."

He said it as if to imply it was not unfavorable to him.

"Oh, dear," Barker replied. "Out with it, then. We shall brace ourselves."

"There is no easy way to say this, Mr. Barker, but I'm afraid your royal warrant has been rescinded."

Barker sat silently for a few moments, then nodded. "Very

well. Thank you for taking time from your important duties to inform us. I hope Her Majesty will not be inconvenienced."

Bigge looked relieved, and even belatedly a bit guilty. He had expected us to become violent, I suppose.

"You may keep the warrant displayed for another month."

"There's no need," Barker said. "Ye can tak it with ye."

There it was. His Scottish accent came to the fore, a sign he was angry. He reached into his desk and retrieved an Italian dagger once owned by the Sicilian crime organization the Camorra. Generally, he used it to open his post. He stood and began to advance upon the secretary. I tried to head him off, but then he veered to the right and walked into our outer offices, continuing out the front door. Rain was pouring down into our small cul-de-sac. Stepping outside, Barker was soaked immediately, but it didn't stop him. He inserted the weapon behind the hoarding and pried it off. It was as wide as the door below it. There had been at least a dozen nails holding it in place. He tucked the dripping sign under his arm and brought it to the secretary, offering it to him. Bigge stepped back. He had no wish to take custody of the sodden board, neither in his expensive suit nor while sporting an umbrella.

"Here you are, Mr. Bigge," my partner pronounced. "It has been a delight to have it advertise our agency, but I suppose all things must come to an end."

The secretary didn't know what to do. I did, however.

"Here," I said hotly. "You can take this with you as well!"

My partner might have been cool in the face of bad news, but I wasn't. I tore the watch given us by the Prince of Wales "For Services Rendered" from my pocket. I couldn't wrest it from its chain, so I gave him that as well, tossing it on the desk in front of the Queen's secretary.

"My compliments to His Highness," I said, standing too

close to Bigge, nearly eye to eye. "Give him my best, won't you?"

"Of course," he said, flustered.

"Have we any other business?" I asked.

"No," he admitted.

"Then get out."

He fled, one arm dragging the board, and his other hand holding my once prized watch. I called him an uncomplimentary name and for once Barker did not correct me.

"Where were we?" he asked, after the blackguard had gone.

"I was typing, sir," I said. "I don't know what you were doing, I'm afraid."

Barker nodded. I returned to my work, while he stared out the window at the rain. There was no sign of anger on his face. He had swallowed it in that stoical way of his.

One would think that would be enough trouble for the day, but one would be wrong. Another fellow arrived a few hours later, when we were about to close our doors. I didn't recognize him, but Barker obviously did.

"Stockton," he said, offering a hand. The man accepted it, but with reluctance. He ran a thumb between his throat and collar and refused to sit.

"Out with it, man," the Guv barked, making our visitor jump. "There's no need to stand upon ceremony here."

Stockton pulled a buff-colored envelope from his pocket, accidentally bending it in the process. He placed it on the desk as far away from himself as he could reach, doing his best to be able to retreat should my partner react to it. He wasn't far enough away, actually. He'd need to be out the window to reach safety.

Barker lifted the dagger I had replaced on the desk, and slit the envelope open in one move. He removed a sheet of paper from it, opened it in a leisurely fashion, and studied it.

"I'm afraid you've been banned from the Knights Templar, sir. Effective immediately. If you wish to defend yourself, you know the proper protocols."

The Knights Templar was a secret society of which Barker was not only a member but had helmed for a few years. He had been much respected there. Great pressure must have been brought to bear to remove him from its membership with no obvious reason.

"I do indeed, Mr. Stockton," Barker replied. "Thank you for coming to see me on so inclement a day. Inform your present leader I have no interest in arguing the matter. Show our visitor out, Mr. Llewelyn. Have you an umbrella, sir? No? You'll be drenched. Feel free to take one from the stand there. Good day."

I kept my temper while our visitor selected an umbrella and left with it. Jenkins was wiping an eye with his handkerchief. However, when I returned to my desk, the Guv was acting as if it were just another day. He taught me another lesson that afternoon: take each day as it comes. Don't fret. It won't be as bad as you imagine, nor will good news be as grand. Above all, control your emotions. They will only drag you into more trouble, or what John Bunyan would call the *Slough of Despond*. That was a body of water with which I was quite familiar.

"Don't you have some notes to finish, Thomas?" he rapped out.

I'd been sitting in front of my typewriter for five minutes, deflated.

"Yes, sir," I said, turning to my document.

There was one change in Barker's behavior, however. The Guv shut the office at three. Jeremy Jenkins was glad to have the rest of the afternoon off, but we both understood why. For some reason, he and I could not look each other in the eye. I hailed a cab, and actually found one, but Jeremy slinked off with his top hat jammed on his head, looking like a wet cat. It's possible the Templar man had taken his umbrella.

When we reached Lion Street, Barker went up to change, while I pulled Jacob into the kitchen and explained why we were home so early.

"My word," he exclaimed. "Both in one day?"

"Yes," I replied. "It's crushing, but he accepted them both without comment."

"I've got the bathhouse heating," he said. "Perhaps a soak would help. Will you stay? He probably needs the company."

"I left enough food for Daisy, I think," I said. "But she'll need to go out soon. I can't stay all evening."

I skirted the garden to the bathhouse where it was very hot inside. I took off my clothes, poured a bucket of water over my head, and scrubbed myself down. Then I poured a second bucket over me and lowered myself into the bath. It was the Japanese way. The steam danced across the surface of the water like a wraith. I reclined on a submerged bench and inhaled the moist air.

Cyrus Barker arrived a minute or two later, wearing a Japanese *yukata*, a bathrobe with rows of blue and black vertical stripes. He was smoking a new pipe, white as bone, carved as a dragon, its claws reaching forward to scratch. It was the largest he owned, and it was belching smoke the way the bathhouse boiler belched steam. I thought it likely he had been saving it for a day like this, to either celebrate or commiserate.

My partner didn't say a word to me. He set down the pipe, removed the robe, and poured the buckets over his head ceremoniously. Then he stepped down into the bath and sat there, turned away from me. It revealed what I privately called his battlefield.

There were tattoos across his back, as well as scars. Lots and lots of scars. I saw two I recognized to be bullet pocks. At least five must have been sword or knife wounds. Finally, there were parallel marks in an arc going down one side, which I surmised were claw marks from some creature. Deep ones. I recalled that Nightwine once kept a pair of large cats. Leopards or panthers, I'm not sure which. They ran loose in his house here in London and slept in his conservatory. One lay in a potted tree overhead, and the other had strolled by me so close that I could feel his breath.

Barker spoke up then, his back still to me. His head was down, and his short hair was spiked from having had water poured over it.

"You realize this is Sebastian's doing, don't you?"

"What is?" I asked. "Be more specific."

"He convinced Prince Albert to take away my warrant. Then, he put pressure on him to force members of the Templars to have me dismissed."

"That is conjecture," I stated. "But it does explain why Nightwine renewed his acquaintance with the Prince. Do you suppose the prince is in any danger?"

"No, they were friends at university. Christ Church, Oxford, I believe he is safe. Sebastian used to brag about the two of them getting on well as upperclassmen. The Queen despaired of her son."

"He's a rascal. Is Nightwine also something of a roué?"

"If he is seeing a woman, you can rest assured he wants something out of her besides conquest. The female sex are not human to him, merely pawns in a game. He makes himself romantic in their eyes, being a handsome rogue, then exploits them ruthlessly. At least one of them killed herself with prussic acid."

"Sofia Ilyanova's mother?"

"Aye."

"If Sofia is in town, it may be proof that he intends to kill someone," I observed.

I could smell his tobacco now, his personal blend. Soon it would fill the moist chamber.

"Could it be the prince himself who decided to remove the warrant?" I asked. "Instead of being Nightwine's idea, I mean."

The Guv looked over his shoulder, his black spectacles fogged. "I cannot rule it out, of course. However, this has been personal so far, and I'm certain Nightwine means me serious harm. You have no concept of his vindictiveness."

"He's not coming after me, surely," I said.

"No? You've gone out of your way to insult and provoke him, and then you seduced his daughter."

"I did not seduce her," I argued. "You've got it backwards. She kidnapped me, stuffed me full of laudanum, and seduced me, no doubt to spite her father. I barely remember the incident, and I wasn't married then."

"I doubt that matters much to him," Barker stated. "Odd that he should concern himself with her virtue, after he trained her to kill men, but he is full of contradictions. His father had much to answer for."

Barker set down his pipe carefully and plunged forward into the steaming water. He emerged on the other side of the tank, sitting on another submerged bench.

I rubbed my perspiring face with a towel. The Japanese way of bathing is steaming hot. Most Westerners can't stand it. I've spent much of my adult life parboiled.

"And she's in charge of a child, whom I assume she's dragging along with her around the world," I remarked. "She must be a terrible mother."

"A mother to your child, Thomas. Have you thought of that?"

"I've tried not to think about it," I admitted. "Of course, I wouldn't want the boy—any boy—to go through that ordeal. She might be torturing him as her father tortured her, although she is not the monster her father is. I can't even imagine what sort of life he is living."

"As Nightwine's father tortured him," added my partner. "That's often the way."

"What a tangle!" I remarked.

"That's Sebastian's modus operandi, lad. He'll tie everyone in knots and abscond with whatever prize he came for, while they suffer."

"Only you outsmarted him, sir," I said.

"Did I?" he asked. "Perhaps it was chance when I stabbed him."

"You do not believe in chance, sir, or in luck."

"Divine Providence, then."

We paused. He removed his spectacles and set them down on the wooden pathway that surrounded the pool. He only felt comfortable doing so around Mac and me. A scar bisected one brow, splitting his cheek, and his eye was damaged, though he could see through it. He took a ladle full of steaming water and anointed his head with it.

"I've missed this," I admitted. "The water and the steam soak the tension away. I've been tied in a knot since the case began."

"Feel free to come over anytime, Thomas," he said, reaching for a towel and running it over his spiky head. "Even if I'm not here. You know you are always welcome."

"Thank you, sir. I wonder where he is now. Nightwine, I mean. What sort of mischief is he getting into?"

"An excellent question," he said, nodding. "That's why I have Mac standing guard outside with his shotgun at this very minute."

"He must be enjoying that," I replied. From time to time Mac likes to drive off intruders with a load of buckshot. It's one of his favorite duties.

"I haven't heard from Hewitt lately, Thomas. I'm growing concerned."

"Don't say that," I protested. "I rather like J. M."

"It's the nature of the work. He understands that any case could be his last."

"Perhaps that's true, but I want the next funeral we attend to be Sebastian Nightwine's."

"I cannot disagree with that, Thomas. Hewitt's a good man. I like him."

I yawned. The tension in my body was slowly easing. Perhaps it would help me sleep that night. Insomnia is the bane of my existence.

"I hope Rebecca is doing well," I remarked. "This must be very stressful for her."

"She'll do well enough, lad," Barker replied. "Mrs. Llewelyn is a very resilient creature, I've found."

"I'll take my one Rebecca over a hundred women. But then I suppose I have."

Barker grunted. It was a laugh of sorts.

"Who would have thought my sending you to be a Shabbas goy for a Jewish family those many years ago would result in your marrying their daughter."

"I don't believe I'd ever met a Jew until you lent me to the Mocatta family."

"That was the intent, Thomas," he stated. "You needed

to expand your knowledge of the world. We all have our own natural fears and prejudices. I didn't want them to affect the enquiry."

"Thank you for the suggestion, sir."

"I didn't suggest it, lad. As I recall, I ordered you to go. However, I didn't order you to take advantage of the daughter."

He immediately submerged his entire body under the surface of the water.

"I never!" I cried.

CHAPTER 18

I doubted that His Royal Highness Albert Edward would recognize us. We had only met him once and then just for a minute or two. Several years before, we'd stopped an Irish bomber from blowing him to kingdom come with a satchel bomb. We had saved his life, and the prince was not in Nightwine's pocket at the time. He'd sent a token of thanks to us in the form of the watch which I'd just returned, along with the royal warrant outside our door. Barker had lent it to me, because he did not approve of the prince's reputation as a libertine, and because he carried an old turnip watch that had sentimental value to him. I thought it likely that the prince no longer recalled the Guv's name and had been coerced by Nightwine into pulling our warrant as a personal favor. If we could enter the event that evening and somehow remain anonymous, we might be able to spy on Sebastian Nightwine and the prince, as well. The Guv's plan of a stealthy entrance and a quick departure suited us both.

I arrived in Lion Street as resplendent as a Llewelyn can be, and was greeted by Mac, who brushed my suit savagely, though I was wearing it at the time. My top hat received similar treatment. Jacob Maccabee has exacting standards, and if I were anything but natty he would hold himself responsible. By the time he was satisfied, the Guv had descended from his aerie at the top of the house, and I was beginning to feel like a beaten rug.

"I thought we were being discreet," I remarked.

Cyrus Barker wore an evening suit with an outsized shirt-front and waistcoat covering his broad chest. He wore a pair of green-lensed spectacles as opaque as jade, which would draw the attention of anyone in the room. If that didn't do the trick, his full opera cape would.

"Discreet clothes are for discreet men," he stated.

"You aren't feeling discreet this evening?" I asked.

"Decidedly not."

Ah, I told myself. His desire for a confrontation had finally shown itself.

Mac assessed him as critically as if he were a painting in Grosvenor Gallery, cocking his head to one side in judgment. He attempted to apply the whisk brush, but his master batted it down the hall to the back door. In response, his factotum proffered his top hat and evaporated like the morning dew. That meant that my partner's emotions could only be vented on me. Barker is like the switch on an electric light. He is either calm or glacially angry. He'd be a joy to go out with that evening.

A cab appeared at the door. It must have been summoned by Mac, now safely barricaded in his butler's pantry. We stepped aboard and settled ourselves in our seats. The horse's hooves dug into the cobblestones, and we were off.

"Where is this event?" I asked.

"St. James," Cyrus Barker growled.

I glanced in his direction. "Where in St. James?"

"Nowhere. The St. James Restaurant in Piccadilly."

We crossed to the Middlesex side of the river. The evening sky was a blanket of gray clouds.

"Oh," I said, trying to keep my spirits up. "So, it's not a royal event."

"Far from it," the Guv replied. "It's probably more a chance for drunken debauchery, but the salient feature is that Nightwine will be present. He is being feted by a few of the prince's friends. The royal family is at Balmoral and there will be no official events until the coming year."

"There is no reason then why we can't join the party," I reasoned. "Unless Nightwine or the prince spies us and we are tossed into the street."

"Aye."

"In that case," I remarked. "You may punch Nightwine if necessary, but not the Prince of Wales."

"Mmph," he replied. He'd consider the matter but offered no promises.

The St. James is one of the most exclusive restaurants in London. Prince Albert is something of a bon vivant, as can be proven by his waistline. All of the men in London society wore the lowest button of their waistcoats undone in deference, because he could no longer button his.

"Do we have an invitation?" I asked.

The Guv shook his head. "It's a private party."

"How do we get in, then?"

"The Templars provided me with a password to guarantee

our entrance. However, it will be the last time I can count upon their good graces."

"What's the password?" I asked.

Cyrus Barker shook his head. "The password to be uttered to the steward is: 'blancmange.'"

"At least they're taking this matter seriously," I quipped. "Our future sovereign doesn't strike me as a serious person."

"Aye, but he's young," my partner answered. "He'll grow into the crown, I trust. That is, I hope he will for the country's sake."

"Young?" I sputtered. "The man's fifty-four!"

"True, but his mother is seventy-six and shows no sign of ill health. He's waited decades to become king. I trust he will be a better sovereign than he is a husband."

We arrived in Piccadilly. The door to the St. James Restaurant was flanked by two guards. One was a sharp-faced fellow, whose duty it was to receive the password, and warn off anyone who didn't know it. The other was built along the lines of a steamer trunk. I assumed he was the one who removed anyone who displeased the first.

"Your names, sirs?" the first guard asked in a glacial tone.

I cudgeled my brain for aliases, but Barker had no trouble supplying our actual names. I wondered who would read the list later, after the private event was over.

"And the password?" the man asked.

"Blancmange," I whispered through my fingers.

"Thank you, sir," he said with a nod. "However, you are not on the approved list. Who invited you tonight?"

I paused, but Barker didn't.

"Sir Arthur Bigge, the Queen's secretary," the Guv replied. "We're also longtime friends of Mr. Nightwine. In fact we were in business together."

We were allowed entrance into Aladdin's cave more easily

than I anticipated. Inside, Barker removed his voluminous cape and handed it to a footman, along with our hats and sticks. Meanwhile, I looked about the room to see if I recognized anyone, particularly Sebastian Nightwine, cursed be his name. The evening was an all-male salon of sorts, the kind that flowed with brandy and champagne. The room was opulent, with glossy wood floors and mirrors on the walls, which seemed to enlarge the room. Tables had been cleared away, and velvet lounges and easy chairs installed in their place at the government's expense. A knot of men played whist in the corner, and there was a baccarat table on the other side of the room. Men discussed business or bragged about their exploits. All the guests seemed to know one another. I thought it was likely some had been university friends of the prince.

I nearly walked into someone I recognized. I couldn't recall his name, but the fellow looked familiar. He was in his early thirties, as I was. I suspected we'd met at Oxford at Magdalen College. He pointed at me and began snapping his fingers, trying to remember my name. Next, he would recall the scandal that sent me down and put me in Oxford Prison. That is, unless I confused him.

"Inglenook," I told him. "Algernon Inglenook. Haven't seen you in ages, old fellow. Staying out of trouble?"

"Er, well, doing my best," he said, looking perplexed.

"Is Bertie about?" I asked. "And that rascal, Nightwine. He owes me a pound or two."

He cocked his head over his shoulder. "They're in the back room."

I nodded. "Excellent. We really need to lift a glass together and reminisce about old times. What larks, eh?"

"Of course!" he said, shaking my hand before the Guv and I continued onward.

"That was impressive, Mr. Inglenook," Barker murmured. "You knew him?"

"I recognize him from my university days, but for the life of me I can't recall his name."

It was a wealthy crowd, though I'm certain a few were getting by on their wits rather than their bank accounts. Too many of the gentry these days are landed but impoverished, hoping to make a good marriage or become friends with a prince of the realm. I recognized a few faces in the crowd from the newspapers. One of the reasons Barker has us read them is to be able to recognize important men and know their histories. The wealthier the guests were, the louder they spoke. Amongst the lot were aristocrats, financiers, barristers, and wastrel sons out for a spot of drink and entertainment. Currently, the entire crowd was male, but I wondered if women would arrive later: singers, actresses, and promising ballerinas, perhaps, along with adventuresses and other women of scandalous reputation. I'd never been to an event like this, despite my obvious savoir faire. But then, I was a married man. This was the last sort of place I should be, especially with the wife away. Being there was dangerous in more ways than one.

I turned as someone pushed his way through the crowd. It was our old friend, Arthur Bigge, who had just taken our royal warrant, may he fall off his stupid bike and break a limb. Fortunately, he didn't see us, despite Barker's flamboyant spectacles.

Another reason we read the newspapers front to back is to be able to discuss a subject with knowledge in case it was necessary. Barker slipped among a group of men and made a remark about current trade with France. He claimed tariffs needed to be more severe. He'd never discussed tariffs with me before, so I suspected he was just blowing smoke to fit in among them. However, he was the tallest of them all, and with his imposing shirtfront and those spectacles, everyone must be wondering who he was. Asking, however, would prove they were not part of the prince's inner circle, and the last thing any of them would admit to was that.

We took champagne from a passing waiter's tray and did our best to be inconspicuous. I noted a few burly men among the crowd who were probably there to protect the prince. Were they from the Foreign Office? The palace? A military escort? There are too many hounds these days with nothing to do but chase their own tails.

Having dipped our feet into most of the groups in the outer room, we wandered into the back and looked about. It was a room much like the first, perhaps a bit more intimate. Near the far wall there was a low divan of crushed green velvet with a man sitting upon it whom I recognized as the prince. It was odd to have seen his image hundreds of times from his youth to his wedding, to his duties in court, as well as trips to various countries for diplomatic reasons. Yet, there he sat, whispering a remark to a waiter.

Barker set his champagne glass on a ledge, untouched. I could see he was about to approach His Highness, but without a second's warning, he suddenly stood face-to-face with Sebastian Nightwine, who was just about to leave the room as we entered. Both men were taken aback, but neither would admit he had been caught out.

"Hello, Cyrus," Nightwine said, gathering his aplomb. "You're looking well."

"As are you, Sebastian," my partner replied. "You look far better than when last we met."

It was true, because when last I saw him, the man was at death's door. I scrutinized him carefully. His formerly blond hair was now snowy white. He had aged, as would be expected, and he no longer seemed the kind of man who could tramp into the jungle like Livingston for six months at a moment's notice. There was something wrong with his torso; it was twisted. One side was concave, and the other convex. Something alarming had happened to him. Perhaps it was the fact that Barker had run him through with a sword. That would certainly do it.

One thing that hadn't changed was Nightwine's taste in clothes. It was late October, but he wore an oatmeal-colored suit in a thick weave, with a green tie. It suited the former big game hunter and explorer but stood in marked contrast with the entire restaurant full of self-indulgent Londoners in identical evening kit. I'm certain he meant it to.

"So I do," Nightwine replied. Both men were being civil, but that could change in a heartbeat. It would only take the smallest spark to ignite tempers. "You look much the same, Cyrus. I note a little gray in your hair."

"Time marches on," the Guv agreed. "What brings you to London? Actually, I know what you're doing here, but I'll give you the chance to make a clear confession."

Sebastian Nightwine shrugged. "A bit of shopping, I suppose one could say. I wanted to pick up a few items that they don't have in China anymore."

"Anyone we know?" I retorted.

Nightwine's golden eyes settled on mine. "Ah, Mr. Llewelyn! Still hiding behind your master? I assumed you were dead by now. At least, I hoped."

"How are the old injuries?" I asked. I can joust with the best of them. The trick is knowing where to point the lance. "You're looking rather diminished, if I may say it. Hunting days behind you now?"

"Gentlemen, remember where we are," Barker warned, breaking into our tête-à-tête. "A prince is across the room."

"That's true!" Nightwine said, a look of pleasure in his eyes. "Come, I'll introduce you."

Before we had time to prepare, Nightwine dragged us in front of the Prince of Wales, the very man whom we expressly hoped to avoid. There was no telling what sort of lies he'd been told. Queen Victoria's son was a stout fellow with a short beard and drooping eyelids. He was taller than I expected and held a snifter of brandy in his chubby hand. A woman was sitting nearby looking bored, I noticed. She was certainly not his wife.

"Your Highness, these are the gentlemen I have been speaking to you about," Nightwine said smoothly. "This is Mr. Cyrus Barker and Mr. Theodore Llewelyn."

"Thomas," I corrected.

"What the devil are you doing at my private party?" the prince demanded.

"We heard our old friend Sebastian Nightwine was in town, sir," Barker replied. "We hoped to renew our acquaintance. This was the only way for us to speak to him, Your Highness."

"You cannot lie to me, gentlemen," Prince Albert continued, red-faced. "You're the common detectives who have been following Sebastian about and badgering him for no reason."

"As I said, Your Highness, I've only just met him now."

"I pulled your warrant today!" the prince sputtered. "I don't know how you earned it."

"We saved your life from an Irish bomber in Pall Mall, sir," I reminded him. "You presented us with a watch, inscribed *For Services Rendered to the Crown*."

"I didn't ask you, Mr. Whatever-Your-Name-Is," Prince Albert replied. "I asked this absurd fellow in the green spectacles."

The prince set his glass firmly on a nearby table, causing it to wobble. "I'm going to speak to Scotland Yard about you gentlemen. You cannot be allowed to invade private parties and harass my guests."

This was not going as planned by any means. It felt as if someone had just emptied a champagne bucket full of ice down the back of my jacket.

"How did you know the password?" Albert continued to thunder.

"I heard someone speak it aloud outside, Your Highness," Cyrus Barker answered.

He had, in fact. The person who said it was me. Barker almost never lies, but he can parse the truth with the best of them.

"Throw these men out!" the prince ordered to no one in particular.

"I'll escort them!" Sebastian Nightwine cried.

The next I knew, we were seized by several men and dragged through one of the nicest restaurants in the city, while Nightwine crowed in our ears.

"I'd have come all the way to England just for this very moment," he said. "I intend to snatch you, but I'll do that later. I'm enjoying this far too much."

Three men had my partner by the arms and a fourth was pressing down on his head. I've seen him toss four men about for exercise, but for some reason he wasn't trying to defend himself. When they reached the pavement, they ran forward in unison and pitched Cyrus Barker into the street. As for me, they seized me by the arms and ankles, swung me back and forth, and then let go. When I hit the cobblestones, pain blossomed everywhere. I lay in the gutter while everyone returned to the party, laughing. The last to go inside was Nightwine.

"I really don't know why I was so concerned about coming here," he said conversationally. "You're obviously past your prime."

We heard the door slam shut. After a moment, as if on cue, it began to rain. Then the door squealed open again and something large fluttered to the ground on top of us. It was Barker's enormous cape. Our hats and sticks were tossed out after.

Slowly, I sat up. Everything hurt, but there was a specific contest between my left elbow and my right hip. It was not the best evening I could recall. It all comes from poor planning, I thought, and overconfidence that we could get ourselves out of any scrape.

Barker pushed himself up as well and pulled the cape off his head. One of his green spectacles was broken, revealing an eye, but it was the one without the outsized scar.

"Why did you let them do that, sir?" I asked. "You could have cut a swathe through that crowd."

"Aye, and put us into serious trouble? We have no friends or organizations to help us now. Flag a hansom, would you, lad?"

I pushed myself to my feet and staggered into the center of the street. A cab arrived just in time, perhaps because the address was known for its generous tips. The cabman helped me boost my partner into the cab. I'm sure he'd done it dozens of times, helping inebriated gentlemen from the curb in front of the St. James. He'd probably have more work here in an hour or two.

Barker had a small cut on his face from the broken spectacles. I handed him a handkerchief.

"What hurts most is having Nightwine gloat," I complained.

"Aye, but we found him, lad."

"What did we gain by that, sir?" I asked.

"Confirmation from his own mouth," the Guv said. "You heard him, lad. He's come shopping. He wants Sun Yat-sen, and the entire crew of the *Osprey*. His relationship with the prince is only a subterfuge. Nightwine has no need or desire for royal friendship. Money is what he's after."

I tried to mull that over, but my entire body was throbbing. I'd try more seriously in the morning.

"Home or hospital?" I asked.

He considered the question a moment, leaning against the back of the leather seat. I almost thought he passed out.

"Home, I think," he said after a moment.

"Mac won't appreciate carrying you up two flights of stairs, sir."

"No, but he's paid well enough."

I saw my partner home, where Mac and I both helped him out of the cab. Afterward, the cabman took me through the glossy, wet streets of Lambeth, bound for the City. I hovered between sleep and wakefulness. When I finally reached Camomile Street, I gave him a good tip for both of us and he helped me to the door.

"You gents really tied one on, sir, if I may say so," he noted wryly. "You'll regret it in the morning."

I unlocked my front door. "I think I might regret it already."

Daisy was at the door, wagging her tail. I stepped inside, locked the two of us in, and went upstairs to the cupboard where the liniment is kept.

There's a saying that any encounter one can walk away from was a success. It's utter nonsense as far as I'm concerned.

CHAPTER 19

We were back in our offices the following morning, aches and pains notwithstanding. Barker was considering a visit to the Savoy to break into Nightwine's rooms, hoping to find his second map of Tibet if he brought it, and burn it as he had the first. Losing one map was bad enough. Losing a second would seem like carelessness in the eyes of Her Majesty's Government. Any plans he might have had along those lines would be scuttled, as well as the slim chance of Nightwine becoming Sir Sebastian for his services to the Crown.

Someone entered our offices then, whom Jenkins allowed through to our chambers directly. It was Hewitt. He seated himself in our visitor's chair, or rather, fell into it. The fellow was in poor condition. One of his eyes was swollen shut, and there was a bruise on his chin and lip. His beautiful suit for which I had given him an inordinate sum was ruined. It had been torn and rent, and the waistcoat had lost most of its buttons. Given, I'd damaged more than one suit myself over the years, but never one so new and expensive. It looked beyond repair.

"My word!" I exclaimed. "Have you been walking down Whitehall Street like that?"

"No," he replied. "I got into my office late last night and slept atop my desk. I just awoke about five minutes ago. Thought I would come in and report before going home for the day. Someone else will have to look after Nightwine now."

"There's no need. What happened to you?" Barker asked.

"I was set upon and beaten by three Chinese men in an alley in Piccadilly, early last night," Hewitt explained. "I'd followed your suspect there. I've been careful. I don't know how they pegged me."

"That sounds familiar," I said.

"This is my fault," the Guv stated. "I should have employed a second man. Sebastian is canny. He must have realized he was being followed. That suit of yours is notable."

"My suit!" Hewitt complained. "My beautiful suit! I'll never afford another like it."

"You needn't worry," the Guv told him. "Our client will order another just like it."

I knew our client was Barker himself, but there was no reason for Hewitt to know that. If my partner felt it necessary, he could tell him later. It was the Guv's money to spend as he pleased, without any input from me. Still, I had opinions on the matter.

"You must go to Charing Cross Hospital and have a doctor look at you," Barker ordered.

"I'm sure I'll be fine in a day or two," J. M. said.

Barker shook his head. "You needn't play the knight-errant here, Hewitt. I can see you're in pain. Go to the hospital."

"It will take more than that to put me off a case. I have rent to pay."

"Well spoken! Now tell me what Mr. Nightwine has been doing. My first question is whether he has been seen with a woman?"

"No, sir," Hewitt answered. "I've seen him in various restaurants, usually with the Prince of Wales and his lot, but he had no female companion the entire time I've watched him. What sort of woman are you talking about?"

"You can't miss her," I said. "Her hair is very pale, and her eyes are a kind of golden color. One can tell she is Nightwine's daughter. Have you seen anyone that meets this description?"

"No," he replied. "I'd have noticed a woman like that. Is she young?"

"Younger than you, but if you do see her, leave immediately. She's dangerous."

The side of Hewitt's mouth went up. "Dangerous?"

"Remarkably dangerous," Barker said.

"Remember when the tsarevich was shot a few years ago?" I asked. "She was the one who pulled the trigger."

"Now you're pulling my leg," he said. "A young, female assassin? What kind of fool do you take me for?"

"He isn't joking," Barker rumbled. "However, we believe Nightwine and his daughter are menacing some friends of mine. Three of them have gone missing. As it happens, the Qing government put out a reward for each of us several years ago. We suspect Nightwine plans to take us back to China for those rewards."

"What about the little Chinese fellow, Sun?" Hewitt asked. "How is he involved?"

"He's a recently escaped revolutionary," the Guv replied, running a finger over his mustache. "His reward may be the largest of all."

I pointed at Hewitt. "You, sir, are bleeding. Jeremy! Bring the bandage kit!"

"I'm sorry, gentlemen," the detective murmured. He looked embarrassed that he had failed. I knew the feeling.

"Have you a change of clothes in your office?" I asked.

Hewitt shook his head.

"We have plenty of clothing in a room in the back," Barker said.

"What sort of clothing?" Hewitt asked with a wry smile. "Not a costume, I assume?"

"Just ordinary clothing," I explained. "Not busbies or opera capes."

The latter was for my partner's benefit.

"Right," he replied.

"Did Mr. Nightwine visit the Chinese embassy recently," my partner continued, while Jenkins applied a sticking plaster to Hewitt's face.

"As a matter of fact, he did," the detective replied. "He walked in the door."

"Which entrance?" Barker asked. "The one on the street?"

"No," he answered, shaking his head. "There was a fancy-looking one in the back with red doors and a carpet."

"Interesting."

"All done here," Jenkins said, surveying his handiwork.

"S'truth!" J. M. said, looking at himself in a hand mirror. "Your clerk used up all the plaster in the kit!"

"I assume you stayed until he returned," Barker remarked, not to be dissuaded from his topic. "Did he seem satisfied when he left the building?"

"He had a smile on his face," Hewitt answered. "I can vouch for it. Hopped in a hackney and trundled off. I had a dickens of a time finding a second cab."

"I see. Has he had any visitors at the Savoy?"

Hewitt shook his head. "Not a one, sir. I've got a room down the hall. I could monitor who comes and goes."

"Did he keep to a schedule?" Barker pursued.

"No, but he was a busy one," he replied. "He must have taken ten cabs in a day. Went to the palace twice."

"The palace?" I asked. "You mean the Palace Theatre?"

"No, Tommy Boy. The palace. Buckingham Palace, that is."

My partner glanced my way. "The man seems to be keeping rarefied company these days."

"I wonder if the left hand knows what the right hand is doing," I said. "The Chinese embassy in the afternoon and the palace that evening."

"It's a noisy crowd he hangs about with," Hewitt said, shrugging. "A tremendous amount of champagne for the ladies, a tremendous amount of décolletage for the men."

"Your duties concerning Mr. Nightwine are concluded. However, I may need you again in a day or two."

"Yes, sir," Hewitt answered from inside his swathe of bandages.

"Is it possible the prince has introduced Nightwine to Her Majesty?" I asked.

Cyrus Barker has sentimental feelings toward the Queen. He won't hear an ill word said against her. Once I had the cheek to refer to her as Queen Vicky and Barker would not let the matter rest for a full week. Our morning exercises were little short of torture.

"I will see that doesn't happen," he stated. I believed him.

I called a cab in Whitehall Street, while Hewitt changed

into a plain-looking suit in our back room that I suspected had been purchased secondhand. It didn't fit him, but then he wouldn't have to wear it for long.

It had begun raining against our windowpanes. I gave Hewitt our last brolly, and helped him into a hackney cab. I ordered the jarvey to take him to Charing Cross Hospital.

"Come," Barker said when I returned.

"Jolly," I remarked. "Where are we going?"

"We need to speak to Her Majesty."

He's mad, I thought. He's worked too hard and now his mind is gone.

"Sir," I said cautiously, "one cannot simply drop by for tea with the Queen. There are protocols."

"Then we will speak to her secretary."

"Oh, no, sir, you don't mean . . ."

"Aye," he said, nodding. "The ubiquitous Mr. Bigge."

"Is it really necessary, sir?"

Barker drummed a finger on his desk. It was not insistent, merely a steady tap every two seconds or so, like the drip of a faucet. He was thinking. I left him alone, awaiting his conclusion. Finally, he spoke.

"Let me consider it further. You remarked on Sebastian's physical condition last night," he said. "I had not the chance to study him. We were eye to eye. What were your conclusions?"

"His body is twisted, sir," I answered. "Probably because of the duel years ago. He's upright and he hides it well, but something is wrong with him. My remark about his hunting days being over hit home, I think."

"If he is permanently injured, he cannot be running about alone kidnapping men like Paul Beauchamp or Ho. I take that to mean he has assistance, one or more people helping him. My former crew must have been physically restrained and smuggled aboard a ship bound for Canton. And I think we both know which ship he'll be using."

"The *Osprey*, sir," I replied. "I also suspect the men who took it are the secret service agents from the Chinese legation."

"Very likely, Thomas. I'm certain Nightwine and Sir Halliday have hatched this plan together."

"Someone must have spotted the *Osprey* by now," I complained. "But there must be a half dozen explanations why it hasn't been seen yet. It might be in dry dock. They could have repainted her or are keeping her in the Channel near Dieppe or Le Havre."

"Perhaps. However, the Qing agents can't be far from their base in London," he argued.

"Unless there are more of them than we know," I countered.

"In a pinch, four of us ran the *Osprey*," Barker said. "And we had done so for years. Nightwine might require a larger crew, especially because he can't help the others in his weakened physical condition, not that he ever helped much when he was in China."

"Perhaps he hired a gang," I suggested. "Sailors from Limehouse or the Docks."

"That's possible. Someone must guard the prisoners, and the Chinese are busy at the embassy."

"So that means there may be as many as eight of them," I speculated. "Those are not good odds for us."

"Remember, lad, they have Ho, who is well-admired, even revered in Limehouse. Some of the sailors and locals will be jumping at the chance to rescue him, as well as receiving the reward. I'm sure K'ing already has men looking along the Thames estuaries."

"This is madness," I told him as we moved through the traffic. "Bigge won't see us."

"Not if we are polite," he replied. "However, he might have no choice if we are a threat."

"You're determined to see us in a cell, aren't you? We've just avoided one by the skin of our teeth."

"You are pessimistic today, Mr. Llewelyn."

"I am, sir. It's how I've managed to survive these many years."

We arrived at Her Majesty's residence, where of course we were stopped at the gate. I noted that the Queen was not in residence. The royal standard was not rippling overhead.

"We have an appointment with the Queen's secretary," my partner stated to the guard in full scarlet jacket and bear hat as if we were in a restaurant and he the maître d'. The Guv presented his card. Then he presented a second. It was Bigge's, the one he'd given Jenkins the day before. I've been told I have cheek, but I stood beside the master.

"They'll never let us in," I muttered.

"Perhaps they will, if only for Mr. Bigge to harangue us again. He took delight in taking our warrant yesterday."

"What's the purpose of our visit?" I demanded.

"You're beginning to sound like the man himself, Thomas. What is it that we do? We collect information and we dispense information."

I raised a brow. "We'll find ourselves in the Tower yet."

"We've been there before. As I recall, you found it interesting,"

"I did, but I don't intend to live there!"

I prayed that we would be turned away, but my maker and I have always been at odds. The guard returned and led us through the palace. On any other day, I'd have marveled at the beauty, brilliance, and history of one of the grandest palaces in the world, but just then I felt the way a mouse does just before the trap snaps down upon his neck.

"Barker, what in hell are you doing here?" Bigge demanded when we stepped into his opulent office.

"You came to visit us, sir," the Guv replied. "I thought we would return the favor."

"I'm calling the guard."

"As you wish, sir, but I've come to warn you that His Highness Prince Edward is in grave danger."

"My eye," he scoffed.

"Very well," the Guv said affably. "If I tell you what I've come to tell you, and you ignore it and the prince dies, then it will be on your head, not mine. We are private citizens, attempting to do our duty to our country, are we not, Mr. Llewelyn?"

"We are indeed, sir," I said, nodding.

Bigge frowned. It could go either way, I thought. I regretted ordering the secretary from our offices.

"Very well," he said between gritted teeth. "Say what you have to say and go."

"His Highness has made a friend recently," Cyrus Barker said. "They've had dinner together several times. He is the newest member of the prince's circle. There may be talk of him being knighted. His name is Sebastian Nightwine. I assume you've met him, since you were at his private event last night."

"What of it?" he demanded.

"I've known this man for many years," the Guv continued. "We were partners in a venture together. He is an utter scoundrel. More important, he is the father of a young woman known as La Sylphide. She was responsible for His Highness's brother being fired upon a few years ago at Kensington Palace, and the tsarevich being shot in the shoulder. She was the shootist, I assume at Nightwine's instruction."

"Why are you wasting my time with this nonsense?" Bigge fairly shouted. "I'm going to call Scotland Yard!"

"Do so, sir, by all means," Barker replied. "They have the full particulars of both incidents. The Duke of York was mistaken for the tsarevich. They look much alike, you see."

"Why should I believe you?" Bigge said, crossing his arms.

"I don't care a whit whether you believe me or not," my partner rumbled. "I've come to warn you that the Prince of Wales is in mortal danger."

"I'm having the two of you thrown out."

"You have that right, Mr. Bigge," my partner replied. "But if the future sovereign's head is blown apart by an expanding bullet, and the government learns you knew of the danger beforehand you'll have the shortest tenure as Her Majesty's secretary of any man who has ever held the office. You may think us mad, but we are not uninformed. Come, Thomas, let's allow the gentleman to get on with his day."

"Get out!" Bigge ordered, but Barker was already leaving the room.

I turned and hurried after him. We were not stopped. No line of royal guards armed with rifles and fixed bayonets were ready to shoot us. In fact, they barely noticed us. None of the royals were in residence that day, and only the sentries in their little boxes at the gate outside stood at attention. We even stopped to view the changing of the guards.

"Inspiring, don't you think?" Barker asked, once the military parade was over.

"Thrilling, sir," I agreed.

I'd seen it at least a hundred times. The road is blocked for several minutes, and there is shouting and solemn marching, and everything comes to a standstill. As a Londoner, I found it an impediment to traffic and a bit of a nuisance, but I knew better than to say so to the Guv. As I said, the man's a royalist to the core.

CHAPTER 20

I arrived in Camomile Street late, and when I unlocked the door there was only a little dog to greet me, though she did her best. She hopped about in circles, jumped at my knees, and barked as if there were a party of strangers in the house. I patted her head and let her into the backyard. Daisy and I must fend for ourselves in the wilds of Bishopsgate. It was cool and dark inside the house, and there was a smell of stale air and dust about the place. I turned up the gas lamp and went to the icebox, where I found a pie on the shelf. Was it for me, I hoped? I looked at the calendar pinned to a corkboard and remembered the bake sale for the Jewish Ladies Auxiliary. She must have baked it for that very reason, but it was mine now. A slice of pie would certainly go down a treat. I lifted it from the shelf and inspected it, sniffing around the edges, trying to discern what was underneath the crust. It was either raspberry or rhubarb and apple. A plain apple pie was preferable, but I could tolerate any flavor. I was ravenous.

I fed Daisy first, a plate of chicken livers, and remembered there was a public house nearby, the George and Vulture, where I went for my evening meal. There I had a very passable roast and mash with Yorkshire pud and a pint or two of Boddingtons Ale. I spent the meal alone, and even when I was finished, I carried my pint to the bar, and sat at the end, hoping no one would engage me in conversation. Luckily, it was a standoffish crowd that night, one that didn't abide strangers almost as much as me.

Afterward I went home, put a small log on the fire, lit a lamp, and tried to interest myself in *The Return of the Native.* However, no one should attempt to scale Thomas Hardy after seven o'clock in the evening. It is too steep a climb; there should be a warning affixed to every copy. I groused to myself about the case, about Nightwine and Sir Halliday bloody Macartney and Chinese bullyboys, and partners I won't mention. In general, I felt sorry for myself. I missed Rebecca who was still sequestered in a private hotel with our daughter and Philippa Ashleigh. She always knew how to make me feel better. Maybe it took a few nights alone to make me appreciate what I had, but I wanted her back immediately. I wanted to watch Rachel play with her stuffed animals. I wanted my family back, and for things to be normal again.

I changed into my nightshirt and brushed my teeth, then climbed into what I estimated was the loneliest bed in London, if not all creation. Daisy jumped up and lay at the foot of the bed. I called her to me and scratched her back, feeling low. If one is going to make an art of self-pity one must really put one's heart and soul into it. However, it was for an audience of one, and the ale I consumed was tossing cobwebs at my head. I wondered what the point was and went to sleep.

I woke a few hours later with one thought in mind. The pie in the kitchen. The bake sale was over, and the ice in the icebox had melted. It was only right that I should dispose of it, since it would spoil by the time my wife returned. I do like raspberry pie. If it were rhubarb I could wait until breakfast tomorrow, but if it was raspberry, that was another matter.

Crawling out of bed, I donned a robe and squeezed into my slippers. Then I went downstairs to the kitchen, concentrating on my newest investigation. I'm a professional enquiry agent after all, so I was qualified for the work. One thing Barker has taught me is that often the most direct approach is the best. Therefore, I stuck a finger into the pie and tasted it. It was cherry. Cherry would do. I cut a healthy slice, out of respect for my wife's skills. There was milk in the icebox, but I suspect it had gone off, so I ate the pie with water, which is not ideal, but after all, one is eating pie and therefore shouldn't complain.

When I finished, I pushed open the kitchen door and suddenly found I wasn't alone. Someone was in my house, standing between me and the front door. It had been raining, and a hooded cloak dripped on the linoleum. The hood lifted, and I realized with a start that Sofia Ilyanova was in my house. The assassin, La Sylphide, that will-o'-the-wisp, who brought death and destruction in her wake, stood before me in my very own house. My throat went dry, and my hackles rose.

"Good evening, Thomas," she said. "How have you been? Prospering, I see."

"Sofia," I croaked. "Have you come to kill me?"

"You probably deserve it, but that wasn't my intention."

My tongue cleaved to the roof of my mouth. I coughed, held up a finger, and retreated into the kitchen. There I went to the pantry and seized a sawn-down shotgun I kept there by the back door. It wasn't a standard item for a pantry, but my work is dangerous. It certainly was at that moment. However, I felt the cold barrel of a pistol against the back of my head.

"Don't be a fool," she said. "I'm not here to kill you, and you certainly aren't going to shoot me. If you try to kick me, I'll be forced to shoot off your kneecap, and then you will have to hobble along permanently behind Mr. Barker. Put the gun down. Now."

The last word was delivered with a tap to my head from the revolver. I turned about. It was a pendulum-style pistol, probably of German manufacture. She always had the latest equipment, even before it is available to the public.

"Are you still using an air gun?" I asked. I dared pour myself a drink of water and drank it before I choked.

"Sometimes, when silence is required," she replied. She looked about the room. "What a nice kitchen. It's all very domestic. Your wife is taking care of you."

"Let's not talk about my wife."

"I'm teasing you," she said. "I missed you, Thomas. Look at you! A beautiful house. A wife and child. A full partner in the agency. You've done well for yourself."

I didn't know what to say. I don't often have conversations with murderers, although far more than most people, generally speaking. "Why are you here?" I asked.

"Your wife is pretty and petite," she continued. "I like her. Oh, and your baby is such a little darling! She would be a wonderful playmate for Dimitri."

"How do you know what my family looks like?" I demanded. "They're in France."

She pointed the broom-handled pistol at me again.

"Temper, Thomas," she said. "You are one of my favorite people, but the first man I killed was my stepfather and I liked him too."

"You mentioned my family," I repeated.

"Let us sit and talk like civilized people," Sofia instructed. "You English are always civilized. Sorry! Welsh."

"I wish to stand," I told her. "But I will talk. How do you know what my wife and daughter look like? Did you enter my home and creep though the rooms, peering at us?"

She shrugged. "I was curious and wanted to see who has replaced me. She's lovely. And the little girl, such a darling! I almost picked her up."

I could have kicked myself. I suspected she was in town. Why hadn't I paid more attention?

"Don't you dare," I said, growing hot. "And Rebecca has not replaced you. You and I were never together."

"We were for a time," she argued. "You should see your son. Dimitri is the very image of you. He'll be excited to learn he has a sister. They should meet."

"They will never meet, Sofia."

"Don't be cruel, Thomas," she stated. Her voice was grave. "You see, I'm being civil."

"You are," I admitted, trying to work out what I should do with my visitor. "What have you been doing in London?"

"I've been busy, I suppose," she answered. "I've just arrived from South America. You wouldn't believe the number of politicians there that need killing these days. You know, you could always join me."

"I could never live your life. You know that."

"You and your moral codes," she chided. "It's so tiresome. I blame Mr. Barker for it. But what will you do if he dies? He will, if my father has his way. Of course, you may end up dead, as well. My father says I have a weakness for you, and he hates weakness in any form."

"It is curious that you act as if you have nothing to do with the matter, yet you would be the one pulling the trigger," I speculated.

"I kill who I'm hired to kill," she acknowledged. "It is my only skill, but I am very talented. The best, perhaps, if I cared about such things."

A thought occurred to me then. "You say you haven't come to kill me, but have you come to shoot me?"

"What makes you say that?" she asked.

"You're here in the middle of the night," I observed. "You're armed. You just mentioned your only skill. I'm not inspired like Barker, but I'm not a fool. I may not be on the list of the crew of the *Osprey* your father created, but I do tend to irritate him. Would he pay you well for shooting me?"

"Father is appalled that my son has your blood in his veins," she replied, "but so far, he hasn't told me to shoot you."

"You would do it, then?"

"Of course I would. I must eat. I must provide for my son. I'd shoot any person I was hired to kill. You might say I was bred for it."

"Oh, come now," I protested. "That man has never voluntarily paid for anything in his life. He has a hundred excuses for not paying his tailor, his bookie, his bank. You need to leave him, you really do."

"Perhaps I will if you come with me."

"I'm sorry, but we both know that's never going to happen," I said.

"Can't you see? You're as unkind as he is!"

She raised her German pistol and shot me in the chest,

near my left shoulder. The blow knocked me off my feet and I landed in a heap on the cold, hard floor.

"Goodbye, Thomas Llewelyn," she said. "You'll never see me again, but at least I've given you something to remember me by."

I heard the door close. It was deadly silent in the hall after the crack of the pistol. Blood dripped down my best dressing gown, ruining it. My body felt slack and numb, except for my shoulder, which was in excruciating pain. Slowly, slowly, lethargy washed over me and I began to think it would be so nice to fall asleep. Sleep, even if it were forever.

The next thing I knew, something was licking my face. It was Daisy, of course. I raised my head and looked about me in a state of torpor. My shirt was slick with blood. I looked at the standing clock in the hall and saw that I had been shot over three hours earlier. Why wasn't I dead yet?

Her pistol must have misfired, I reasoned. I opened my nightshirt and looked at the wound. It was red and swollen, but only a trickle of blood had issued from it. I couldn't believe I could be so fortunate as to be shot by an assassin and survive. As I said, in the past she used experimental equipment. Perhaps this one had been defective. However, whatever had happened, my shoulder was still injured. I decided to drag myself upstairs and examine the wound in a mirror.

"Some watchdog you are," I complained to Daisy as I staggered by, not that she heard the remark. The poor old thing is deaf as a post and missing half her teeth.

I went upstairs, sat in a dressing chair, and examined the wound closer. The skin was churned and angry-looking. Something had pierced the skin, but what? I reached behind my back to make certain a bullet hadn't passed through but there was no wound on my back.

My head was aching, and I could barely stand. I thought of calling Barker. Then I thought of a hospital. Yes, I'd better go to a hospital first. I'd call the Guv later.

Putting on my trousers took at least three minutes. My limbs were like rubber. After several attempts I gave up any thought of tying my shoes. I threw on the first shirt and coat I could find. Rebecca has sometimes called me a fop. She would change her mind if she saw me now.

I nearly broke my neck falling down the stairs. Once outside, I staggered toward Commercial Road, and when I finally arrived, raised my arm for a cab. The next I knew, one was at my feet.

"You've had a snootful, haven't you?" the cabman asked.

"For your information, sir, I have been shot," I replied. "Take me to London Hospital, if you don't mind."

I held open my coat to show him the blood, but he didn't seem particularly impressed.

"I'll take you, but if you get that on my seats, I'll shoot you again myself."

The ride was excruciating. However, the cabman helped me into London Hospital, and complained about me to the orderly at the desk, which was helpful. Apparently, being shot takes precedence over lesser wounds, so I was taken to see the doctor immediately.

An old fellow appeared a few minutes later. He wore a spade beard. He took my chin in one hand and examined my face.

"Have you been taking drugs?" he asked. "Opium, perhaps?"

"No, sir. I despise the stuff. Why?"

"Your pupils are dilated," he said. "What month is it?"

I tried to think, but nothing came to mind. I shrugged.

The old gent opened my coat and examined the wound. "Shot, you say?"

I nodded. "Bang. It went bang. Ripped my nightshirt. My best one."

He seized a lens and examined the wound closely.

"It was a projectile of some sort. A slingshot, perhaps?"

"Bang," I repeated.

"Did you come here directly?"

"I changed clothes," I told him. "After I slept on the floor for a while. A few hours or so. What's wrong with me, Doctor?"

He shook his head. "I'll admit I can't quite work it out. However, I can dress the wound."

The next I knew there were three other doctors in the room examining me. There were opinions given but no consensus among them. The doctor gave me a few stitches and sent me on my way. I paid the bill from Barker's wallet, since I'd forgotten my own. I'd consider it an expense, being in the line of duty and all that.

I vaguely recall being taken back to Camomile Street, feeling less light-headed. The doctor said there was no need to give me any more drugs.

Coming through the door of our home, I found Daisy on the floor, unmoving. I called her name, then rushed over to her. I thought she was dead, but her heart was beating. There was something beside her that she must have been chewing. It was a small cylinder the size of a bullet. Something projected from the tip, a pin, very short.

The dog would sleep it off. In fact, so would I, but first I had to call the Guv. For safety's sake, I made certain that the front and back doors were locked and bolted. Then I stumbled out into the hallway and made a telephone call.

"Barker residence," a voice answered, with a note of disapproval. Who would dare call at this hour? The voice could only belong to Jacob Maccabee.

"Mac!" I said, a trifle loudly. "Let me speak to the Guv."

"If you'll wait a moment, I'll get Mr. Barker."

I heard the telephone receiver being set down on the shelf in an alcove. Soon came the clomp of Barker's boots as he came down the stairs.

"Lad," Cyrus Barker rumbled into the receiver. I didn't think it politic to remind him not to call me lad. "What has happened?"

"Sofia Ilyanova was here at the house a few hours ago. She shot me."

"She shot you?" he repeated.

"Shot, yes," I replied. "She also claimed she sneaked into the house last week to look about. She was in our house, sir, watching us. She could have slit our collective throats in our beds."

"You sound strange, Thomas," he said. "Have you been drinking?"

"No, sir, not drinking. The doctor said my pupils are dilated. And I found a strange little bullet. Daisy's licked at it and now she's passed out."

"Are you certain Miss Ilyanova has left the premises?" he asked.

"Yes, sir," I told him. "Locked the door, I did. Unless I locked her in."

"Good. Where were you shot?"

"In the foyer, sir. Or is it foy-ay? I can't recall. Oh, I was also shot in the shoulder. Left side. Skin's all chewed up. Now I'm going to have to explain everything to Rebecca about that damned woman being in the house. She won't be pleased. It's a touchy subject."

"It would be, Thomas. I know you'd be tempted to say nothing for the good of your marriage, but it's best this way. Everything must be honest and aboveboard."

"You know what sort of fellow I am, sir."

"No one is blaming you, Thomas. I know you are a gentleman."

"What kind of man raises his own child to be an assassin, sir?" I asked. "It's monstrous."

"As I understand it, Nightwine's father was just as monstrous," he replied. "Perhaps it is passed down through the blood. In that case I wonder about her child, and what shall become of him as he grows. Did Miss Ilyanova mention Sun Yat-sen?"

I shook my head and almost dropped the receiver. "No, sir, but she may not have been privy to his plans."

"I should like to have met her," he rumbled. "If you recall, I've never had the opportunity. She must be remarkable."

"Can you imagine the sort of woman who kills people for money! She was in my house, sir, skulking through our bedrooms while we slept! She even looked in on the baby!"

"Calm yourself, lad. You've had a narrow escape, but kept your head. We must look over our shoulders from now on, and not just the two of us. Her arrival complicates matters."

I was going to say something else, but I heard the receiver being hung up and the call ended.

Daisy staggered into the room and looked up at me. I put her on the bed, where she promptly fell asleep. I settled into my pillow. However, for the rest of the night I woke every quarter hour or so and looked for Sofia Ilyanova hiding somewhere in the shadows.

CHAPTER 21

There was a jangle at the cell door. Sun Yat-sen sat up in his cot and then stood when he saw who it was. Macartney was back again, after several days. The councilor was well-dressed, reminding Sun that he'd had no change of clothing and no bath since he had arrived at the embassy. Cleanliness mattered to him. It was another way to beat him down and break his spirit.

"I demand to see the ambassador!" Sun insisted.

"Alas," Sir Halliday replied, shaking his head. "I'm afraid he's out of town."

"Because of me?" Sun asked.

Macartney smiled. "How self-important you are to think he has anything to do with you. He has no concern for your welfare, and in fact, I have very little myself. In a day or two, you'll be tossed onto a ship, and it will be as if you never existed at all. I'm leaving for my estate this afternoon. I hear it will be good weather for grouse shooting. We shall both be far away when you are smuggled aboard a ship bound for the Suez Canal and the China Seas. I only wish I could be present when you are beheaded. You are an idealist, an intellectual troublemaker, and China will never be the way you want it to be. It was naïve of you to think that by your whining little missive to the emperor you could change anything. Had you not been raised so far from your native country you'd have realized that."

"Then why are you so eager to see me on my way?" Sun asked. "Why leave town on my account?"

"Deniability, Doctor," Macartney replied. "It is wise for all officials to be out of town during such an event. It saves embarrassment should something go wrong."

Sun crossed his arms. "So, something could go wrong, then. Your well-laid plans could fail!"

"Come now, you are Chinese," Sir Halliday said. "You understand, one must prepare for any contingency. One of the junior ambassadors at the embassy will be put in charge temporarily and willingly take the blame should your plight become known. Then he would be sent back to Peking to a hero's welcome. Meanwhile, you shall be swatted like a gnat and be forgotten quickly. No one will ever remember the name Sun Yat-sen. It would have been better had you never been born. You will die in disgrace, and your mother and father, your sisters and brothers, will claim they never heard of you. You'll be a failure in the world's eyes."

Sun could take it no longer. He lunged at the counselor but one of the men who had brought him to the embassy stepped around Macartney and clouted the doctor on the head. Yat-sen collapsed and was thrown back on the bed. The Englishman looked pleased, and the Chinese guards chuckled.

"You really are quite useless, you know," Macartney continued. "How did you come to write such an incredibly stupid letter? Were you coerced by revolutionary friends? If so, they took advantage of you. Why, the very fellow who gave your note to His Imperial Majesty has been demoted and locked in a cangue, for people to walk by and spit on. At least you deserved your punishment. You might even say you have earned it. Goodbye, Doctor. By this time tomorrow you'll be in the Channel nearing France, and I will have bagged my first pheasant at a shooting party in Greenwich. If someone mentions the name Sun Yat-sen, I won't even recall who you are."

Sir Halliday Macartney turned and waddled out of the narrow chamber. Once he and the guards were gone, Dr. Sun moved to the slops bucket and was violently ill again. Soon there was a hand on his back, a tentative but helpful hand that belonged to Cole, the caretaker.

"It ain't right, them thumpin' you like this," he muttered. "You ain't done nuffink 'cept write a bleedin' letter. Nobody deserves to die for writin' a letter. Sorry, I was in the hall and couldn't help listenin'. I'll bet it was more important than they let on or the ambassador wouldn't have Macartney down here talkin' to you. They ain't only tryin' to convince you that you ain't important, I reckon. They're a-tryin' to convince themselves."

"Thank you," Sun Yat-sen murmured.

He'd lost the contents of his stomach, and his chest was heaving. At that point he didn't care if he lived or died. The revolution seemed unimportant. Was it worth imprisonment? Was it worth beheading?

"By gar, that tears it," Cole continued. "My missus talked me out of it, but it's the right thing to do. I'll speak to your doctor friend tonight and tell them where you are and how poorly they're treatin' you. A nice fellow like you, who went through all that readin' and studyin' to become a doctor shouldn't be hurt for doing what he swore an oath to do. It makes me ashamed to work here, even if it is just moppin' the floors and emptyin' slops. You don't deserve to die for no letter. It ain't civilized, and it ain't bloody English!"

"Thank you!" Sun Yat-sen mumbled. He became ill again.

"There you go," Cole said, stroking his back. "Get it all out of you."

He helped the sweating prisoner to his cot.

"Maybe I shouldn't have written the letter," Sun admitted.

Cole shook his head. "None o' that. You wouldn't of writ it unless it was important. You didn't do nuffin' wrong. It were the ambassador and his lot, and Macartney ain't helpin'. You get yourself some sleep now. Leave the rest to me."

Sun Yat-sen was not so confident. The punishment had frightened him. He had been bullied as a child. The native Hawaiian boys didn't like the Chinese. Neither did their fathers. He'd been beaten several times, which forced him into an isolated world of study. Soon, he excelled, which only resulted in more cruel treatment after school. He had anticipated that adulthood would be better. However, it wasn't, and now the bullies were larger, and more malicious.

I'm going to get out of here, he told himself, anger starting to build inside him. *I'm not going to die; I'll escape somehow, and when I do, I won't just write a letter of protest to the emperor, I will shake the walls of the Forbidden City.*

CHAPTER 22

There had been too many factors involved in the case for me to join Barker in antagonistics the next morning. Although I reached the office at exactly seven thirty, according to the tolling of Big Ben, the Guv looked at me as if I had disappointed him a little. That might have crushed me a few years earlier, but now I thought he was entitled to his own disappointments. I had things to do, and the garden would still be waiting there for me tomorrow.

"How are you feeling this morning?" my partner asked as I came in and went over to my desk.

"A little groggy, if I may say so," I replied, fishing in my pocket until I came up with a handkerchief wrapped around the bullet that had struck me the evening before. "Take a look at this."

I set it on Barker's blotter while he retrieved a lamp from

the corner and brought it to his desk. The bullet was a brass lozenge about an inch long, which the Guv immediately pried apart with his knife. Inside was a thin barrel, a needle, a tiny syringe, and a charge at the back. A small tailpiece had been chewed by Daisy before it put her to sleep.

"Ingenious," the Guv said as he examined the tiny device.

"Be careful," I warned, "or you'll prick your finger, and I'll have to call for an ambulance."

"If I did, I would deserve it," he growled.

Just then, a small ragamuffin with no shoes shot into our outer office and bounced off the front of Jenkins's desk like a bee in a glass jar. Our clerk exchanged the slip of paper the boy brought for a ha'penny, and the tyke was gone in a trice. They are stock-in-trade for enquiry agents, boys delivering and receiving messages. Many Londoners still do not trust the telephone, or do not have access to one, and when we were away from our chambers the devices were hard to come by even for us. Boys, however, and even girl messengers, were legion.

Jenkins took the missive to the Guv on his salver and offered it to him. My partner took the note with a nod and read it while our clerk returned to his desk. I believe Jenkins was even more proud of our offices than Barker himself. Ours were the most professional-looking chambers of any agency in London. Our clerk loved working here and took every opportunity to add to the tone of the rooms.

I glanced at Jenkins as he returned to his desk with a look of satisfaction, then turned to Barker, who was reading the note and frowning. One learns to decipher expressions in our profession. Sometimes it can be a matter of life and death. My partner's features wavered between surprise and disapproval. He rose to his feet immediately, and therefore so did I. We threw on our coats and hats, took our sticks and hurried out the door. I didn't question him. There were clouds rolling in from the sea, so to speak. The wrong word and he'd have bitten my head off.

Barker bawled "Mayfair" to a cabman at the curb, and we bowled off. Then he passed the slip of paper to me. The message was one word written in a florid hand, "Brown's."

"The hotel?" I asked, handing it back to him.

"Presumably," he replied. "There is a Brown's haberdashery in Savile Row, and a boot repair shop in Poplar, but I don't believe we are being summoned to either of them."

"A feminine hand," I noted. "Surely Sofia Ilyanova hasn't written us."

"Unlikely," he agreed.

I could have speculated until lunch, but Barker looked a trifle nettled.

We reached the elegant façade of the oldest hotel in London and jumped down. Having paid the cabman, I hurried inside, and none too soon. Barker was walking briskly from the front desk. Brown's had not yet installed a lift in the old pile, so I followed him up the elegant staircase.

"Suite 409," he called over his shoulder, as if that would tell me everything. We hurried down a long hallway, and when we reached the numbered door, I knocked first. My partner has not mastered the art of knocking without making the occupant of the room think Scotland Yard was outside coming for an arrest. There was a pause, and then the door was flung open. It was answered by the last person on earth I expected. I immediately recognized that mischievous dimple.

"Thomas!" she cried, and promptly jumped in my arms.

"Rebecca!" I exclaimed. "What are you doing here?"

Barker stepped around us and into the room. Philippa entered from an adjoining chamber and smiled. When they met, she pecked him on the cheek, which caused his face to turn red. Had he known he'd have been kissed in front of strangers, by which I mean me, he would not have come.

"What are the two of you doing in London?" he demanded, closing and locking the door behind him.

"There has been a change of plan, I'm afraid," Philippa said. "It couldn't be helped."

The woman is imperturbable. She was every bit his equal and was not afraid of one of his outbursts.

All of us sat. I wasn't prepared for the depth as I sank into one of Brown's plush chairs. I wondered how much these exclusive rooms must have cost per night.

"We were chased away," Lady Ashleigh explained. "We thought it best that we return to London since Paris is no safer."

"What happened?" I asked.

"Etienne has disappeared," she replied. "He was harvesting the last grapes of the season in his vineyard and went missing yesterday morning."

"How did you hear of it?" Barker rumbled.

Philippa turned to the Guv. "From his wife, Mireille Dummolard."

"You let her know you were on the Continent?" my partner asked. "That was thoughtless and dangerous."

"I am never thoughtless and there was no danger," she replied. "I called her on the telephone when we arrived in Paris. She and I are acquainted, and she sent me the exchange number to their family home last year. When she called yesterday, she was distraught. I promised her you would take care of the problem. You do intend to take care of the problem, don't you?"

"Of course," he replied. "Did she offer any idea of what might have happened?"

"His brother, Robert, saw marks in the dirt where Etienne

had been dragged away. You know he is a very sturdy man. There were also furrows at the end of the row where a horse and cart had stood. It's obvious he has been taken."

"How did you arrive here?" Barker demanded, crossing his thick, muscular arms. He was upset. He had taken her almost three hundred miles to keep her safe, and now here she was again, endangering her life and my entire family's.

"We boarded the Paris-to-Calais express, took a ferry to Dover, and the train brought us here," Philippa said. "Sebastian is resourceful, but I don't believe even he is able to watch every port in England."

"They might have followed you," Cyrus Barker reasoned.

"Rebecca and I are not incompetent," she stated.

"Far from it," Barker agreed.

"We are educated women," she continued. "We didn't attend finishing schools merely to learn embroidery and how to find a husband. We fully understand the danger we are in. Etienne was taken no more than an hour away from the hotel. You are the one who claimed Paris was safe. Unfortunately, you were wrong, so we made the decision to come back to London."

"At tremendous risk to your safety," he argued.

"Do you think I can't defend myself?" she asked. "I always carry that dainty little pistol you gave me, and you purchased a James Smith umbrella for me, as well. It is a formidable weapon. You told me so yourself."

"Enough, woman!" he said, raising his hands in surrender. "Very well. You were right, and I overreacted."

Philippa Ashleigh suddenly smiled. She could be magnanimous in her triumph. *My*, I thought, *these aristocrats have style.*

"Your apology is accepted," she said. "Now, Etienne is gone. How will we find him?"

"That makes three of my crew who have been kidnapped. Etienne, Paul, and Ho, who was taken from his restaurant last week. And as you know, the *Osprey* has vanished from her moorings. I have put out a reward but haven't received any word about what has happened to her."

Philippa studied him for a moment. "What's going on, Cyrus? We deserve to know."

The Guv heaved a sigh. "There has been a reward for all our heads in China, but probably only two or three men on earth recall that fact. Unfortunately, Sebastian Nightwine is one of them. Also, there is a doctor in London named Sun Yat-sen, whom we suspect is a prisoner in the Chinese embassy, who also has a price on his head. Sebastian visited the embassy this very week. I believe he intends to snap us up and sail to Peking."

"He's an industrious fellow," Lady Ashleigh responded. "I suppose you are the only one left free with a reward upon his head, then."

"I am."

"Yet you were concerned for our safety and not your own."

Just then, the door of a bedchamber was pushed open, and my daughter rushed in, calling me. Rebecca excused us and led me into an inner room. There I kissed Rachel and lifted her onto my lap. Rebecca sat next to me and told me everything that had happened to her since she left London, some important and most not. A weight was lifted from my mind just seeing them again.

I knew it was too early yet to tell Rebecca that Sofia had invaded our home, but I would have to tell her soon. She would naturally be upset. The woman's name is not spoken in our home.

After a few minutes, we rejoined the others in the sitting room, where the argument between Lady Ashleigh and

Barker, if that's what it was, was momentarily set aside. However, they were still behaving in a formal fashion, as they always did in public. They were a curious couple, but I was not the first to say it, and I most certainly wouldn't be the last.

"Do you still believe it was necessary for us to go all the way to Paris?" Philippa asked.

"Of course," he replied. "The fact that three of our friends have disappeared is proof that it was necessary."

"We are no danger to Sebastian, nor an enticement," Philippa replied. "We haven't any reward from the Chinese government upon our heads."

"Perhaps not," Barker replied. "But he does have a fascination with you and has since our days in Canton."

"Cyrus is of the opinion that Sebastian orchestrated my husband's death," Her Ladyship explained. "Hal stumbled coming down a harbor stair on the island docks and fell to his death on the stone dock below. It was ruled misadventure, but that is merely a legal term. Hal was the least adventurous person you'd ever meet. Even descending a stone staircase on the harbor, buffeted by native sailors and laborers, would have been too much for his nerves. He would have been on his guard. To be successfully knocked from his perch is suspect, particularly with Sebastian in the vicinity. There was no evidence against him, and he claimed he was in Shanghai at the time, but how difficult would it be to hire someone to nudge an Englishman off a rail-less harbor staircase?"

"Yet he still attempted to propose to you, with all your suspicions?" I asked.

"More than that, he went about as if I had agreed to marry him when my grieving was over. He told half the compound at Shameen Island. I didn't hear of it until weeks later, by which time it was considered common knowledge. I was furious, of course, but he merely shrugged his shoulders as if there were nothing to be done about the situation. There was no proof he had anything to do with Hal's death, and of course he denied the charge. Cyrus and I weren't together then."

They were hardly together now, I thought, although he'd slip off after work on a Saturday afternoon without comment and be back in his house in Lion Street early Monday morning. As closely as the two of us worked together, their relationship was none of my business. Rebecca found it delightfully scandalous and a bit romantic, as well. Scandalous certainly, but the romantic bit was hard to swallow in a man who didn't speak her given name in our presence.

They sat in leather chairs side by side, though a comfortable sofa was in the room. Rebecca would claim they were communing together, whatever that meant. To me, he seemed as romantic as Inspector Javert in *Les Misérables*. In turn, I was certain the Guv found me overly demonstrative with my wife, but of course he wouldn't mention it.

I turned my attention back to the enquiry. I was a trained agent now, but I only had a little experience with that devil, Nightwine, or knowledge of their relationships in far-off Canton. The Guv and his crew were very close, but they never spoke of their time on the Pearl River with me. I was shut out of all of it. Perhaps they were so secretive because of the price on their heads, but there was no way for me to imagine myself in their place, no handle for me to grasp. The most I could do was to be at his command and jump without question when he told me to, but that was my duty even on a normal day.

Rachel had acquired a stuffed hedgehog in Paris and treated it as if it were her baby. I had missed them. It angered me that my family might be in danger from Sebastian Nightwine and his abominable daughter. I doubted anyone else would have considered harming a man's family, but few are as venal as the pair of them. My family had been forced to flee. Now they were back on English shores, and once again in harm's way.

"Are they safe here?" I asked the Guv, sotto voce, as my daughter played and the women talked.

"No more or less than in Paris," he replied. "I admit I was caught out to hear that Etienne has been taken. I had not considered Sebastian's need for vengeance would be so rigorous. More likely it is the need for funds."

"Do you suppose Nightwine is doing this himself?" I asked. "Miss Ilyanova can do many things, but carrying a man Etienne's size would be beyond her abilities. Do you suppose the Imperial Secret Service is involved? In that case, he and Macartney would obviously be working together. Unless of course you have another enemy that you haven't told me about. Someone from your boxing days in China, perhaps?"

He did not rise to the bait. He is a difficult fish to bring to the net.

"I made no other enemies of whom I am aware," he answered icily. "Certainly no one willing to travel half the world to find me. However, as you say, he could hire someone if he was willing to share part of the bounty. That is, until his daughter shoots his accomplice and returns the money to her father or keeps it for herself. It always comes down to pounds sterling with them."

"I think it likely that she lives on the money she makes assassinating people."

He nodded his head. "That may be the case. I hadn't considered the matter."

"Could we have been followed here to the hotel?" I asked, still concerned for my family.

"I saw no one while we were traveling across London, but you are wise to be cautious."

"I'm not as worried about myself as I am about my family," I told him. "I've never asked you this before, but were you against my getting married? You yourself are a lifelong bachelor."

"I understand your need for a wife," he replied. "I had not expected you to live as a monk. And though I have not married since coming to England that does not preclude the possibility that I might at some time in the future. Each of us has the freedom to do as he pleases."

I tried not to glare, but he is a very canny Scot.

"Don't read anything into that, Thomas," he warned.

"No, sir, of course not. It's none of my concern."

"Aye, lad. Truer words were never spoken."

The conversation ended there. However, I wondered if he suspected I was doing a Highland fling in my head at that very moment. I couldn't wait to tell Rebecca. Perhaps I could get her to winkle more information out of Lady Ashleigh.

Now that was an enquiry I was willing to solve.

CHAPTER 23

Dr. Cantlie walked into our offices that afternoon, accompanied by a downtrodden fellow we had never seen before. The doctor looked a trifle more jubilant than when we last saw him, so I expected good news. Barker stood and shook our client's hand, but the other fellow was too timid to shake Barker's. Whoever he was, he was wise to be cautious.

Our visitor was a little taller than I, with a weak jaw and scanty hair. He looked a typical hardworking East Ender. He wore a neckerchief under his shirt, and his shoes were worn, but the shirt was as white as mine. I surmised he had a wife who cared about his appearance.

"Gentlemen, you were correct!" Dr. Cantlie exclaimed. "We have news of Sun Yat-sen!"

"Excellent," the Guv replied. "So, he is indeed being held at the Chinese embassy."

"Yes, he is there. This man can attest to it."

"And who is this helpful fellow?" my partner asked.

"Albert Cole, sir," the visitor answered, mangling the flat cap in his hands. "I'm a caretaker at the embassy. I clean Mr. Sun's cell. He convinced me to go to Dr. Cantlie's flat. They were a-beatin' him something fierce."

"It is to your credit that you came, sir," Barker replied. "Others might not want to help their fellow man for fear they'd be sacked."

Cole nodded. "I'd prefer not to be, as well, Mr. Barker, but Sir Macartney had no right to keep a fellow locked in a cell with all his friends lookin' for him."

"How is he faring?" the Guv asked. "Has he been mistreated?"

"Yes, sir," the caretaker answered. "The Chinamen who work for the embassy, the bodyguards or jailers or what-have-you, have cuffed him about the head now and again, for no other reason than the enjoyment of it. Mr. Sun don't look used to such treatment, you see."

"And you?" my partner inquired. "Have you experienced it yourself?"

The hat made another revolution in Cole's hands. "Yes, sir, every now and then, when I don't move as fast as they'd like. But I was more worried about Mr. Sun. Them Chinese guards knock him about to show they're serious. And they taunt him mercilessly."

"Taunt him?" I asked from behind my shorthand notebook.

"That's the word, isn't it? They tell all about what it's like to have your head cut off, and that he's only a week or two from havin' it done. Said there'd be no waitin' unless the emperor wanted to come see it for himself. Torturin' him, they are. Made me sick. They're bad people, Mr. Barker, I hope you remember that. They don't play by our rules and human life h'ain't worth nothin' to them. Live, die, it's all the same to them. And Dr. Sun bein' an educated man and all."

"You like him," Barker stated, a faint smile on his lips.

"Never 'ad any use for celestials before, sir, but he's all right. Treats me polite-like, and don't look down on me for emptyin' chamber pots."

"Have you been amply compensated?" my partner asked.

"Amply what? Oh, yeah, Dr. Cantlie took good care of me."

"Excellent," Barker replied. "But you've made our work at this agency easier, as well. Thomas?"

I handed Cole a five-pound note. He was more than grateful. Cantlie sent him off lest his absence be noticed.

"Well, gentlemen, what shall we do now?" Dr. Cantlie asked.

Barker leaned forward in his chair. "Thomas, set this down in shorthand: Scotland Yard, *The Times*, *The Star*, *The Illustrated London News*, *The Gazette*, and the *Daily Chronicle*." He turned to the doctor. "Tell me, have you time enough to visit these places in the next day or so? Inform them there shall be a demonstration soon at the Chinese embassy. We'll let them know the exact time later."

"Of course," Cantlie agreed. "What is this about?"

"Mr. Llewelyn and I are going to Limehouse to speak to some leaders there," he replied. "They won't want the embassy mistreating one of their own."

"Won't you need an interpreter?" the doctor asked.

"Sir, I may be a Scot, but I was raised in Foochow."

He gave my partner a look of surprise. He had underestimated Cyrus Barker. I suspected Sir Halliday Macartney had as well. We saw Dr. Cantlie to the door. Once he was gone, we prepared to leave.

"Shouldn't we alert the Foreign Office?" I asked.

Barker shrugged as we stepped out onto the curb.

"Why?" he asked. "Hesketh Pierce had us arrested. I'm not inclined to offer him any favors today. Nor the Yard, for that matter. Cab!"

Limehouse was as bedraggled as ever, but we stopped at the Grapes, one of London's best public houses, founded in 1583, believed to be by the site where public hangings took place a few centuries ago. It was but a street or two from Ho's. I wondered where Barker's shipmate had been taken and whether Ho had been injured in the tunnel blast. Barker stopped here, I suspected, because this was about the time he generally stopped at Ho's tearoom for a meal and advice. I tried to question the Guv about our next move, but he put me off. He wasn't in a talkative mood. We drank our stout in silence. I could see that he was thinking, which is generally a good thing, so I left him to his thoughts.

Afterward we looked at Limehouse Kiln Street, where the tunnel once stood, and then he led me deeper into Dockland, intending to speak to K'ing, who would want to know our progress.

In the Inn of Double Happiness, which I always assumed referred to gambling and opium, we cooled our heels for a quarter hour drinking tasteless tea. Barker tells me I haven't a subtle palette. It all tastes like bilgewater to me. A meeting was taking place in K'ing's office, and I wondered if it was related to our work. A group of young Chinese men came out of K'ing's office and went down the stairs arguing with one another loudly. We stood to ascend the staircase.

"It's the young men, Thomas," the Guv said in a low voice.

"They are impatient to throw off the yoke of the Manchus. God grant it happens this time."

"Two hundred and fifty years is an awfully long time to be subjugated, sir," I answered.

"The English did the same to Scotland in 1650, lad," he reminded me. "Don't think we've forgotten the matter."

"The Welsh have you beaten, sir. It was 1282 for us. I grew up speaking my native tongue and am proud of it!"

We climbed the stairs and went into K'ing's office. A guard relieved us temporarily of our weapons. I did not kick up a fuss because I still carried a weapon no one could take away from me: my training in Chinese boxing.

"Gentlemen, sit," K'ing ordered.

Our host wore a well-tailored English suit, but a Chinese robe had been thrown over it. The desk he sat behind was lacquered to a high gloss, with a European desk pad atop it. K'ing was smoking a cigarette in a jade holder. I noted a bowl and chopsticks at one end of his desk. He had been working through a meal. He was a very busy man.

"What has happened, gentlemen?" he asked. "I assume you haven't come to chat."

Barker cleared his throat. "As we suspected, Sun Yat-sen is incarcerated in the Chinese embassy. We found a note from him in the area, and a servant went to Sun's mentor to tell him."

"Has he been mistreated?"

"By Sir Halliday Macartney, certainly," the Guv replied. "According to our witness, the Imperial Secret Service have given him a drubbing. Thomas and I had a difference of opinion with them recently ourselves."

"I'd have enjoyed witnessing that," K'ing admitted. "There is no love lost between Sir Halliday and myself."

"Perhaps you shall yet," Barker remarked. "We came here

to suggest that there be a public protest in front of the embassy in a day or so. The public must be informed. We'll need British citizens, radicals and anarchists, the press, and of course, Sun's native kinsmen, I hope. A small contingent might be best."

"We are eager to participate."

"A contingent of Chinese in Portland Place—" Barker began.

"Is none of your concern," K'ing said, finishing his sentence. "He is a Chinese national. You found the doctor, and for that, we thank you. Let us handle the matter from here."

"I am involved because I was hired to be involved, by Dr. Cantlie, and because my crew has been taken by Nightwine, with whom I have a long history. You may have political concerns, but they aren't relevant to my enquiry."

"I understand that," K'ing conceded. "But you must understand that Southern China is in turmoil."

"Aye," Cyrus Barker replied. "I received a letter from my boxing master in Canton, informing me of recent events. He is a member of the Heaven and Earth Society, as am I."

K'ing set down his cigarette. "I am aware that Wong Fei Hung is a member. Do you want credit for freeing Dr. Sun? Is this to be an English matter? I have fought against the Manchus for most of my life. The fall of the Qing government has been my chief purpose for living!"

The conversation began to get heated. Both men leaned forward in their chairs.

"We need to have the British public behind us, supporting Yat-sen," Barker countered. "Her Majesty's Government has a great deal of power in China. The palace may sway public opinion and Parliament."

"Macartney and the legation dithered too long," I put in, hoping to be included in the conversation. "Had they put the doctor on a ship immediately, no one would have been able to say what became of him. Does it matter who rescues him?"

"It does!" K'ing insisted, tapping the table with a polished and overlong fingernail.

"Suppose Dr. Cantlie gets credit for releasing him here in London, while the Society takes credit for rescuing Sun from British imperialism and execution in China?" I suggested.

"I am unable to make that decision for myself," K'ing replied. "I must take counsel."

"Dr. Sun is not in our hands yet, man," Barker growled. You take counsel and he'll be on board a ship passing through the Suez Canal tomorrow!"

"Ngoi fu," K'ing murmured. "We would never let that happen."

That was one I hadn't heard before. I memorized the phrase. I'd have to ask the Guv what it meant later.

"Damn and blast!" Barker growled. "Where's my ship? I'd go to China myself to straighten out the matter if I had it."

"Sir," I pointed out. "They want your head there, as well. There is a reward."

"I don't care," he replied. "A captain's responsible for his crew."

"Which you lost," K'ing reminded him. I thought it a low blow, and not helpful in light of the circumstances.

"Look, gentlemen, this is counterproductive. I'd like to know what we're going to do in Portland Place, and when."

"I agree, Thomas. Something must be done immediately." The Guv looked at the Chinese leader. "What do you say about tomorrow? Is it too early?"

There was a pause as K'ing leaned back in his chair and tented his fingers.

"If we work all night, it might be possible," he replied. "We'll protest outside the embassy, obviously."

"A vocal Chinese presence," Barker agreed. "Then we shall gather socialist groups and possibly a sympathetic church or two. I have a clerk who can make placards and banners overnight. We'll make enough noise to attract a crowd, which shall inevitably get the attention of Scotland Yard. The public will see the protest and wonder what the commotion is all about, and I'm certain the protestors will have their photograph in *The Illustrated London News*. A copy or two of that newspaper may even find its way to Peking."

"One or two?" K'ing asked. "We'll buy out the edition! They'll be forced to publish a second printing. We'll smuggle it all over Southern China. It will encourage the masses to revolt, because if the stupid English can free imprisoned protestors, why can't we? I mean no disrespect, Mr. Llewelyn."

"None taken," I replied. "I'm Welsh."

"Are we agreed, then?" Barker asked the den owner. "Tomorrow?"

"I still must take counsel with our elders," K'ing repeated. "But, I think I can make them agree to the plan. Many of the exiles here are patriots."

"'Destroy the Qing, restore the Ming!'" I cried.

K'ing frowned at me. It would have been acceptable if the Guv had said it, but as I had just pointed out, I am a mere Welshman, who had never been to China.

Five minutes later we were on the streets of Limehouse again. A fog had risen; ribbons of vapor crept in from the river, and the few streetlamps had a nimbus of light around them. I could hear an erhu being strummed nearby. Somehow, a common London fog made this drab area of Limehouse appear more picturesque and exotic. I thought of the opium den in Dickens's *The Mystery of Edwin Drood*.

"What did K'ing mean when he called you *Ngoi fu*?" I asked.

"Father-in-law," Barker explained.

Mr. K'ing was married to my partner's former ward, Bok Fu Ying, whom the Guv had taken on when she was given to him by the Empress Dowager to look after Harm. She was the dog's slave, his property. As its caregiver, she somehow found herself on that fateful flight to the West with the Guv. Afterward Barker had placed her with a kind Asian family and visited her regularly. When she grew older, she took over grooming Harm, arriving at Lion Street twice a week in widow's weeds to hide her oriental ancestry. Her Eastern appearance would make tongues wag even more than they already did about Number 3 Lion Street. Stupid Englishmen, indeed.

"Shall we look in on Fu Ying?" Barker asked. "She owns a telephone set, and I have many calls to make."

"Of course," I replied.

We walked through the streets of Limehouse to Three Colt Lane, where Barker slapped the knocker on the door of Fu Ying's house. A maid arrived with a curtsy and took our coats. It was an unusual house for provincial London: the maid was English and the mistress Chinese. We were shown into a parlor lined with Hong Kong silk walls, and miniature Asian villages carved out of cork at one's elbow.

A little doll of a girl in black pigtails with a satin suit of pale green came to Barker, taking the corner of his coat and holding it without saying a word. Fu Ying had trained her daughter well regarding this monolithic benefactor. She communed with the Guv silently for a few moments, then ran over to me and grinned, showing that her two front teeth were missing. I picked her up and gave her a peck on the cheek. Soo and I were old friends.

Bok Fu Ying appeared then in a blue Parisian dress and stylish shoes. She bowed to us both and invited us to sit. Like any English lady, she rang for tea.

"It's good to see you," she said to Barker, sitting on the very edge of the sofa by him, as enamored of him as her daughter. What odd little lives all of us touched by Cyrus Barker lead. We circle in his orbit like planets. "And you, Thomas? How are you? Are you well?"

"Very well, thank you," I assured her.

"And how is Rebecca?"

"You must find out for yourself. She would enjoy a visit from you," I said. "It's been a while, although it will have to wait until this case is over."

"I would love to see her," she said.

"Things shall settle soon," I assured her. "Call her in a week or so. She and Rachel had a recent adventure in Paris."

"Have you spoken to my husband?"

"Aye, we have," Barker replied. "About the Sun matter."

"That poor man," she remarked.

"I'd like to use your telephone set, if I may," Barker requested. "I have several calls to make."

"Of course," Bok Fu Ying said, although I could tell she was disappointed. "You know where it is."

They spoke only once or twice a week. He treated her in the traditional Asian manner. When the Guv had left, Fu Ying and I talked of the case. K'ing kept his wife well-informed, though he treated her in some ways as callously as Barker. It wouldn't occur to him to ask her opinion about anything. They were one of the most unusual couples in London. The man is very nearly a warlord, a revolutionary, and a drug peddler, while his wife is one of my wife's best friends and our daughters play together.

Cyrus Barker was gone for almost an hour. Bok Fu Ying was another student of Barker's, so she showed me a few moves he had not taught me while her daughter played with a deck of cards on the carpet.

Finally, Barker returned and gestured to us. There was work to be done before tomorrow. He and his ward bowed stoically at the door as we left. I wondered if it would ever change. Perhaps it never would unless I spoke to him about it.

CHAPTER 24

By late afternoon, I realized I needed to speak to Rebecca about Sofia Ilyanova. Normally in a crisis I weather the storm and delay a discussion, but Nightwine's daughter was another matter and needed to be discussed. Barker and I made our way to Brown's Hotel. Rachel took a nap while I pulled her mother into the private sitting room we had used earlier.

"What is it, Thomas?" Rebecca asked. "I can see from the look on your face that something has happened."

My encounter with Sofia Ilyanova tumbled out of me, from her entering our home to being shot by the dart. She took the news stoically, but I could see that she was hurt and somewhat angry.

"And there is one final matter," I added, dreading her

reaction. "It appears that she had broken into the house sometime last week."

"When?" she asked, sitting up ramrod straight.

"Before we left for Paris," I replied. "She said she stole about, looked at everyone sleeping, then left, or so she claimed. I didn't believe her at first. I assumed she was making it out of whole cloth. Now I'm not so certain."

"The house?" Rebecca asked, her face growing pale. "She was in our house? My house?"

It was indeed her house. It had been willed her by her first husband, though they had been married less than a year when he died. It had taken me a while to be willing to move into it, being another man's castle, so to speak, but she loved that house, and I would do anything to please her. Now it had been desecrated.

"So she claimed." Every muscle was clenched, and my stomach was swimming in acid.

She literally reached up and seized the curls on both sides of her head in agony.

"That was a message for me," Rebecca insisted. "It says she can reach out and take whatever she pleases—even you—and there is nothing I can do about it. I own no air rifle and the only art I have been taught is stitchery. I don't know how to kill someone and wouldn't if I could. Not even her. She's not as mad as you claim, Thomas. She can intrigue as well as any woman. You must do something about her, or I can never return to Camomile Street again. She has violated our home. My house has been tainted. I cannot return."

I thought to argue, but a voice told me this couldn't be rectified in five minutes' conversation.

"I don't feel safe, Thomas," she continued, "and I certainly do not feel comfortable bringing Rachel home. That odious woman could have stolen our baby in the night!"

I nodded my head.

"She could have kidnapped you again! You were unconscious. You could be in her web this very moment!"

"That hadn't occurred to me," I admitted. She could have.

She gave me a withering look. I must do something, take some initiative, or we'd be living a gypsy existence for who knew how long.

"I'll have the house fortified like Mr. Barker's," I promised. "Double locks on the doors."

"Do you promise to shoot her if she breaks in again?" she asked.

I couldn't tell if she was serious, but I held up my hand. I'd do whatever was necessary.

"I promise."

She looked at me with some degree of skepticism. Then she changed the subject.

"She has a young son," she began.

I clapped a hand to my face. "I'm sorry!"

"We have to discuss it, Thomas," she replied. "She is a professional killer. She shoots people and poisons them."

"Yes," I said, waiting for her to make her point.

"She travels around the world, or so you've claimed."

"Yes, she mentioned South America."

"What of the child? Who is watching him while she's murdering monarchs? Certainly not his grandfather."

"She implied he travels with her," I replied. "He was certainly with her in London during the Romanoff business. I saw him for the briefest second."

"It's cruelty," she stated. "Dragging him about from one continent to the next. What kind of mother must she be, who holds her son's life in so little esteem?"

"A terrible one, I'm sure," I said. "You know I've been concerned about her mental state. One cannot do what she does without receiving some kind of damage to her psyche."

We stopped, lost in our thoughts. She fell back against the pillows on the settee.

"Tell me again what happened when she shot you."

"She owns some sort of prototype gun that shoots darts containing a drug," I answered. "I was unconscious for hours, and I suspect that's what she did to the rest of Barker's crew."

"Did it pierce the flesh?" she asked.

"I had to go to London Hospital for a stitch or two. Here," I said, opening my jacket.

She shook her head. "Stop! Show me later. Or after it heals. Or never!"

"I thought you'd be glad this one wasn't fatal," I replied.

"Let's not fight," she said, by way of a response. "Our friends are in the next room."

Rebecca took my hand and drew me into the main room, where Barker and Lady Ashleigh were sitting by the fire.

"Thomas was shot last night," she said. "By that horrid woman in our own house."

"In your own house?" Philippa echoed.

"Worse yet, she's been creeping about, watching us sleep."

"No!" Her Ladyship cried. "What will you do?"

"I don't know," Rebecca said. "I may sell the house. I can't live in a home where a woman has been standing over my child in the middle of the night like a vampire."

"I've promised to increase the security at the house," I replied.

She crossed her arms and glared at me. "It doesn't matter. It's been tainted."

"We should discuss this tomorrow when we're not so tired," Philippa said.

The Guv nodded gravely.

"A great deal will depend on how this case is settled for all of us," I said.

"I think Thomas and I should be on our way," my partner added delicately. "We must bring this case to its conclusion so all our lives can return to normal."

He walked to the door of the suite and donned his coat and hat. He turned to the ladies and gave them a formal bow. Then he raised the bowler to his head and walked out.

I kissed my wife on the cheek and attempted the same, but I don't possess his gravitas. It looked more like I was fleeing.

Once we were back in our chambers in Craig's Court, my partner stared at the floor for twenty minutes. He hummed to himself off-key and swiveled back and forth in his chair. Once or twice, he reached for his telephone set but thought better of it. For a while he rooted about in Jeremy Jenkins's scrapbooks of old clippings and smoked three pipes in a row, lining them on his desk like artillery. Finally, he jumped to his feet.

"Blast!" he said. "I shall run mad! I'm about to track down the man and strangle him. I want to see his eyes start from his head."

"You're in a bloodthirsty mood," I noted.

He brayed, making me jump. It caught me off guard.

Nightwine seemed to bring out his impatient side. Gone was the wise philosopher from the East. He could be as Western as . . . well, me. Impatient, preoccupied, undisciplined; all the things he accuses me of in our private lessons every morning.

My partner stared out the window at that blessed wall for another ten minutes. Finally, he rose to his feet.

"I am in need of inspiration," he said. "Come."

I stepped into the outer office and gave him his stick and

hat. As I said, it was good to anticipate him, even if only a second or two. We stepped out into the court. No one shot at us, but there was a prickly feeling between my shoulder blades as if I were being watched through the scope of a rifle from a great distance.

We took a cab to a building in a part of Lambeth that had seen better days. Barker unlocked the door with a Georgian-era brass key, and we stepped into a cobwebby vestibule. Climbing the stair, the Guv unlocked a second door, which led to another set of stairs. At the top was a garret room with two windows, shrouded in dust, though I had cleaned them once years before. This was the room the crew of the *Osprey* had rented that fateful day they arrived from China.

I recalled something from our first visit to this small flat and picked up a book from the table. It was printed in Chinese, and when I opened it, there was what my partner once called the Kong, all four of them, in a faded sepia photograph. They had come halfway 'round the earth, escaping an armada from China, with a fabulous fortune, and yet they still glowered up at me from that frozen moment in time. Barker, Ho, and Etienne were thinner than they were now, though Paul Beauchamp was much the same. Barker looked so much younger, but then he must have been near my current age.

Continuing to flip through the book, I found a second photograph I hadn't noticed the first time I held it. It was a photograph of two Chinamen, one seated and one standing beside him. The seated man wore a long coat with a mandarin collar. I recognized him as Barker's instructor, Dr. Wong of Foochow. The young man who was standing had his head shaven in the traditional manner, and I'm sure he wore a queue behind him, but the round spectacles in brass and quartz were unmistakable. It was Barker, of course, a thinner, less muscular version of him, wearing a dark shirt without sleeves. It was the standard photograph taken of a student and teacher in that far-off land, proof of one's martial pedigree, otherwise anyone could claim a champion like Wong Fei Hung as their teacher.

"What are we doing here, sir?" I asked.

"I keep this place only for the direst of emergencies," he replied. "But I wanted to see it again. It brings back memories from our arrival in London, matters I may have forgotten."

He threw something at me, and I caught it, if a bit clumsily. It was cold and milky and the size of a walnut. I suspected it was a diamond, but I could not be certain because it was uncut. I was about to say "Jings!" but stopped myself. A diamond of that size could purchase another mansion perhaps, but I had no idea. I handed it back to him cautiously.

"You still have some of the jewels from the Pirate Queen, then?" I asked incredulously.

"Aye," he replied. "Most have been turned into notes, but we each have a few baubles left over from Yi-Sao's treasure."

"The Pirate Queen! I can't even imagine how it must have felt to find them," I said. "And now I can understand Nightwine's desire to get his hands on the entire prize."

"As usual, he was greedy and manipulative," Barker said, nodding. "He argued that the treasure was his by rights, since the ship was his, even though he'd done nothing to earn it. He came to us one by one and wheedled and bullied, but we stood firmly together. That was what made us the Kong. We were as one man."

"What happened next?" I asked.

"He read an official notice from the Forbidden City that the Empress Dowager was being poisoned," the Guv continued. "She was ill, but she did not trust the government or the eunuchs who intrigued against her. Therefore, the palace called for someone to investigate, and one by one the candidates were eliminated for various reasons. Nightwine suggested my name, inventing a list of my exploits. It was a gamble, and I assume a substantial bribe had to go with it. Sebastian reasoned that my punishment afterward would make the others from the Kong release the remaining treasure."

"And?" I asked.

"And the rest is . . ."

"Indelicate," I muttered. "I know. You are going to tell me sometime, aren't you?"

"Perhaps," he said. "Someday, if you work hard enough and impress me."

CHAPTER 25

Have we made any progress?" I asked.

"We have," my partner said, as we made our way onto an omnibus bound for Aldgate. "The protest shall begin at noon tomorrow. I've spoken to various clubs and political organizations in London and even warned a few MPs that something would happen. Jeremy will be painting placards all night, and I've mentioned to a few of the more progressive newspapers that something newsworthy might occur tomorrow by the Chinese embassy. *The Times* refuses to cover it, but I've spoken to *The Globe*, which tends to snap up the crumbs *The Times* is not willing to print. They promised to consider an article about Sun's detainment even if it is vague. That should attract attention."

"What about Scotland Yard?" I asked. "Surely they must do something at this late date."

"As I understand it, lad, they continue to drag their feet, but the case has been passed to Inspector Jarvis, a competent detective who brooks no nonsense, as I recall. He answers only to the commissioner. I assume he has been ordered to go ahead. However, with the embassy involved, we must proceed with caution. There are political matters to consider. I left a message for Jarvis to read in the morning. We are in a good position."

"What of the Chinese ambassador?" I asked. "What has he been doing for the last week or more?"

"The embassy claims he's been on holiday, but that is the standard Chinese excuse in such situations, so as to avoid embarrassment."

I shook my head. "Saving face, and all that?"

"Precisely, lad. It helps to know a government's methods."

"Shall we go to the embassy to see if anything is happening?" I asked.

"I think not," the Guv replied. "We don't want to tip our hand. I appreciate your enthusiasm, however."

We returned to our offices, where we sent Jenkins off to gather materials for protest signs. Knowing him as I do, they would be professional and easily readable in a photograph for the sake of the press. A few hours later, Hewitt slinked in the door. His eye was not so swollen, I noticed.

"Your boy visited the embassy again," he said, referring to Sebastian Nightwine. "He was in there over an hour. I doubt he and Macartney have been playing whist."

"Did you note any change in Nightwine's behavior when he left?" the Guv asked.

"No, not really," Hewitt answered. "He walked in and out through the front door, with no attempt to hide himself."

"Was anyone milling about? Reporters, for example?" Barker asked.

"Not a soul. Dull as a sermon out there."

"Where is he now?"

"At a luncheon with the prince," Hewitt replied. "He's trying to gain an introduction to the Princess of Wales I think, not that I blame him. She's a stunner. Must dash, gents. I just thought you should have this information."

The Guv nodded. "Thank you, J. M. Stay safe. I don't want to see you beaten again."

"Too late, Barker," he replied. "It's personal now."

We spent the rest of the afternoon preparing for the protest. Barker made more telephone calls but stopped after lunch because he didn't want to tip his hand. If Macartney or Nightwine caught wind of our plans and Sun Yat-sen were moved, it would be extremely embarrassing for the agency and catastrophic for the Chinese doctor.

After shutting our doors, we surreptitiously made our way to Philippa and Rebecca's hotel suite again. We had dinner brought in and afterward discussed the case. Barker was not above asking two intelligent women their opinions of events. I compared his behavior now with how he treated Bok Fu Ying in Limehouse. His former ward might have had some observations to contribute, being Chinese. I was certain Rebecca would agree. If only the Guv realized it. I would have to approach him sometime, but it was like trying to give a lion medicine. No one goes unscathed.

Later, I went home and was greeted by the dog, who missed her routine and her family, as I did. I let her out and fed her, then I spent the evening with her in my lap as I read. I needed plenty of sleep for the next day. Trollope did the trick. I locked up the house and fell asleep with Daisy at the foot of the bed and *Barchester Towers* perched on my chest.

At five thirty the next morning, I appeared at Cyrus Barker's front door. Mac made a remark on the stairs about the 'calm before the storm.' There would be no exercise that morning. We had a full day ahead of us.

Barker was up in his aerie, scribbling notes about the enquiry that only he could decipher. There were enough factors in this enquiry to require putting them down on paper.

"I spoke last night to Hesketh Pierce by telephone," he said. "We've had several setbacks. Dr. Cantlie visited the Foreign Office asking for an acknowledgment that Sun Yat-sen had been kidnapped, there was not sufficient proof for Pierce's superiors."

"Blast," I said. "What did he say?"

"He was obviously upset," the Guv replied. "There was a discussion at the Foreign Office last night but Pierce's request for an appearance at the embassy was refused. He suspects the Colonial Office might have had something to do with it. I'm beginning to suspect they have been . . . what is the phrase, lad?"

"Got at, sir?"

"That's the one. Also, a writ of habeas corpus was lodged against the embassy at the Old Bailey yesterday afternoon, but the judge didn't agree with such an action, and it fell through. Sir Halliday Macartney has friends in high legal circles. This is why I don't work hand in hand with the government, Thomas. One never knows what they will do. Let your yes be yes, and your no, no, I say."

"Tell me there is some good news," I said.

"The reporters from *The Globe* finally appeared at Dr. Cantlie's door, *The Times* having utterly refused to write about Sun. They had only scant information regarding Sun, but the doctor soon apprised the reporter of all the pertinent facts. Macartney can no longer keep this out of the newspapers."

"Finally," I said. "When will it be published?"

"It should be coming off the presses even as we speak."

"Is there any other news?"

"No," he replied. "But I'm certain that reporters from other newspapers will sense a story. My beloved *Times* shall be last, alas, but they had their opportunity and lacked courage. It shall be a lesson I hope the editors take to heart."

"Is that all?" I asked.

"Isn't that enough?" Barker retorted. "I pulled Hewitt from following Nightwine and hired a hansom cab for him to watch the embassy. This might be the day they try to move Sun onto a ship. In fact, I'm planning on it. Matters are swiftly coming to a head."

"What shall we do?" I asked. "I don't like sitting on my pockets when others are sopping up the credit like Christman gravy."

"What do you say about a frontal assault? We'll beat . . ." He stopped himself, and I could practically see his mind churning. "Thomas, wasn't there a door in the back of the embassy, near the alley where we escaped?"

"Yes, sir," I answered. "A gaudy one, red and gold. Why?"

"Think like the Chinese," he said. "Taking Sun out the front door would be a sign of acquiescence to the whim of the British government. Sending him out the back door would be an insult to our young doctor, as well as to us. It's a disgrace in Chinese culture, but the embassy will consider the English too stupid to understand what's going on."

"For once I won't make a derogatory remark about the English today," I stated.

Barker nodded. "It's probably best. Let's go to Devonshire Street. We'll see what Hewitt has to say and whether anyone has arrived to protest."

"Without breakfast?" I asked.

"Unfortunately, Etienne is not here to make demands upon our time," he said. "Let us take a bun and go."

We crossed the river and were soon close to the embassy. At our request, the cabman dropped us nearby on Weymouth Street, and we sauntered closer with our hands in our pockets, just a couple of blokes taking the air on a Friday morning. Storming the Chinese embassy? Why, we never heard of such a thing!

We came up on Hewitt from behind. He wore a woolen coat and a low-crowned top hat that had seen better days. Gone was the foppish man about town and in his place a respectable example of the industrial working man. He had borrowed our hansom cab, with my mare, Juno, in its traces.

"Hello, gents!" he called. "I've been besieged. Every reporter in town wants to hire this cab."

"Has anything happened yet?" Barker asked.

"It's just started. There's a group of Chinamen down the street with banners that no one in the West End can read but you, and there's another group who have taken over a coffee shop on that corner there. Can you see it? Reporters are milling about near the front door, which I suspect has been barred from the inside."

"Thank you, Hewitt." My partner said, then turned to me. "Thomas, we've suddenly been promoted to reporters. Come."

"Demoted, more like," I muttered to Hewitt, before I turned to follow the Guv.

In the street, we sauntered by as if it were an ordinary day, although we were watching everything along Portland Place. We studied the reporters across the street, whose supervisors had sent along hoping for content about a ridiculous rumor that the Chinese embassy was holding a hostage, but they didn't believe it. Surely that couldn't happen in London in this modern age. The Chinese wouldn't dare.

There was no sign of disorder in the street. There were no protesters. In fact, I began to wonder if this protest would come off at all. The Guv could call for help as he had last night, but there was no certainty anyone would come.

Ahead of us, a man in a worn coat and a flat cap was walking. It looked as if he was going to pass between us, but at the very last second, he stopped. He stood face-to-face with the Guv.

"You're Barker, right?" the man asked. "We're just around the corner in Harley Street."

The stranger turned and began walking with us.

"How many people are with you?" my partner asked.

"Twenty-five, maybe thirty," he replied. "Done the best we could. More may come."

"Thank you, Mitchell," Barker said to the man, whom he obviously knew. My partner had friends in all the wrong places. "I knew we could rely on the socialist cause."

As we reached Portland Place, I saw a knot of men a few hundred yards from us coming our way. I did not have to look at them to know whom they represented. They were K'ing's people. They carried tall, narrow vertical signs with Chinese lettering on them. I was certain Sir Halliday Macartney would be reading the placards from a window.

We met them at the corner, where Barker spoke to their leader for a moment in Cantonese. He nodded and they continued along Portland Place.

"Mr. K'ing sends his regrets about the smallness of the group and the fact that he could not be here with us," the Guv translated. "The price on his head is greater than mine. However, he has sent another contingent waiting on the other side in Devonshire Road. No one is making a protest yet. They'll wait for a signal from us."

"That's good news," I remarked.

"Is that everyone?" the Guv asked.

"For now, Mr. Barker," the Asian leader answered. "Mr. K'ing wants this protest to attract as many onlookers as possible."

He pointed over his shoulder, and I turned to see what was happening. The door was being unlocked. Reporters stepped out from under awnings and building fronts because there was a light drizzle, and sprinted forward like pigeons searching for bread. However, a man passed through it and the door was locked again.

If there were an equal ratio of Chinamen to socialists there would be close to seventy protestors present. The fact that some of the crowd didn't speak English added to the cacophony. The Chinese brought stout drums on wheels and began to beat them with sticks. Still, it wasn't enough. Not yet. However, Barker was confident.

Placards were raised above the crowd, painted in Jenkins's skilled hand: FREE SUN YAT-SEN! they read. FREE DR. SUN! RELEASE OUR BROTHER! FOR SHAME!

Cabs and omnibuses along the crossing thoroughfares slowed for the spectacle. People stepped into Portland Place from omnibuses to see what the commotion was about. The reporters rushed about searching in vain for someone to interview. Meanwhile, Barker and I went into the coffeehouse on the corner and watched the spectacle from behind a large plate glass window, availing ourselves of large cups of coffee.

"How long will this go on?" I asked.

"Until Scotland Yard arrives to find out what's causing the commotion," Barker answered. "We may be here until teatime."

"Will there be arrests?" I asked. "I'd prefer not to add another to my file at the Yard."

Barker shrugged his burly shoulders. His file was far larger than mine, but then he was unwed, and didn't give a tinker's damn what others thought of him.

A church delegation arrived, took up a few of the more genteel-looking signs, and began singing hymns. Curious onlookers gathered to observe the proceedings. Most everyone had no idea what the protest was about, but this was something novel to do, and when articles were published in the next editions, they could brag that they had been there. That poor little Chinese doctor, they'd say, the one they'd never heard of this morning.

"Ah, here we are," the Guv remarked, sitting up in his chair.

A few constables appeared, working their way through the crowd to observe what was happening. It was a peaceful protest so far, but there were socialists about, a bad lot in their opinion, who always enjoyed a good scrap, and the Chinese were very serious about having their comrade-in-arms rescued.

"Look, there's a vendor's cart," I said in surprise. "They're going to sell sausages!"

"He's entitled to sell his wares, Thomas," Barker reasoned. "People get hungry."

Someone dropped a flyer outside our window. I stepped out into the street and retrieved it, noting that it explained what was being protested, and who Dr. Sun was. He was being introduced to London for the first time.

"I recognize more of Jenkins's handiwork," I said. "Did you write this?"

The Guv shrugged. "I may have written an edifying message to those who might wonder why we are here."

"You should have asked me to write it, sir," I said in an arch tone. "That's my bailiwick."

"It is," he agreed. "But I didn't realize I would need an explanation for the crowd until late last night. However, the confusion is a tool in itself." Barker pointed over my shoulder. "Look."

Two men in front of the embassy were pushing their way through the crowd and ducking the signs being carried by the protesters. One was Macartney, his features as red as a tomato. He shoved through the crowd of Chinamen, activists, and choir members. The other man was Sebastian Nightwine himself. If I'd needed any proof that the two were working together, here it was. He wasn't as visibly upset as his partner, but he didn't look pleased.

"Is the Imperial Secret Service with them?" Barker asked.

"Let me see," I said.

I went to the picture window and looked out, one hand resting on the pane.

"Yes," I replied. "There's a fellow arguing with K'ing's group who has just punched someone. Now a constable's getting involved. What larks, eh?"

The glass in front of me suddenly splintered. Barker tossed over the table between us and pulled me away from the window. A bullet ricocheted around the room until it spent itself.

"Good god!" I exclaimed. Then I looked at my partner. "Sorry, sir."

I'd taken the Lord's name in vain in front of a religious man.

"Sofia Ilyanova has shown herself at last, I see," Barker replied, pulling me into a chair.

"If she aimed at me, she missed," I said, but my hand was shaking.

"Lad, you know she doesn't miss," he replied. "That was

a greeting of sorts to you, a message, perhaps. She's still about."

The manager of the coffeehouse began running about, angry as a hornet.

"You seem to have bewitched the woman, Thomas," he commented, peering into the street. "Most assassins would have simply shot you."

"I'd rather be dead than in the clutches of Sofia Ilyanova again, thank you," I said.

Cyrus Barker raised a brow. "Be careful what you wish for, Thomas."

CHAPTER 26

When we returned to the embassy, something had changed. Sir Halliday Macartney had disappeared through the embassy's front door. The Chinese considered this a good omen and had begun beating drums and banging cymbals. A more festive atmosphere had begun. The crowd needed a diversion, and this was just the ticket. Of course, none of them had even heard of the young doctor from Honolulu, who had dared express criticism to an emperor who believed he had a mandate from heaven, but it was a proper spectacle, no mistake.

Barker and I saw Doctors Cantlie and Manson coming down the pavement toward us. Manson was in his usual terse mood, but Cantlie was exuberant.

"I feel it, sirs!" he said. "Yat-sen shall be a free man by day's end."

"I hope so," Barker answered. "Macartney's return is a good sign. I suspect he planned to be out of town by the time news of Sun's imprisonment reached the newspapers. The Chinese ambassador had been conveniently missing since before Sun was taken, but Sir Halliday was not so fortunate."

"Indeed," Manson replied. He seemed to be energized by the chaos. "He's stepped into a trap."

"Where do you think Sun will meet us?" Dr. Cantlie asked.

Barker nodded. "I doubt the young doctor will be released through these doors. Macartney may use the front entrance, but Sun would be led out the doors at the back of the compound. Few know what an insult that would be to him save Mr. K'ing's contingent and the four of us. However, I expect Scotland Yard and the Foreign Office, who have been appallingly slow and reluctant during this case, will scoop up the final hand and claim the glory."

"They've been no help at all, as Dr. Cantlie will testify," I added. "And look across the street! Those are reporters from *The Times*, whom you have pestered unsuccessfully since yesterday."

"Should we go around the back now?" Manson asked.

"Not yet," Dr. Cantlie said in his Scot's accent. "This kind of release takes time. There are preparations to be made, and a decision must be reached about who shall take the blame."

"It was a misunderstanding," Manson suggested in a falsetto voice. "Mistakes occurred because of an amateur translator. Had the ambassador been here this wouldn't have happened."

"That will be the story told to the press word for word," Barker agreed.

I decided I liked the doctor, despite the gallbladder incident. I looked up at the roofs nearby, seeing if I could spot Sofia Ilyanova, but she was nowhere to be found.

"Sir," I said to my partner, "Is it possible Miss Ilyanova has been sent to assassinate Sun Yat-sen?"

"What?" Cantlie demanded a little too loudly. "What's this about an assassination?"

Every reporter in Portland Place heard the doctor and came sprinting toward us.

"You are on your own, gentlemen," the Guv remarked. "Come, Thomas."

Barker seized my shoulder, and we left before the flood of reporters confronted the panicking doctors. The Guv drew me down the alley where we had combatted Tang and his band of Imperial Secret Service bullies.

"It's too early for Sun to be released, isn't it?" I asked.

"Perhaps," he said. "However, I believe that matters are happening apace inside the building. Calls are being made, and telegrams winging their way to the ambassador. Fortunately, the embassy has no more than one or two guards of their own, for ceremonial occasions, aside from the Imperial Secret Service."

"What do you suppose they'll do?" I asked.

The Guv shrugged. "It's all in Macartney's hands. We'll look about the docks when this is over. It's just possible the doctor has been smuggled into Limehouse already, and this entire escapade is a subterfuge. You understand why the *Osprey* was stolen, don't you?"

"Wait!" I exclaimed. "Surely you're not saying it's moored somewhere near Limehouse under our very noses?"

"I've tried to think like Sebastian," Barker said. "Should he return to Canton with his former crew in chains, and the latest rabble-rouser, Sun, aboard the very ship that outran the Imperial Navy, he'd be a hero. Then he'd have his ship back and be rewarded with all the repairs and the fixtures and fittings he might wish. He could either use it or sell it for a tidy profit. What wealthy Mandarin would pass over such a worthy prize?"

"Meanwhile, it's just sitting here in London somewhere, while people are hunting the coasts for it?" I asked.

"It may be, Thomas. It could be under a tarp, or in dry dock. They might even have affixed another name to the bow."

I tried to take it in. "So, you're saying that Ho, Etienne, and Paul might be nearby in chains at this very minute?"

"We can't know for certain," the Guv replied. "As soon as this matter is over, we must search for the ship ourselves. I paid him for it, made significant repairs on it, and if he thinks he can sail off with my boat, he doesn't know Cyrus Barker."

My partner led me out of the alleyway to the back of the embassy.

"But first, we must retrieve Dr. Cantlie's student," he said. "As you yourself have asked, what need does an embassy have for a barred window?"

"Exactly," I said, thinking it was nice to be vindicated.

Someone jostled my elbow. Several reporters had followed, evidently thinking Cyrus Barker was a commanding fellow who seemed to know his way about. Also, we were seen leaving the coffeehouse with a broken window. Leaving the front door of the embassy was a risk for the reporters, and had their editors been there they'd have laid into them, but it could eventually earn them dividends.

"The Chinese are canny," Barker said in a low voice. "They may be planning to do something inadvisable, and perhaps even illegal, but they hope to avoid exposure. For example, Macartney may deny to the skies that he doesn't have Sun Yat-sen in custody, but most of these reporters will know he is lying. The tide would turn in either direction, if something happened which either gave Sun credit or showed him in a good light."

"I see what you're saying," I said. "Next week in the newspapers there might be an article about how well the Chinese are assimilating themselves in London, or an event had occurred attended by the leading Chinese diplomat, who spoke with the prime minister, all in order to deflect from this incident."

"Precisely," my partner replied. "It's a system of checks and balances. All governments do it, but the Chinese have a specific knack for it. It's been their forte for thousands of years."

The ornate door to the back of the building opened abruptly and a short Chinese man shuffled out into the afternoon sun, holding a hand up to shield his eyes. I saw flashes of magnesium light from the reporters' cameras, but we quickly realized this was not the noble Dr. Sun. Instead, he was one of the men the Guv and I had fought, a scrawny fellow with bad skin. He waved us away with his arms as if we were pests.

"Go 'way!" he cried. "Go home!"

In response, the reporters made rude, jeering noises. They weren't going to be put off by a skinny Chinaman. Someone threw a cobblestone at him, and he just avoided it. Imperial Secret Service agent or no, he hurried back into the building.

"Negotiations are taking place inside," Barker explained. "It should take some time. The Chinese are in no hurry. However, the demonstration in front of the building is an embarrassment to them. Macartney is probably waiting for a telegram from the ambassador. He cannot make such a decision by himself, being only an advisor. Why don't you see if

Dr. Cantlie and Dr. Manson are in the area? They will need to be here when he's released."

"Yes, sir," I replied.

Portland Place was crowded with people of all sorts: Chinamen in their silken *changshan* jackets, English ladies off to one side peering at the chaos, and dozens of men with mustaches and bowler hats pushing their way through the crowd. Many carried the signs of protest that Jenkins had made, and somewhere in that crowd was a pair of physicians, wearing respectable top hats.

I inserted myself into the melee. I was at a disadvantage, being shorter than many of the men, but I had done this sort of thing before and knew most of the dodges. The best thing to do was to press both hands together in front of you and pretend to be an icebreaker ship pushing its way through an arctic ice flow.

In Portland Place again, I thought I spied my quarry, but they proved to be a pair of clergymen being buffeted by the crowd. I moved them to safety and struggled on my way. I finally found the two doctors in the very same coffeehouse where we had begun. The glass where Sofia Ilyanova had shot at me had finally shattered, but it was out of the chaos.

"Gentlemen!" I exclaimed, stepping inside. "Have you finished your coffee? Mr. Barker believes he has found the door where Dr. Sun will be released. He is waiting for us, but there is no especial hurry."

"There rarely is in Chinese government circles," Dr. Cantlie said, waving for the bill.

"I've never seen such riffraff in a West End street," Dr. Manson observed. "I've a mind to clout someone just for sport."

"Don't encourage him, Mr. Llewelyn," his friend warned. "He'd do it, too."

Cantlie paid the bill, and we slowly made our way through the crowd. Manson didn't strike anyone, but the peppery physician employed his elbows rather freely.

People stood chockablock in front of the embassy and some had begun chanting, "Free Sun Yat-sen!" However, I suspected most didn't know who he was, or what the rally was for. I've noticed the English have a natural affinity for public protest.

By then, it was half past three and I was famished. If someone had told me our vigil was ending soon, I could wait, but with no idea when this would end, my stomach protested. Having delivered the doctors to the back door, I returned to the coffeehouse and found it besieged. I queued for half an hour and there was very little left when I reached the counter. I purchased a few buns and left.

A hansom cab came slowly along the street, forcing the crowd to let it through. It stopped at the front door of the embassy and disgorged a passenger and a police sergeant. The passenger's face was familiar to me, a fellow approaching sixty, but hardy and ramrod straight. He adjusted his cravat and hat as if he were standing alone, then walked into the building. I wondered where I had seen him before. He was obviously an inspector, but which one? I knew the Guv would want to know. I ran through the names of every inspector I could recall. He couldn't be from any of the branches, because he looked too important.

Dr. Cantlie scurried up and spoke to the inspector. The latter pulled him inside.

"Oy!" someone called. I looked up and saw they had been delivered by Hewitt and Juno. I patted the old girl under the muzzle and tipped a wink to the detective.

I turned the corner into the alley. It was advantageous that Barker hadn't given up our spot near the front, because the back alley was now full of people. I reached my partner, and he stuffed the roll I handed him into his mouth. Food was mere fodder to him. Beef Wellington and jellied eel were all the same in his eyes.

"An inspector just arrived and went in the front door," I said. "He took Cantlie with him."

"Which inspector?"

Of course he would ask. I probed my brain, running through a dozen names of inspectors I knew.

"Jarvis," I said after a moment. That was his name. Of course, I knew it all along. Good old Inspector Jarvis, my old friend. I was so glad I recalled his name that I tossed a hungry-looking reporter my last bun.

"Good man, Jarvis," Barker stated.

"I'm glad Scotland Yard finally sent someone," I replied. "Something's bound to happen soon. He must be speaking to Macartney now."

If we had attempted to go through the front door, we'd only be bounced onto the pavement again, but Jarvis was another story. He carried the whole weight of the Yard behind him. He'd be the darling of the press by morning, as would Sun Yat-sen and Dr. Cantlie, if all went according to plan. But does anything ever go according to plan? Not in my universe.

"Hewitt better not try to bring that cab back here," I remarked. "He'll block the alley."

A half hour later the back door finally opened again, and Inspector Jarvis and Dr. Cantlie stepped out again, both supporting a slight young man, as if he were too weak to stand. It was Sun Yat-sen. It had to be. He was young and had a mustache and an English haircut. His suit jacket hung on his shoulders. Later, one reporter called him "emaciated."

The young man was shocked by the reception. His eyes

grew large, as cameras flashed and the area filled with smoke. Spontaneously, Sun hugged his old friend, Cantlie. Everyone forgave him for his informality. The poor fellow had been through an ordeal.

There was no sign of Sir Halliday Macartney, nor of any of the Imperial Secret Service. I saw it, now that Barker had explained it to me. Sun had been brought out the back door rather than the front, a humiliation for him. Think of it as the back end of an alimentary canal. The ambassador had scored a victory over the English, though he was far away. The embassy would call it a triumph. Each side believed that they had won and harmony had been achieved. Chinese dignity was maintained.

Sun was being braced by both doctors now, as he tottered across the back lot, then through the alleyway to the front. Everyone was cheering, but it was nothing compared to the tumult when he reached Portland Place. Manson raised Sun's hand, which made the crowd call even louder.

Finally, the door to Hewitt's cab opened, and the doctors bundled the frail young man inside. Then they bowled off through the crowded street amidst a storm of cheers.

"I'm hungry, lad," Cyrus Barker said when they were gone, and we were at loose ends again.

"I suppose I could eat a little something," I replied.

"What say you, lad? Prospect of Whitby? The Clarence?"

"What about the Mitre in Greenwich, sir?" I asked. "My treat."

"Aye, your treat, my wallet."

"Blast," I said, raising my arm for a cab. "I was hoping you wouldn't notice."

CHAPTER 27

Sun Yat-sen was trembling when he reached his rooms at the Lincoln Inn that evening. When he collapsed on the bed after his rescue, and he and his mentor had discussed the events of the last few days, he became overwhelmed. He hadn't thought so at the time, but both Dr. Cantlie and Dr. Manson saw that he was near the breaking point and would suffer an attack of the nerves that would require rest. In fact, if he didn't get hold of himself, he might need to be sent to a sanitorium to recover.

Sun kept his eyes open for fear he'd find his rescue just a dream, that he was back in his cell again with Macartney railing at him and the Qing guards cuffing him on the head. He listened to Big Ben tolling the hour somewhere in the distance, feeling disembodied, as if nothing were real.

It was a relief to be left alone. He lay on the bed, his shoes and jacket off and his braces hanging from his waist, staring at the ceiling and going back over the events of the last two days.

October twenty-second had begun like any other day of his captivity. Tang ran a stick along the bars of his cell and berated him for being a layabout. Sun had risen and knotted his tie, then slipped into his jacket. He was distressed that after wearing it for so many days, it was growing tatty and worn. He fancied that at that moment he was the most ill-treated man on earth.

Like his other days in captivity, he wondered what he was going to do to occupy his time. There was nothing to read, and nothing to do. He began by attempting some exercises. He was not trained in anything physical, having always been a reader and a dreamer. Why would one willingly join in a sport which might end with one bleeding from the nose? Instead, he performed what calisthenic exercises he recalled from his youth at school.

Cole unlocked the door and stepped in with his coal scuttle. He replaced the full scuttle for the empty one in the cell. There was a fire, but it was far too weak to fight the cold October breeze. Sun met his eyes with a kind of ferocity in a desperate plea for help. Cole looked away. Then he did something that interested him. He glanced back at the coal scuttle he'd set down.

A moment later, Tang came up to the bars of his cell and complained that Cole was dawdling. The caretaker hurried into the hall and went his way without looking back. Sun Yat-sen looked at the scuttle. Should he start a fire? Would it bring help? Surely a fireman would release him from the cell. He reached for it and saw something lying on top of the coal. It was a newspaper. Yat-sen quickly stuffed it into his suit and acted disinterested as one of the guards walked past.

When the man was gone, the doctor ripped the newspaper from his jacket and began to read. It didn't matter what it was. His mind had been stultified from having nothing to do. Eagerly, he perused the copy.

It was an edition of *The Globe*, a newspaper with which he had no familiarity. It had been printed that very morning and the first story read:

"Chinese doctor kidnapped in London! Held hostage at the Chinese embassy!"

Sun's heart began to beat faster. At last, his ordeal attracted some attention. Surely, something must happen now. Good old Dr. Cantlie had not forgotten him. In fact, the more he read the more he understood the debt he owed his old mentor. The press had become involved and for the first time in almost a week Sun had a feeling of hope.

He comforted himself that something was being done which would end in his release. The British public would not accept a visitor to their shores being snatched off the street, particularly by a foreign embassy. Sun was certain about the fairness of the British justice system. He'd read about it in dozens of novels.

He dressed and did his best to improve his appearance. He was aware that he needed a shave and a bath. The hours dragged by, then at four thirty in the afternoon one of the guards unlocked the door and said, "Macartney wants to see you downstairs. Put on your boots and hat."

Sun did as he was told, and then stepped out of the cell, a feeling of panic seizing him. This was Chinese land, or so they claimed. Were they going to behead him here and now, instead of sending him back to China? A cold sweat crept down his back and he couldn't breathe.

The guard marched him down the steps one by one. His knees knocked together until he feared they would fail him.

It worsened when they passed the ground floor and continued to descend. They were heading into the basement, he realized, as fear overtook him.

Get hold of yourself, Yat-sen, he thought. *It can't be as bad as you fear.* Perhaps Macartney was planning to hide him while the authorities searched the building.

Then he saw two men standing in the corridor watching him. One of them was his friend, Dr. Cantlie. Sun almost cried out in relief. The other was a man of Cantlie's own age and seemed to be a man of authority. Macartney was nowhere in sight, which was a good sign if he followed the Chinese rules of behavior. He might release his prisoner but would not be seen doing so publicly. The Englishmen wouldn't understand the behavior, of course, but Sun did.

The two men continued to study him. He hadn't eaten much since being placed in the cell. He'd lost weight, and his clothes didn't fit him well. He needed his hair cut. He felt ashamed of his appearance in front of strangers. Then his mentor came forward and shook his hand.

"Yat-sen, we're so sorry you've had to go through this ordeal," Cantlie said. "It has been difficult to find you and to attract enough public interest to battle the inertia of the British government. This gentleman is Inspector Jarvis of Scotland Yard. We're here to release you."

At that moment, a rather red-faced Sir Halliday Macartney came down the stairs.

"I hand this man over to you," he stated brusquely. "And I do so on condition that neither the prerogative nor the diplomatic rights of the embassy are interfered with."

Sun had difficulty comprehending the words. In his dazed state, they sounded senseless. Abruptly, Macartney seized his hand and shook it, then did the same to Dr. Cantlie. Sun thought it very like a Judas kiss.

"You are a free man," the counselor said, although Sun could see the loathing in his eyes.

A door opened ahead of him, and he followed Cantlie outside. A mass of people was clustered there, cheering. Cameras were being ignited with magnesium, and everyone seemed to be talking at once. Some began firing questions at him. He felt dazed. Dizzy. The inspector held his arm, sensing he might collapse.

Sun looked over his shoulder. He had been ushered out by the back entrance, which he understood was an insult on the part of the embassy. To the English, he had been freed by the evil Qing government, but to the Chinese, he and the English had been made to look like fools. If the front entrance of the building is the mouth, the back exit could only be the bowels.

The inspector escorted them to a waiting hansom cab. Inspector Jarvis looked cautiously about, carefully studying the crowd, and the thought came into Sun's head that someone might try to shoot him. It would be a long time until he felt safe again. The inspector shoved him into the cab, and he and Dr. Cantlie climbed in on either side of him.

"Damn!" Jarvis growled, looking up overhead.

"What is it?" Sun Yat-sen asked, as nervous as a cat.

"Reporters have jumped on top of our cab."

"Won't they be hurt?"

The inspector chuckled. "They'd gladly break a limb for a good story, and you, sir, are a good story."

"I didn't mean to be," Sun replied. "If I had known what trouble I caused by writing a single letter to the emperor—"

"You probably would have written it anyway," the Englishman finished. "You seem to be the sort who cannot abide oppression."

"Perhaps," Sun admitted. "I only think people should be willing to listen to reason."

"That'll be a first, no mistake," Jarvis replied.

The cab rattled across London to Holborn and stopped at Ye Olde Mitre, a public house. A second group of reporters followed in another cab. After they were seated inside, two men Yat-sen had not seen before sat at their table. Cantlie explained they were the private enquiry agents he had hired to find him and had done so. One was sturdily built with a mustache and Chinese quartz spectacles. The other was slight and seemed to defer to his elder. The larger of the two came forward and greeted Sun in Cantonese.

"It appears I owe you thanks, sir," Sun Yat-sen said over the raucous crowd.

"There is no need, Dr. Sun," the man replied. "We are professional agents and were glad to have been of service."

The reporters had waited long enough. They launched volleys of questions at him. They took apart his tale the way a watchmaker strips a watch. Inspector Jarvis, having done his duty, went off to file a report, nodding at the two men. The detectives had temporarily become Sun's bodyguards.

"Gentlemen!" the larger one said to the crowd of reporters. "Dr. Sun has had a trying few days and is exhausted. He should sleep in his own bed tonight, I'm sure you'll agree. Thank you for your patience. You waited for hours to get your story, and it does you great credit. I'm sure Dr. Sun will be eager to answer more questions tomorrow. Until then, go! Write your preliminary stories. I look forward to reading them all in the morning. Good luck to you!"

No one argued with him. The large man with the dark spectacles spoke with authority. One man made a half-hearted attempt to get a private audience with Sun, but the smaller detective ushered him out of the building with an arm twisted behind his back. Sun began to wonder how many men Dr. Cantlie had hired and how much this cam-

"But he was released by the embassy," I reasoned. "If he were to be taken by them again it would cause an international incident. The newspapers would be glutted with complaints and Her Majesty's Government would demand to know where Sun is."

"Aye. Which means?"

"Nightwine has taken him," I said. "Macartney would have no qualms about taking Sun prisoner if he were delivered to a third party. No one but us has twigged his plan."

"Very good. And your conclusion?"

"Wherever Sun is, the *Osprey* shall be leaving tonight, fully loaded for a long voyage. It's ironic that Nightwine should return to China on the very vessel that helped you escape. How do you think they took Dr. Sun?"

"Perhaps he was shot by one of La Sylphide's dart bullets," Barker said. "How she lowered him to the ground I cannot work out, but she is a most ingenious woman. Perhaps the Imperial Secret Service helped her."

"If only we knew where the *Osprey* was berthed," I replied. "It has to be in London."

"There was a message here when I returned home this evening," he said. "She has been found by some of K'ing's people. She was down the river in Rainham for a while but has left her berth."

"Not in London proper, then," I remarked. "If we had searched for her here, we'd have stopped at the city's edge. But what can we do, sir? They must have gone by now. We've got little chance of reaching her."

"We can try, Thomas," he replied. "I've explained to the Thames Police about the kidnapping, and they should have a launch ready for us in Limehouse Reach."

"I'll meet you there."

We rang off and I mounted the stairs and began throwing on clothes, but it seemed a fool's errand to me. They could be miles away by now.

I met Barker at the Thames Police constabulary near Limehouse Reach, where four constables were waiting with the launches. The Guv took the first vessel and I the second. We had no more jumped aboard than the little boats flew off and I nearly fell over the side. Perhaps we might catch up to the *Osprey*, after all, I thought. The officers looked very keen.

"Thomas Llewelyn!" I called to one of the officers behind me.

"Sergeant Partridge," the man at the tiller returned. "This fellow is PC Bobby Sykes!"

"Pleased to meet you," I replied. "Do you think we can get some speed out of this pretty little vessel of yours?"

"You just hold on to her, Mr. Llewelyn," he called. "There's been talk of scrapping the service and we've been dying for a test to show those men in the House of bloody Lords what we can do."

The next I knew we were flying over the water. The sergeant thought it his duty to catch the other boat. If we weren't racing against time, I'd have thought it a fine jaunt. However, I noticed that another fog was beginning to roll in.

"I don't want you to damage your fine launches!" I called.

"Bless you, sir, but we know every inch of these banks," Partridge answered without looking my way. "We'll do this blindfolded if necessary."

Our launch pulled ahead of Barker's, but the other captain wouldn't stand for that. Thus, it became a contest between both vessels. Meanwhile, the tentacles of fog began to reach across the Thames like a nightmare out of Jules Verne. Perhaps, I thought to myself, we didn't need to go so very fast.

We were the only boats on the water. All other watermen

and lightermen had monitored their barometers and knew better than to be out on the river on a night like this. We were the only fools attempting it, but we'd been called that too many times to count or care.

In spite of our progress I wondered if we were too late to find the *Osprey.* I hoped that her crew, whoever they were, might be unfamiliar with the area and therefore cautious. They may have already had a near miss along the river. Then I realized what I'd been hoping for: that Barker's beautiful ship, his pride and joy, would run aground. If I had entertained such a thought, I wondered what Cyrus Barker was thinking. The moon ducked in and out of the clouds above as we sped along the river.

After a quarter hour, we came around a corner of the Thames's snaky coil and Partridge sang out.

"Thar she is, sir!" he called. "Pretty little ship she is, too. T'would be a shame to spoil her."

"I hope it doesn't come to that!" I called over my shoulder. "I know you gents aren't allowed incentives, but I might mention that Mr. Barker is a wealthy man and a generous one. He might even take you on a sail around the Channel, which is where his ship is usually berthed!"

"Hear that, Constable Sykes?" Partridge asked. "We can't let those tossers Jamison and Burrows make us look like layabouts. Put the blooming kettle on!"

The PC increased the steam pressure, and we began shrinking the distance to the *Osprey* ahead of us. The tendrils of fog had long since met in the middle of the river, and we were shrouded enough that we could barely see the other vessels. I made out the figure of a man standing on the deck of the other launch with something in his hands, which he spun in a circle above his head. Then it flew from his hand, and the last I saw, it snatched him over the side.

"Barker," I muttered to myself. No other man would be so foolhardy.

"Stop your vessel and prepare to be boarded!" an officer in the first launch called out to the *Osprey.*

There was a pistol shot in response.

"Blast!" I cried.

"Look!" Partridge said. "They're firing on the launch."

As we watched, the vessel ahead of us struck the *Osprey* at an angle, bouncing away again. We were in danger of hitting it next, so close were we on their tail. Partridge steered a wide circle around both vessels, spraying an arc of water against the hull on the port side. The deck of the *Osprey* was far over our heads, however, so it was difficult to see what was happening on deck. I wondered if Barker had succeeded in climbing aboard, assuming that Sebastian Nightwine was on that boat, and possibly Ilyanova as well. Nightwine must have some sort of crew to run the vessel. It was impossible for one man to helm it alone, even with the latest steam boiler Barker had installed on the ship.

I heard shots. Someone, presumably Nightwine, was armed. It hadn't occurred to me to wonder whether Barker was armed as well, although I presumed he was. It also answered my question as to whether he was on board. Nightwine, an accomplished marksman, would not waste bullets.

"Pull away!" I ordered Partridge. "I want to see what's happening on deck!"

We drifted back as the *Osprey* continued onward. Then Partridge swung our launch away from the vessel, far enough for us to get a better look at the deck. No sooner had we done so than a man fell over the side of the *Osprey* and disappeared into the water.

"Is that Mr. Barker, sir?" Sergeant Partridge asked.

"No," I replied. "Nor was it Nightwine. It must have been a crew member."

"That poor sod won't be getting out anytime soon."

I told the sergeant about Nightwine's attempt to collect a bounty on Sun Yat-sen's head.

"Bit of a rotter, eh?" Patridge said.

"That's it in a nutshell," I agreed. "A complete rotter."

"You say his old crew and the Chinese fellow are down below tied up?"

"They have to be."

"Let's go, then. Ain't got all night!"

He had a quick grasp of things and knew what to do about them.

"Do you have a grappling hook?" I asked.

"We do, sir," he said, handing it to me from a pile of rope beside him.

"Can you see anything up there?"

Partridge shook his head. "Not a blessed thing."

"I must get aboard," I told him. "My partner needs me."

"Best let me throw the grappling hook, then, Mr. Llewelyn," he replied. "You don't look like much of a deckhand, if you'll permit my saying."

"True, but I am good at steam. I can steer this tiller and monitor the temperature."

"We're not supposed to give control of the launch to a civilian, sir, but if you keep mum about it, I will."

We changed places. I steered the launch closer to the *Osprey* while Partridge began spinning the grappling hook. A random thought that came to me then was how often I found myself in desperate situations like this. I maneuvered the craft parallel to the *Osprey*, as close as possible. It took nine tries for Partridge to finally land the grappling hook precisely, but I didn't complain. I tugged at the rope, then looked at my companion.

"Into the breach," I muttered, jumping overboard.

By the time I reached the deck, I had been half submerged. It was a mathematical problem. I jumped so far, but the rope was not at its height, and the ship rolled from one minute to the next. I hate getting soaked, almost as much as a cat, but finally I pulled myself over the side and stood at the far end of the ship. I drew my pistol, hoping it would fire after the unexpected bath, and crept along the deck. From where I stood the area seemed deserted, then I heard a pistol firing nearby. I edged closer and closer and then stepped out of the shadows.

Barker was crouching behind a crate, while across the deck, Nightwine stood in the shadow of the cabin. He was unscathed, but I could see Barker had been shot. Between them were two of Nightwine's crew members, one dead, the other writhing on the deck in pain. I had no wish to join either one. I fired my Webley No. 2, but the entire ship was rolling. It seemed possible that no one was steering the ship anymore. There was even a chance we might run aground at any minute near the narrowest point of the Thames.

I fired a shot at Nightwine, which splintered the corner of the cabin door beside him. Then I bent low and scuttled to where my partner was kneeling. He'd been shot in the arm and had used his necktie as a tourniquet.

Barker nodded at me and fired, but his wound threw off his aim. Sebastian Nightwine made a living with his gun. He was a remarkably accurate shot and equally fast. I was neither of those things, and Barker, as good a shot as he was, was no match for his old rival at that moment, which meant we had to be crafty.

"Both at once, sir!" I cried and we did, hoping to catch

Nightwine in the crossfire. Unfortunately, I carried no bullets besides the ones in my pistol, and I suspected the Guv didn't, either, whereas Nightwine was keeping up a withering fire and so must have had a supply of ammunition in his pockets.

"You're starting to bore me, Cyrus!" Nightwine called. "Shooting from behind a crate is more your brother Caleb's bailiwick!"

I fired again, and once again struck the doorframe, but shards of wood splintered into Nightwine's face. He cried out, but it was more frustration than pain.

"Come out, Nightwine," I called from the shadows.

"You're a danger to doorframes but little else!" he replied.

Cyrus Barker was now circling the ship to where Nightwine stood, hoping we could catch him in a crossfire. I knew that eventually his eyes would penetrate the gloom, so I crept forward, to where Barker had been crouching behind the crate.

I pulled the trigger at the same time as Barker. I heard a loud sound as Nightwine staggered back and collapsed to the deck. The Guv and I froze, wondering if our nemesis was injured or dead.

Cyrus Barker ran forward and leaned over Nightwine's prone body, reaching for his wrist. "He's dead, Thomas. An excellent shot."

"I don't think it was me, sir," I answered. "You shot him."

"Not I. I was surprised to learn I was out of bullets," my partner rumbled. He stood and looked toward the shore. "Either way, it's finally over."

He walked to the side of the boat and waved at the waiting launches. Then he crossed to the cabin door and opened it.

"I'll give you scurvy rascals five seconds to get off my boat before I turn you over to the River Police or shoot you dead!"

he shouted at the remaining crew. It was bluff. I knew his gun was empty. "One . . . two . . ."

There was a scurrying sound and then splashes from the back of the boat. They might have been the Imperial Secret Service men, but I couldn't see in the fog. I hoped Partridge would round them up, even if they had diplomatic immunity, and prove to the powers that be at Scotland Yard that the River Police hold their end of the line well and needed to be better funded.

There was a moment then when all action seemed to cease. My partner leaned forward and closed the man's eyes. Then he seemed to sag a little and sat with his head bent between his knees.

I stepped down into the cabin and looked about in the gloom. They were all there below me: Ho, Etienne Dummolard, Paul Beauchamp, and young Dr. Sun, laying in the hold, trussed like Sunday geese at market. The last looked even more relieved than the rest. They were all gagged and chained, so I found a tool chest and went to work freeing them. One by one we helped them up on deck. It didn't help the situation that the manacles were very difficult to open without a key. When we finally removed Ho's gag he had a thing or two to say about his confinement.

"What have you been doing?" he bawled. "We've been here for days! Did you even try to look for us? You would have been here faster if you had crawled on your knees! No more free food for you from now on. No! Strictly cash. If I let the two of you in at all, that is. We are not friends anymore!"

It wasn't true, at least the friendship part. However, at that moment, he was in his element. Ho enjoys nothing more than having something to be incensed about.

Barker came down to help rescue his crew. Etienne kissed each of our cheeks and hugged us in a bearlike grasp, Dr. Sun looked dazed, and Paul, well, Paul tugged on his forelock and stepped out on the deck, to inspect the damage to the boat. It seemed minimal to me, but I knew he'd have a long list of repairs to see to before the *Osprey* would meet his exacting standards. I didn't point out the splintered doorframe.

Sergeant Partridge and his men came aboard then, examined the body, and took down everyone's statements, a process which took almost an hour. Afterward, Barker and his original crew took control of the *Osprey*. I was left out of the action, so I sat with Dr. Sun.

"Is it always this dangerous here in London, Mr. Llewelyn?" he asked.

"This is a slow day," I replied. "You should see one of the corkers. I've got to say I'm impressed, Doctor. You've been kidnapped twice in one week. You must be a very popular fellow."

He looked a trifle shocked. He was one of those grave individuals devoid of a sense of humor. Jokes, jibes, and flippant remarks soared over his head like spent embers from a fire.

After much discussion it was suggested that the *Osprey* would be berthed where it had been the last few days, then the "Kong," the original crew, would sail to Dover and around the South Coast to Seaford.

A short while later, I found Barker sitting on a crate, looking dazed, though I saw his wound had been tended to. I sat beside him.

"Are you all right, sir?" I asked. He'd lost all his aplomb.

"I thought I was, when I believed he was dead all these years," he replied. "But this is profound. I'm like a dog who's been tormented much of his life and then finally set free. I don't know what to do with myself. It will take a long time to accept that the man is finally dead."

Then Nightwine was carried by. At Barker's request, they

stopped to let him examine the body. He opened the shirt and examined the dead man's torso.

"He was shot in the back," Barker said. The bullet went through him and exited the front. None of our pistols could do that. It punched through bone."

Cyrus Barker had been shot in the meat of the right arm, according to a doctor at the London Hospital an hour later, although "meat" doesn't sound very specific, or Latinesque for that matter. However, knowing the size of his brawny arm, it seemed an easy target. The Guv considered it a nuisance and refused a bed at the hospital, preferring his own. When he was released, I hailed a cab, which drove us to his home in Newington in the wee hours of the morning, and to the competent care of Jacob Maccabee. Then the driver took me to my own home. There was only a dog waiting for me, though she tried her best, frisking about the carpet upon my return. Still, I was relieved more than I could say. The ruddy case was over, which meant I could collect my family from that dratted hotel, and we could begin our lives over again at our snug house in Camomile Street. I was nearly as pleased as the dog.

CHAPTER 29

The following morning, it took several telephone calls to branches of Scotland Yard for me to locate Sebastian Nightwine's remains. I found the whole thing suspicious. The responses I received from every division were vague, and there was always a pause before they answered, which suggested they didn't know where he was for certain, as if he'd merely stepped out for a cigarette. My first concern was that perhaps he wasn't dead, after all, but Barker had pronounced him so, and I had no reason to believe otherwise. Unless, of course, one considered the fact that Nightwine had already escaped the mantle of death once before.

Nightwine's body finally breached the door of Scotland Yard, "A" Division. The Guv and I went to have a look for ourselves, so we made our way to the Body Room, where corpses are brought that haven't died of natural causes. We were friends with the cold, dragon-like coroner, Dr. Edward Vandeleur, or at least willing to suffer his cold manner and ill temper. We opened his door at "A" Division and stepped into the room.

"Out!" Vandeleur barked before either of us had said a word.

"We're looking for the body of Sebastian Nightwine," Barker replied.

The coroner cocked his head in the direction of a maze of gurneys, with still forms lying under crisp white sheets. He was elbows deep in a bucket full of what looked to be intestines. I didn't want to look any closer. Moving to the back, I uncovered three bodies before finding the one I was looking for. Sebastian Nightwine lay stripped of his clothing and his dignity, clad in only a sheet. How the mighty have fallen, as King David once said.

"What happened to his chest?" Vandeleur demanded, still staring into his bucket of guts. "It's all mangled, but it had healed long ago."

"You've looked at him, then, but haven't started an autopsy?" I asked.

"Of course I haven't started the autopsy," he snapped. "Has his body been opened? Do you see an incision?"

"We fought a duel several years ago," Barker explained, ignoring the outburst. "I stabbed him with a sword all the way to the hilt. We believed the man dead, but obviously, we were mistaken."

Vandeleur looked up from what he was doing. wiped his hands on a towel and came to look at the body. The new wound in Nightwine's chest was about four inches from the previous one. I assumed it had struck the aorta.

"This is a strange question, I know, sir, but humor me,

please," Cyrus Barker said. "Could you officially assert that this man is dead? He cannot be revived somehow?"

Vandeleur nodded. "I can safely assert that he is what is called in Latin 'mortuus.'"

"What caliber was the bullet?" I asked. "I'd like to know if I was the one who shot him."

"What's your pistol?" the coroner asked.

"A police issue Webley," I told him.

"Hmm," he murmured. "That's a .455 caliber. And Barker's?"

"Colt .45, British-made," the Guv said. "But I was out of bullets."

"Then neither one of you shot him," Vandeleur pronounced. "The bullet was a .303 caliber, and it punched a hole through him, back to front. I suspect it may have been from a Martini-Enfield rifle. English-made, or something similar."

"We were on the side of the cabin, protected by a gangway," I stated, looking at my partner. "Who could have shot him, and how?"

"You're the detectives, not I," Vandeleur said. "Do your own investigation. But for now, get out! You're impeding my work!"

That was Vandeleur. We could put up with his aristocratic tone and famed irritability if he provided the proper information, but only for so long. We stepped out of the reeking room and made our way up the stairs and through to the street, where cold, sweet oxygen encircled us like a mother's blanket and drove the stench from our clothes. Most of it, anyway.

"Could it be possible that neither of us shot him?" I asked Barker as we walked back to our chambers. "It doesn't sound likely."

My partner frowned. "We haven't got all the information.

I assumed the policeman in the launch fired, as well, but they don't carry rifles. What time is it?"

"I have no idea," I replied. "I gave my watch to that odious fellow, Bigge, remember?"

We stepped into the cool of the Shades Public House in Whitehall and ordered a cider, a beef sandwich, and some chips. I loved the ornate, bottle-shaped building. Inside it was dark and cool, allowing us to think.

"Well, Thomas?" the Guv asked. "What's your conclusion about the matter?"

"The bullet passed through him about four inches lower than the last wound, sir," I replied. "Shot him in the vitals."

"Who do you think shot him?"

"That's just it, sir. It was neither of us. The bullet was a .303 caliber round. Could there have been someone else aboard the *Osprey*? Or someone shooting from the bank?"

"Such as?" he inquired.

"Perhaps someone from the Foreign or Colonial offices," I replied, shrugging my shoulders.

"It's doubtful," Barker answered. "We found the *Osprey* on our own, as you recall."

"The only other possibility is that one of the River Police fired on him, but I saw no rifle."

The Guv ran a finger over his mustache and took a sip of cider. "We'll inquire about that later."

The thought occurred to me that I had met many quirky and difficult men in London, knife-edged and hard to approach, like Barker and Vandeleur. Perhaps it is because we lived in a capital city where important people discuss important matters. They were brilliant but not easy to please, driven from within but not for any obvious reason. It would be wonderful to be a Newton or a Disraeli, I thought, but it sounded exhausting.

"How's the arm?" I asked when we had returned to our chambers and taken our seats.

"Tolerable," he grunted. One would need to physically probe the wound with something before he complained.

"What is the next step, sir? Sun has been rescued. Shall I put the enquiry to bed?"

That meant setting down a record of everything that had been said or done since Dr. Cantlie had entered our premises on the first day. This has occasionally come to fifty pages or more. I would present it to Barker for discussion, which could take a full day, and sometimes involved an argument or two. See "difficult men" in the above chapter. After that would come the billing and another possible argument. The man has no head for business. The itemized account would then be proffered, and the enquiry would cease to be of interest to the Guv.

"Go see what deviltry that little rascal is up to, will you, lad?"

"Rascal, sir?" I asked. "What rascal?"

"Sun Yat-sen, of course. One little letter and he has disturbed three continents so far, if one includes North America."

"I don't know if he's a rascal," I replied. "You yourself believe that the Qing government must fall."

"Let us blame youth, then," he said. "Neither the emperor, Guangxu, nor Dr. Sun has reached the age of thirty-five. With age comes wisdom."

"I hope so, sir," I muttered.

He chuckled, then grunted. That arm was bothering him, but he would never admit it. "Best get along and see after our client and Dr. Sun. Find out their plans."

"Yes, sir."

"And when you're back, see if anyone has come forward to claim Sebastian's body."

I was out the door in a minute. London seemed to have

acquired every leaf in England, encircling my feet like pigeons, then flying off to Hyde Park.

"Lad!"

I stopped in my tracks and turned. Cyrus Barker was standing in the doorway to our offices.

"Yes, sir?"

"Stop by the London Hospital as well and see if they can retrieve the bullet they removed from my shoulder," he said.

"There was no bullet," I answered. "It passed through."

The Guv frowned. Then his brows lifted to within an inch of his hairline. "Passed through? Like Sebastian's?"

I shrugged. "I suppose so."

"So, in fact, we both could have been shot with the same rifle."

"Yes, sir," I agreed. "It's possible. Anything else?"

I noticed I was leaning against the wall, with a boot against the flat of it, which was the exact spot where he had first seen me the day I was hired.

"Stop at the Foreign Office then, and tell Hesketh Pierce that I'd like to see him at his earliest convenience," Barker said. "Leave a note if you can't reach him."

"Of course."

"Don't start your report," he ordered. "This enquiry isn't over yet."

I went directly to the Foreign Office building and attempted to speak with Pierce, but no one seemed to have heard of such a person. They took a message which I suspected would be dropped in the rubbish bin the moment I left. However, word would reach Pierce's ear, which was all the Guv cared about. I had done my part.

I took an omnibus to Portland Place, the scene of all the recent controversy. I made my way to Cantlie's address and knocked on the door. A servant answered and within a few minutes I was ushered into our client's parlor, where he and Sun Yat-sen were drinking a very civilized cup of tea.

"You're just in time for a cup," Cantlie said.

"No time, I'm afraid," I replied. "However, Mr. Barker would like to see you at your earliest convenience."

"Ah," the Scotsman said, smiling. "Time to pay the piper, is it?"

"No, sir," I said, smiling. "My partner merely likes to tie up all the loose ends. You may call him if you wish and speak to him yourself, to arrange a time."

I glanced over at the cause of all this drama. Dr. Sun was in a well-cut suit now, with a crisp white collar and a yellow tie. His short hair was immaculate, and he looked far less hollow-eyed than when I saw him last.

"Mr. Llewelyn," he said. "I haven't had the chance to thank you and your partner for what you have done. You have literally saved my life."

"It was all in the line of duty, Dr. Sun," I replied.

"Where shall we see Mr. Barker?" Cantlie asked.

"In the offices in Craig's Court, sir."

Cantlie leaned forward in his chair, frowning. "Did he go to work this morning? I'd heard he'd been shot!"

I nodded. "He was, sir. And he did."

"Zounds! If he were my patient, I'd tear at him like a fox-hound. The man has no business being out of bed."

"Feel free to tell him so, with my compliments," I told him.

"He merely wants to discuss the case?" Sun asked.

"That is what he told me, yes."

"We'll call him on the telephone within the hour," Cantlie said.

"He'll be glad to hear from you."

I bade my adieus and went on to my final task, which just happened to be in Camomile Street. Our maid, Lily, greeted me at the door and took my stick and hat. Delicious aromas were wafting in from the kitchen. Rachel was having a rest after lunch, and Rebecca clasped me as soon as I stepped inside.

"I missed my house," she admitted.

"I knew you would."

"It's so good to be home. They can keep their stuffy old Paris!"

"Nothing to do or shop for there," I agreed.

She nodded. "Tell me it will be a while before something like this happens again, or I shall make you a baker instead of an enquiry agent."

"Don't make me a baker," I pleaded. "I'd swell up like a balloon on teacakes and it will a be all your doing. Oh, it's so good to see everyone home again."

"How long are you here for?" she asked.

"Only an hour or so, I'm afraid. I finished some errands quickly, but I have to get back to the offices."

"Well, you've arrived just in time," Rebecca pronounced. "I've got a pie in the oven. But you could probably smell it in Whitehall. It's apple."

"Apple?" I asked. "Not rhubarb?"

"I only make rhubarb for the women's socials," she replied, pulling me toward the kitchen. "It's a silent protest. I'm hoping they'll stop asking."

"Is that fresh coffee I smell?"

"Yes, I just made some."

"Ah," I said. "Nectar of the gods."

CHAPTER 30

Fortified with coffee and pie, I left the underground at Charing Cross and passed along the familiar buildings of Whitehall with my hands in my pockets, bound for Craig's Court. The fog had blown into the North Sea and was someone else's problem now. As I neared our offices, I saw someone coming toward me from the other direction. It was the long, loose-limbed figure of Hesketh Pierce, clad in his customary gray. We both turned in at Craig's Court. I opened the door, and we stepped inside.

"What's going on, Cyrus?" Pierce asked. "What have you been about besides getting yourself shot?"

"What have I been about?" Barker complained. "Saving my crew, as well as Dr. Sun Yat-sen. Single-handedly, I might add. That's what I've been about."

I decided not to take offense at the remark. He was making a point.

"That and getting a friend of the Prince of Wales killed," Pierce countered.

Barker toyed with a pen on his desk.

"I didn't shoot him," the Guv objected. "Did you shoot him, Thomas?"

"I did not, I assure you," I replied, turning to Pierce. "Do you hear what sort of bullet killed him?"

"A standard .303 rifle round, yes," he stated. "But we believe the tip had been scratched to fragment upon impact."

"The same caliber Dr. Vandeleur claimed," my partner stated. "I do not own a rifle, save for an antique arquebus hanging on the wall in my home, that probably cannot fire. Also, neither of us could have made such a shot. I myself had already been wounded at the time, and Mr. Llewelyn was on the starboard side of the *Osprey*. He would have had to shoot through me to kill Sebastian Nightwine."

Pierce nodded. "We are aware that La Sylphide has been in London. In fact, she has been to Mr. Llewelyn's home. While his wife was away, in fact."

"Have you been following me?" I asked.

"Not us," Hesketh replied, shaking his head. "Blame the chaps in the Colonial Office. I'm sorry to say you did not impress them."

"I'm crestfallen," I answered. "And how did you know they were following us?"

"Because we were following them, obviously. A trifle dense, those Colonial Office boys."

Pierce lit a cigarette and crossed one leg over the other before he continued. "By process of elimination, neither of you killed Sebastian Nightwine. Your entire crew was in the hold with Dr. Sun Yat-sen. However, as I said, La Sylphide did visit Mr. Llewelyn. Did you hire her to kill her father? Was this at your request, Barker?"

"I have never met the woman in question," the Guv replied. "And of course I wouldn't hire her to kill anyone. If someone needed killing I'd do it myself."

"Don't think we haven't considered that. What about you, Llewelyn?"

"I am acquainted with her, I'll admit, but I didn't hire her. Are you saying you believe she killed her own father? What would cause someone to do such a thing?"

"I'm not an alienist," the Foreign Office man answered, "so I cannot comment. The Colonial lads followed her and took her into custody."

Barker grunted. "How did they know to follow her in the first place?"

"It was just by chance that they received a tip regarding the woman and she led them straight to your ship."

"A tip?" I asked.

"Someone at the hotel where she was staying recognized her and mistakenly informed the Colonial Office."

I shook my head. "So, the Colonial Office was unaware that she was an assassin? You didn't happen to say something to them, did you?"

Pierce gave a chilly smile. "If they knew, they certainly didn't hear it from us. We never share secrets with other agencies."

"Even when they are in the same building?" I asked.

"Especially when they are in the same building."

"What has become of Miss Ilyanova?" the Guv asked, wincing as he moved his arm.

Hesketh shrugged. "She gave the dunces the slip, as a matter of fact. An unconfirmed rumor has it she boarded a steamer to Marseille. One of the Colonial boys said that she purchased a ticket. I have an operative in France who will meet the ship when it reaches port, but what do you suppose are the odds that she will be aboard when it docks?"

"Slight, I would imagine," Barker replied.

"I agree, and no doubt there shall be a general reprimand by Her Majesty's Government for the Colonial Office." Pierce turned to me. "Thomas, I'll say this politely: what was an assassin doing at your private residence in the middle of the night?"

"We were once acquainted," I said. "She wanted to let me know that she was in town."

"A professional assassin is an odd acquaintance to have," Pierce said, raising a brow. "We may need to bring you in for an interview."

I shrugged. "You know where to find me."

"That I do. Every minute of the day."

"Has the prince been informed of Nightwine's death?" Barker rumbled.

"Yes, and we made His Highness aware of what occurred aboard the *Osprey*, but he wasn't satisfied with the explanation."

"What precisely did you tell him?" the Guv asked.

"We thought we would try the truth," Pierce answered. "Well, some of it at least. Nightwine was shot by an infamous assassin. We didn't mention that it was his own daughter."

"We've viewed his body at the morgue, or we wouldn't believe it ourselves," my partner said in a low voice.

Pierce put out the cigarette in the crystal ashtray on Barker's desk, though it was only half smoked. "He had only a little money with him when he died. Unless we find another next of kin, he'll end up in a pauper's grave."

"If it comes to that, let me know," Barker replied. "I will

pay for a grave myself. He may have been a bounder, but he was something of a friend once."

"What about the prince?" I asked, appalled at my partner's statement. "Wouldn't he give his friend a burial?"

"I understand Her Majesty has refused," Pierce continued. "Nightwine has become another black mark against her son's reputation. Of course, the palace will distance him from any scandal."

Barker nodded. "Of course."

"Oh, and one last thing," Pierce said, fishing about in his pocket. "I was told to give you this."

It was the watch that Barker had been given for saving the prince's life. I could see the inscription: *For Services Rendered to the Crown.*

I took the watch and tossed it into the cubby of my desk. It had lost its appeal.

Pierce rose to his feet. "There's that sorted. I thought you should know that the matter is officially closed."

After he nodded and slipped from the room, I turned to the Guv.

"She did kill him, didn't she?" I asked. "It couldn't have been anyone else."

"Aye, she killed him all right," Barker replied. "Perhaps she'd reached the time in her life when she had to get away. I wonder if Sebastian knew it would happen eventually. He raised her to be a cold-blooded murderess, and so she finally turned on him."

I sighed. "What's the verse about whirlwinds?"

"'For they have sown the wind, and they shall reap the whirlwind.' Hosea eight, verse seven. Very good, Thomas. By the way, we have an appointment with Dr. Cantlie this afternoon at three."

"Settling his bill?" I asked.

"Your favorite part of every enquiry."

"Nothing puts paid to a successful case like a closed account," I remarked. "I'll type the invoice, then."

We decided on a late lunch, and afterward, I prepared the paperwork. Promptly at three o'clock, our client arrived. I could see the strain on the old gentleman's face. Dr. Sun came with him, along with a third gentleman. I couldn't see who it was at first, then the men parted. It was Mr. K'ing, the last person I expected to ever see darken our door. As he entered, he looked about our chambers. I tried to interpret the dynamics of the room, and in particular the mood of Dr. Sun. I'm certain the Guv did the same.

"How are you feeling, Mr. Barker?" Dr. Cantlie asked. "I heard you were shot. Were I your physician, you would be at home in bed recovering."

"I heal quickly as a rule, but there'll be no tussling for a while, thank you."

"That was quite an unexpected ending to this entire matter," he continued.

"Aye, sir," the Guv replied. "But the late Mr. Nightwine dealt in the unexpected."

"Who was he, and how was he involved in the case?" Cantlie asked.

I noticed that K'ing had a masklike expression on his face. I turned to Sun, being naturally curious. He looked expectant, even excited. Three visitors together, with three completely different emotions. I glanced at Barker, but he leaned back against his seat, his features as guarded as K'ing's. As for me, it was hard-won but I'd learned not to reveal every emotion in front of clients.

The Guv explained in a general way that Nightwine was a criminal who had followed Sun Yat-sen from China in hopes of earning the reward the emperor had offered for his head, in this case quite literally. He didn't mention his own relationship with his former friend, or the rewards offered for the arrest of himself and his crew. Cantlie and Sun swallowed the tale whole. K'ing did not change expression in the slightest, but I'm certain he and Barker understood every nuance of the matter, as I never could. I might learn Cantonese, but I would never think like a Chinaman.

There was a vague, general discussion of matters afterward, during which Sun discussed the details of his incarceration at the Chinese embassy. I had fought the Imperial Secret Service and understood what they were capable of. A few minutes later, the bill was set before Dr. Cantlie and a check was written, which was generous. I could only wish all our clients were so forthcoming.

"Thank you," Cyrus Barker said, accepting the check and handing it to me without even glancing at it. No head for business, as I said. "Tell me of your plans, Dr. Sun. What is next for you?"

"I'm returning to China, Mr. Barker."

In the silence of the room, I dropped my pen.

"China, then," Barker said, as if Sun Yat-sen had said he'd stop in at Chipping Campden.

"Against my wishes!" Cantlie added.

"I would imagine so," my partner purred from the interior of his green leather wing chair. He turned to Dr. Sun. "What do you plan to do there?"

"I'll go to Canton to meet with supporters."

K'ing gave a hint of a smile, while Barker glanced in my general direction. Subtlety was the order of the day. I knew who Sun was talking about: the Heaven and Earth Society, of which both K'ing and my partner were members. Its chief goal was to break the Qing's grip on their country. They were a dedicated bunch, composed of soldiers and sailors, itinerant people, and a few rabble-rousers who led them. It was not a place for intellectuals like Sun, however. They were willing to die for their cause. In fact, this group would make up the bulk of the soldier class who would eventually come to be known as the Boxers.

"Madness," Cantlie murmured.

"I fear I must agree," Barker admitted. "The chances of your survival are no better than when you left."

"Oh, but Mr. K'ing has promised to protect me."

Barker swiveled his chair toward his ward's husband. "Has he? That's a tall order."

"Yes," Sun Yat-sen said, his face slightly flushed. "The accounts of my incarceration are in newspapers all over the globe, and the Qing government has been humiliated. My name is on everyone's lips in China, though newspapers are suppressed there. The latest editions are smuggled in from the outside world through Hong Kong. I know I was unworthy and of little significance until I wrote that letter to the emperor, but Mr. K'ing has promised to introduce me to others who can help the cause."

Madness, I agreed, but then it wasn't my concern. Therefore, as difficult as it was for me, I kept my own counsel. However, Barker didn't.

"How do we know, sir, that the letter you wrote last year wasn't written with just this intent?" the Guv asked.

Sun's jaw dropped. The idea had not occurred to him. That is, unless he was a good actor, and this had been a ruse from the beginning.

"I don't know how to defend myself against that charge, Mr. Barker," Dr. Sun admitted. "I suppose some have thought that very thing. However, they must be in the minority. But, the Manchu may make such a claim! Thank you for warning me, but I cannot provide proof to refute your accusation."

"Not at all."

I could hear the irony in my partner's voice. Sun had ducked the question as far as he was concerned.

"I know my concerns are of little consideration, Dr. Sun," Barker continued. "I am a stranger to you, but I have taken a bullet in your defense. I must agree with the doctor here. You should ponder this solemnly for several days before a decision is made. You're gambling with your own life, and your cause as well."

I glanced Mr. K'ing's way. Again, the man made no remark, although his position was obvious. However, he hadn't shown the menace I have seen in his features before. He'd pulled in his claws, so to speak. Personally, I thought K'ing was untrustworthy, and was probably manipulating Sun for his own purposes.

The meeting ended then. Everything that could be said had been said. We shook hands all around and our now former clients left our chambers.

"Thomas," Barker said, reading my expression after our trio of visitors had left our offices. "What was that remark the character Shylock made in Mr. Shakespeare's play, *The Merchant of Venice*?"

"'A pound of flesh, which I demand of him.'"

Cyrus Barker enjoyed having a scholar for a partner. Also, he would find it scandalous to be able to recall a verse from a frivolous play until he had memorized the entire Holy Bible, both Old and New Testament, which I believed he very nearly had.

Then another quotation from the Bard came to me. Lady Macbeth said, "Screw your courage to the sticking place."

"Sir, I would speak to you a moment on a private matter."

"Oh?" he asked cautiously.

"It concerns Bok Fu Ying."

"Continue."

"Well, sir, I couldn't help notice you treat her in the formal Chinese manner, as if she were a servant."

"She is a servant, of sorts," he reasoned.

"Yes, but Mr. K'ing clearly implied that you are considered by Fu Ying as a father. She has no family to fall back upon but you, sir."

The Guv frowned, but did not respond, save to retrieve a pipe and light it. That was a good sign, I thought.

"You know she and my wife are friends. We both suspect that your ward is dreadfully unhappy. You ignore her and treat her coldly."

"That is how it is done in China," he reasoned.

"It is, sir. I agree. However, Fu Ying barely remembers China. She was raised in England. She has British friends, and converses with them in English. She reads British newspapers and often dresses like an Englishwoman. However, both you and her husband, Mr. K'ing, treat her, well, sir, I shall come out and say it. Abominably. Now she has begun training her daughter, Soo, and I think it is a sore trial for her. Little Soo came up to you and you barely noticed. She—"

"You are right, sir!" he suddenly shouted. "I have been a knave. How stupid of me! It didn't occur to me, but now that I see it, it must be so. I'll speak to her. Thank you for bringing it to my attention. I know it must have been a difficult decision for you."

"You have no idea," I said. "I thought it might end with my being tossed into Whitehall Street."

"On another day I might have. I am in your debt, Thomas. I don't know how to repay you."

"Don't worry, sir," I replied. "I'm sure I'll think of something."

CHAPTER 31

There were a few final matters to resolve before the enquiry could be relegated to my files, but I didn't know what they were. Barker knew; I could read the signs on his face. He looked dissatisfied, though not extremely so. It was a reserved dissatisfaction. He was trying to be patient.

"Has Dr. Sun left London yet?" I asked the Guv as we settled into our chairs a few mornings later.

"He has not," my partner replied. "Dr. Cantlie has convinced him to take some rest after his ordeal."

"I hope his friend can convince him to abandon his suicidal plan to go back to China."

Barker harrumphed. He is a strong believer in autonomy. He would not tell another man what to do with his life. Unlike me, for example, who had done precisely that.

He ran a thumb back and forth under his chin. I could hear

the stubble rasping under his thumbnail. He did so for five minutes, wallowing in his outsized chair. Then he stuffed a pipe but forgot to smoke it. It sat charged and ready in his crystal ashtray. He reached for the telephone set a couple of times, and just as decisively set it down again.

"Is everything all right, sir?" I asked.

"I'm concerned that Her Majesty is aware of my existence," he replied. "She definitely took His Highness in hand on our account. There's seems to be one piece to the puzzle missing."

He picked up the pipe and went to stand at the window, staring out at the iron gray sky. I shrugged and turned to my desk to organize my notes. It was always a pleasure to go through the facts of each case when it has reached a satisfying conclusion. We had started with a missing doctor and had managed to help secure his release. Our compatriots and friends had been menaced and kidnapped, but they were now back to their normal lives.

Ho was reconstructing the tunnel to the entrance of his restaurant, which would be partially operational within a fortnight. In fact, the Guv and I had already been permitted back on the premises for a hearty meal of fried rice and prawns in soy sauce as we discussed how he had been captured and rescued. His rage had subsided somewhat as he channeled his energy into repairing the tunnel.

Etienne and Mireille were back at Le Toison d'Or, bickering as always, and of course, the chef was back in the kitchen at Number 3 Lion Street, where just that morning, I had enjoyed the flakiest croissant to be had in all of London. Not least, Mac was relieved to be released from cooking duties and back to his normal schedule, as well.

Paul was true to his word, sailing the *Osprey* back to Sussex with his sons and was in the process of making repairs to

Barker's beloved ship. He promised us a proper tour of the Channel when the vessel was deemed worthy to sail.

"What should I call the case?" I asked as I held up my notes. "The Sun Yat-sen Enquiry? Or should the title concern Nightwine himself?"

"The first is agreeable but include a note for the Nightwine folder. We have finally put his career to bed. Although, of course, I said that last time."

"Yes, sir."

"Let's review the main facts of the case," Barker said. "The enquiry began when Etienne entered our offices claiming Sebastian had visited Le Toison d'Or with the Prince of Wales. Since he was galley cook aboard my boat, the *Osprey*, and had participated in our treasure hunting days many years ago . . ."

"Or piracy days," I added. "But continue."

"As I was saying," he said, clearing his throat, "Etienne thought it politic to take his family to his ancestral *maison* in Dijon. We immediately informed the other members of the crew living in England. True?"

"Yes, sir."

"Capital," he remarked. "Then Lady Ashleigh arrived with the news that Nightwine had confirmed his presence in London by sending her a letter. We agreed it would be best if Lady Ashleigh, and Mrs. Llewelyn along with your child, be sent to the estate in Seaford."

I wondered at the time if my partner's brain had even registered Rachel's name. He tends to dismiss children who aren't messengers or street arabs. Even if he was their godfather.

"Next," he continued, "Dr. James Cantlie, who had recently returned from his duties of hospital administration in Hong Kong, hired us to find a former student recently arrived in London, who had disappeared. Sun Yat-sen had written a letter to the emperor criticizing policies. We deduced that there was a connection between Nightwine's reappearance in London and the disappearance of Sun Yat-sen."

"A reward was offered by the Qing government for his head," I added. "Years ago, a similar reward had been offered for yours and your crew from the *Osprey*. Mr. Nightwine was known to be in constant need of funds and was a man without scruples."

"Too true, lad," Barker rumbled. "We reconnoitered the area near the Chinese embassy, a possible place for his disappearance, and found a note claiming that Sun was being held on the premises. Then we interviewed another acquaintance of Sun's, Dr. Manson, who suspected his former student was more politically active than he appeared."

"That certainly proved to be true," I said as I consulted my notebook. "His incarceration has since made him famous. It may work in his favor if he does return to Canton, but I wouldn't risk it."

"The *Osprey* was stolen, and Paul was kidnapped," Barker continued. "Within a few days, Etienne was also kidnapped in France, and Ho's tunnel was bombed."

"Nightwine couldn't have done all this himself," I stated. "We saw his physical condition in the Body Room of Scotland Yard. He was in a weakened state, which meant the kidnappings were done by Sofia Ilyanova, possibly with the help of the Imperial Secret Service agents."

"Three men attacked us when we were reconnoitering the area around the Chinese embassy," my partner continued. "Mr. K'ing agreed to work with us to stage a protest, which was successful in making Sun's dire situation known to the press. Pressure from the public forced Sir Halliday Macartney to release Sun.

"That same evening Sun was kidnapped a second time, and taken to the *Osprey*, where the ship's crew was being held, just outside of London. During the attempt to escape, Sebastian Nightwine was killed by his daughter."

"Should I make that 'may have been killed by his daughter'?" I asked. "We have no actual proof of it."

"Do so," he agreed. "But we are of the same opinion. Continue."

"Miss Ilyanova eluded arrest and has fled the country," I replied. "Is that all, sir?"

"For the most part. Good work, Thomas."

"Thank you. Have I missed anything?" I asked.

"Only a couple of minor matters," Barker said. "When the secret service agents attacked us in the alley, it was with the intent of capturing us as well. I was the first trophy he intended to take back with him to China. You came close to being kidnapped as well."

"So I did," I admitted, looking over the file. "Anything else?"

"At first I believed that the escape of the *Osprey* on the Thames was another attempt to assassinate me, which very nearly succeeded. However, Miss Ilyanova shot me, but she didn't kill me. Therefore, I suspect she felt she had fulfilled her contract with her father by shooting me, and then she turned on him. But I still don't understand why."

Barker finally lit the pipe that had been laying in its crystal ashtray since the day before, and blew a smoke ring, watching it float across the room. "Perhaps she wanted to escape after all those years under his control. Who knows what she has been forced to do and to endure because of that man's quest for money and power."

"I agree. Anything else?"

"One last matter, Thomas, though it is only conjecture.

There is no need to include it in your report. It concerns the drugged dart that hit you."

"Yes?" I asked, scribbling away in my notebook. That day I would add a typed copy to our records.

"One would need to know the ways of the Forbidden City," the Guv continued. "The empress and her son only dine upon the rarest of creatures, often brought from foreign lands. I am speaking of animals exotic to China, such as gazelles or giraffes. They would be transported alive to Peking and end their lives far from their home country."

"So, the animals would have been shot with the drugged dart!" I reasoned.

"Continue."

I cudgeled my brain. "That meant the dart was never intended for humans, but for animals."

Barker nodded. "Aye."

"Which meant the person hunting animals on the savanna must have been Nightwine himself, which explains where he has been all these years since your infamous duel."

"Precisely."

"So, in a way, we were all being hunted like animals," I continued.

"I believe that the dart she used to shoot you was meant as a message to us," the Guv said, returning his pipe to the tray. By then the chamber was as thick as a London fog. "It explained how everyone was kidnapped during this case."

"Wouldn't Nightwine have wanted to shoot you himself?" I asked.

"He would have, but he was occupied with influencing the prince."

"That was good luck, sir."

Cyrus Barker shook his head. "Now, Thomas, you know I don't believe in luck."

"No, sir. My mistake."

An hour later, the door to our chambers opened and goodness and light stepped in, in the form of Lady Philippa Ashleigh. She was wearing a smart-looking long coat in a logan green plaid color that I suspected Rebecca would swoon over.

"Hello, old things," she said as she waved to us all, slipping into one of the visitor's chairs.

Barker observes the proprieties, and so we stood a moment, even after she'd been settled.

He sat and looked at her carefully, as if she were a puzzle he was trying to solve, which was exactly what she was. She in turn was eyeing him as well.

"I was going to call you," he said.

"I was out," she countered. "On your behalf, in fact."

"In what way?" he asked.

"You've ruffled a few feathers at the palace," she said with an air of world-weariness. "Not for the first time, I presume, and I doubt it will be the last."

"Out with it then, ma'am," he rumbled. "Mr. Llewelyn will tell you that there is no need for hemming and hawing here. What has happened?"

"The prince is displeased about your involvement with Nightwine's death," she replied. "He thought you should be put in a cell, but the commissioner tactfully told him you had not done anything obviously criminal. Nightwine had poisoned his mind against you."

"I didn't shoot him," Barker said. "Not that I wouldn't have. But of course, I was shot as well. Shot first, in fact. If that doesn't exonerate me there's no hope."

"Of course, Cyrus," she said tactfully. "But as I said, the prince is displeased. He called you a bounder, I understand."

"I've been called worse," the Guv said with a wry smile.

She raised a brow. "But not by such an exalted person.

You do realize that he will be the king one day? And in addition to that, you also caused a stir with Mr. Bigge."

"Now there's a bounder for you," I remarked.

"It would have been better had you not stuffed your signboard under his arm and sent him on his way, Cyrus," Philippa continued.

Barker tensed his jaw. "My blood was up."

Lady Ashleigh turned to me. "And you, Thomas. Your little watch trick didn't help matters. You were like Dr. Sun, tweaking the nose of the emperor. Don't think the prince didn't hear all about it."

"Sorry, ma'am," I replied.

"What you do has consequences, gentlemen."

I wanted to say Bigge started it, but such a remark would only make us look more like schoolboys.

"I spoke to Mr. Pierce of the Foreign Office this morning," Barker said. "He implied that Her Majesty was kindly disposed to us, which I found curious. What has happened at court that I don't know about?"

Philippa removed her gloves and settled them on her lap. "Sebastian was attempting to blacken your names in government circles. It is to your advantage that Queen Victoria holds the opposite viewpoint from her son on just about every subject."

"That's all it is, then?" he asked.

"It is," she replied.

"Aye, but is it, though?" he asked, leaning forward. "What has suddenly made Her Majesty my champion?"

She looked down and away, not meeting his eye.

"Tell me what has happened, Philippa."

His voice was low but tender, and for the briefest second, I saw a different Cyrus Barker than I had ever seen before.

"I agreed to become a lady-in-waiting," she confessed.

"Och, no!" my partner exclaimed, stamping his fist upon the desk, which thankfully did not shatter this time. "You didn't want the position when it was offered you before. You said it would take you away from Sussex overlong."

"Her Majesty doesn't travel much anymore, being in her seventies," Philippa replied. "I would have far more freedom now than I would have five years ago when I was first offered the position. I am one of her favorites at court, and she's old and in poor health."

"I don't want you to sacrifice your freedom on my account," he stated. "It isn't right."

"There are two ambitious ladies only too glad to pick up any slack I might leave behind," she said breezily. "Everything will turn out for the best. You'll see."

"But you hate court," Barker argued.

"I've merely said that I find it a bit tedious at times," she countered. "It's not a great imposition. It is expedient and it's already settled. The prince has been silenced due to a tug from Her Majesty's purse strings, and Mr. Bigge has learned a hard lesson."

"I hope so."

"Oh, I've brought your warrant sign. A footman put it in my hansom and the driver carried it to your door."

All this time I was listening. Any movement I made might alert them that I was still in the room. I wished I were a chameleon who could blend in with the wallpaper behind me.

Barker's head suddenly lifted like a pointer's.

"Haven't you something to do, Mr. Llewelyn?" he demanded.

Jumping to my feet, I bowed to Philippa, then hurried into the outer office. There, Jeremy was looking as astonished at the conversation as I was. I crouched beside him.

We heard my partner say, "That's it, then. I wondered why

Her Majesty had suddenly become so accommodating. Is she playing Cupid on our account?"

In return, Philippa replied, "If marriage is repugnant to you, I know several gentlemen who would be willing to accommodate me."

I seized my bowler from the stand and retreated into the relative safety of Whitehall Street, stepping into Cox and Co. to deposit the check from Dr. Cantlie now that the case was officially over to his satisfaction. Afterward, I loitered on the pavement trying to discern whether Mrs. Ashleigh had left the office. There was no cab at the curb, and her private coach was nowhere to be seen. However, I didn't want to take the chance of interrupting them if she were still inside. It had been awkward. Therefore, I stepped into the Shades Public House for a coffee and some relative peace.

I had accidentally uncovered a few dynamics of the relationship between Barker and Mrs. Ashleigh. I wasn't going to speculate about it. Rather, I would take the salient points and pass them along to Rebecca. She would make speculations for both of us. Perhaps she would take notes. Graphs were even conceivable. I'd leave it to her to work it out.

Back in the office, I saw that Philippa had gone and the Guv was putting on his coat.

"Are we going out, sir?" I asked.

"I've promised Lady Ashleigh I would help her move her luggage to her town home," he replied as he stepped into the outer chamber. "You've done exemplary work this week. It is Friday noon. Meet me here on Monday morning. Good afternoon, gentlemen."

He was gone in a trice, still buttoning his coat in Craig's Court. Jenkins and I stared at each other. Then we both gave a whoop. We didn't need to be told twice. Jenkins put a sign on the door and we donned our hats and coats. Then I locked the agency up tight. We ran to Whitehall Street like students on holiday. I didn't bother to call Rebecca with the good news. I hoped to surprise her, perhaps even with some flowers.

CHAPTER 32

Rebecca Llewelyn is not easy to surprise, but for once, I managed to do so. On the way home, I stopped in Tottenham Court Road and purchased a bouquet of roses. When I opened the door, I found her in the sitting room, working on her embroidery. She lay the sewing aside and jumped to her feet when she saw me.

"You're home in the middle of the day!" she exclaimed.

"Would you believe I've been given a half day today, and we will have all tomorrow and Sunday to ourselves?" I asked, holding out the roses I had just purchased for her inspection.

"Thomas, that's wonderful!" she said, taking them in her arms and holding them to her nose, smelling them deeply. "I love white roses. They'll be perfect in this room. Sit down while I put them in some water."

A few minutes later, she returned, placing the vase of

flowers triumphantly on a table, turning it this way and that until she had arranged it precisely the way she wanted it. I loosened my tie, looking at the sitting room. Despite the name, I rarely sat in it. The furnishings were all pink damasks and chairs never intended for sitting. They seemed to shudder when I attempted such a thing.

"You must have finished the case early," she remarked when she sat down beside me.

I nodded. "Mr. Barker has gone to help Philippa pack. Has she told you about her plans?"

"She called a few hours ago," my wife answered. "I have to say, I am looking forward to having her in town a little more for a while."

Lily brought in Rachel, and I helped her play with her small stuffed hedgehog, while Rebecca told me about her morning, after having been banished from her home for over a week. The whole of Jewish London society seemed to have ground to a halt during her absence. The euphoria of a brief holiday settled into a warm glow. That evening, we ate dinner, which included curry, the source of the fine smells from the kitchen. Afterward, we had coffee with custard tarts, a favorite of mine, before we went to my study where Lily had put on a fire. Generally, we discouraged our tiny daughter from the room because some of the books there were quite old. We also discouraged hedgehogs as a rule, but we relaxed all prohibitions that evening.

After putting Rachel down, we sat in my study for an hour and talked over nothing important. We discussed going to Kensington Gardens the following day, and walking along the High Street, where there were several shops Rebecca hoped to visit. Then there was a knock on the door. She and I looked at each other with some dismay. Who could that be, I wondered?

Our maid, Lily, answered it. I heard a man's voice say, "I wish to speak to Mr. Thomas Llewelyn, please."

I rose from my chair and went into the front hall where Lily stood looking at me in a rather helpless way. A man stood in the doorway, a commissionaire, every bit the retired officer. He was an impressive fellow, six feet tall at least, in a black frogged jacket and matching trousers. His boots gleamed though it was eight o'clock at night, and the bill of his cap was just as shiny. He even wore a cloak.

"Sir," he asked with great seriousness. "Are you Thomas Llewelyn?"

"I am," I admitted.

"Let me be precise, sir," he said. "Are you Thomas Llewelyn of the Barker and Llewelyn Agency in Whitehall Street?"

I felt as if I were being interrogated. "Yes, I am he."

He handed me a small clipboard. "Sign here, please."

When an impressive fellow hands one a clipboard, one signs it.

"You accept receipt of this?" he asked.

It was then that I noticed an envelope in his hand. "Yes, yes, I do."

"Sign for this as well, please," he said.

I did. Anything to get on with it.

"Here you are then," he said, handing me the envelope. "Enjoy your evening."

I stood looking at the official-looking envelope in my hands. And the small boy.

Rebecca was looking over my shoulder. I heard a sharp intake of breath.

As I said, he was a small fellow. I'm not good at guessing children's ages. Six, perhaps? His hair curled in every direction. His coat was too long and his pants too short. He had a forefinger stuffed into one corner of his mouth, and he looked terrified. He'd been taken from wherever he was by a strange man, and now that man had left him here with two more strangers. They were looking at him intently, and it made him nervous.

Rebecca pushed me to the side and bent low, so the two of them were face-to-face. Meanwhile I opened the document. It was full of wherefores, and I wasn't in the mood for wherefores at the moment. There was a handwritten letter in the envelope, however, which I tore open. It read:

Dear Thomas,
I cannot care for our child anymore. He is in danger traveling with me. I have found him with bullets in his hands, and once a knife. He has reached the curious stage now. My father has begun making plans for his future, as he did mine, so I decided that it is better that he lives with you. You recall I visited your home? Of course you do. It wasn't done out of mere curiosity. I wanted to see if it was a safe place to raise a child. Naturally, it is. I should have known better. You and your wife are obviously good parents. Your daughter seems to be thriving.

Dimitri deserves good parents, which I most certainly am not. I kill people for money, but like my father, the money slips through my fingers. I cannot save anything, so I have been forced to do the only work I am trained for. But suppose one day Dimitri sees me kill someone, and discovers what kind of mother

I really am? My nerves are giving out, and it would be best if I were alone in a place where I can think and heal.

After I shot my father, I returned to my hotel and dismantled all my weapons, which I put into a pillowcase and dropped into the Thames. Now I will start over. I will go someplace far away, somewhere I may find myself, even if it is at the bottom of the Volga. No one can stay too long with my father and not be irretrievably ruined. The ones he has hurt and deceived and driven away, they are the lucky ones. Yes, there are other Nightwines, but they escaped. Only I was weak enough to stay.

I took advantage of you when we were young. I wanted to have something that was only mine, even if it ruined you. Now I realize you have scars of your own. Not physical wounds, perhaps, but they are there, nonetheless. I am sorry for causing you pain.

Your wife seems a very kind person. The question is how kind can she be? Could she accept a small boy from a brief indiscretion? Will my son's presence in your home raise too many questions in her ordered world? Will she hate Dimitri? If so, then give him away. I wouldn't want him in a household where someone hates him. He has scars, too, you see. Give him away or put him in an orphanage. Anything is better than being with me. I will only ruin him. You are his only chance for a real future.

You need not worry that I will appear on your doorstep as I did. You will never see me again.

you won't find me in your pretty home like a ghost in the middle of the night. I won't be peering in your windows. You are another painful memory to me.

Goodbye, my dear Thomas. Stay alive. Be well. Raise Dimitri if you will. Be kind and don't think ill of me. I could not take that.

Sofia

I tried to hand the letter to Rebecca, but she pushed it away. She was still eye to eye with the child.

"His name is Dimitri," I said. "His mother . . ."

"I know who his mother is," she said.

"We could takc him somewhere."

"Don't you dare!" she cried, rounding on me.

The child began crying silently then, tears rolling down his cheeks. He had Llewelyn features but his mother's gold-flecked eyes, like fireworks in a Whistler painting.

"I am thinking of you, not of me," I said. "We can't raise him. How will we explain him to society?"

"He is your late sister's son," she stated, taut as a bow-string.

"And what about my family?" I asked, my hands on my hips.

"He is my late sister's son."

"And what if people work it out?" I asked. "Imagine the scandal."

"I don't care," she replied. "People have skeletons and embarrassments in their lives. You may give me the letter now."

I handed it to her. She took the boy by the hand and led him into the study, where she sat in my chair and read it through twice.

"But you've only just met him," I argued.

I wasn't against taking him, but I didn't want the boy reminding her every day of my past indiscretion, deliberate or otherwise.

"I don't care," she responded. "He's ours now. He's mine. No one else will take care of him."

It had been difficult for us to bear a child. We had lost one. It had been hard, especially on her, of course. I tend to skate through life on other's misfortunes, I think. I don't mean to, but it happens even so, especially to Rebecca. She had been through a lot of pain on my account. Therefore, I would deny her nothing, certainly not one small boy.

"What about the staff?" I asked. "What about Lily?"

Our maid had been lent to us by Rebecca's mother after our marriage. She had originally been sent to spy on us, but was gradually subsumed into our household, cutting ties with the woman I referred to as "the Dragon."

"If she says a word to my mother I shall sack her without references," Rebecca replied. "She will find herself unemployable."

"You're adamant," I stated.

"No," she argued. "I am adamantine. I can crush stone!"

"You're a fierce little creature," I remarked. "All five feet of you."

She smiled. "You have no idea."

The gold-flecked eyes of the young boy were still moving from my face to hers, as if in a tennis match.

"If you want him, then I want him," I stated.

"Do you?"

"Of course! Any man would like a son. He's a handsome little fellow or will be after a bath and some new clothes."

"Clothes," she murmured, savoring the word. She'd been given another doll and now had a set. "And he needs a bedroom. We'll put him in the room next to Rachel's."

Rebecca turned and looked down into his small, earnest face.

"You're a good boy, aren't you, Dimitri?" she asked.

The boy nodded. He still hadn't said a word.

"Your mother has gone away, and we are to take care of you. Do you understand?"

Again, he nodded.

"Dimitri, do you speak English?" I asked, trying to be as gentle as I could.

"Yes," he answered. "Yes, sir."

"Dimitri," Rebecca said, grasping the cuff of my shirt. "This is your Uncle Thomas, and I'm your Aunt Rebecca. We have a little girl who is your cousin Rachel. We are your new family, and you'll never have to leave us ever again."

"You'll live here," I said. "And you won't have to move from place to place anymore."

"No boats?" he asked.

"No boats," I replied.

At this late stage our dog entered the room and realized there were too many people present. She began to bay, and Dimitri jumped.

"This is Daisy," I explained over the din. "You must be kind to her. She is old, but she doesn't bite, because she hasn't any teeth."

Rebecca took his hand and let the dog sniff it.

A thought struck me. "My word. Mr. Barker will have to know!"

"Silly," Rebecca said. "You call yourself a detective. Mr. Barker already knows, or he isn't Mr. Barker. Don't you think it strange that he should give you these days off? Can you recall the last time he did so?"

"I can't," I admitted.

"He looks like you, you know," she said.

"Mr. Barker looks like me?"

"No, Thomas. Be serious, as a father should." She smiled at Dimitri. "I'm going to draw you a bath and Uncle Thomas will brush your clothes. We'll get you some new ones tomorrow."

The boy and I both followed directions, and after his bath, she wrapped him in one of my shirts with the sleeves rolled up and offered him dinner before putting him to bed. He wolfed it down as if he were half starved. We'd have to work on his table manners. Afterward, Rebecca sat beside him until he fell asleep.

A short while later, she came back downstairs and found me in my study. I put down the book I was struggling to read and looked at my wife.

"You really want him, this son of a woman you've hated for years?" I asked. "This symbol of my shame?"

"I really do," she answered, sinking into a chair. "I think I need him, Thomas. We've wanted children for so long."

I will never understand women, no matter how long I live. They are a perpetual enigma to me. But sometimes they can bring out the best in a man. In my case I hoped it would be so.

"He's ours, then," I told her.

CHAPTER 33

Sun Yat-sen was aware that he was inconveniencing his British friends. He was at the center of a vortex of events over which he had little control. Reporters followed him about, asking questions to the point that he had to be brusque with them. Strangers stopped to offer moral support, and people murmured whenever he entered a room or shop. He was unaccustomed to being observed and commented upon. People recognized him in the street from articles in the newspapers. Sketches of him had appeared in illustrated magazines. Yat-sen understood that he would be forgotten quickly, unless he took the horse by the reins. He must capitalize on this fleeting fame, but how?

Every day but the Sabbath, Sun took himself to the Reading Room of the British Museum to study, write, and think. He had begun a brief account of his experience in the cell within the Chinese embassy. It might become an article in *Blackwood's* or another popular magazine, or he might even expand it into a book-long account.

Sun Yat-sen was a naturally shy person, but he had been placed in an unusual situation. Mr. Shakespeare speaks in *Twelfth Night* of those who have greatness thrust upon them. Certainly, he was not a great man. He was aware of his own shortcomings and didn't consider himself an orator, or a great thinker, but he had a grasp of what his natural skills were, and what he could achieve. He wasn't a fiery orator, but he could write clearly enough. He suffered a thousand torments in his cell, but he could control what he said and how he represented himself. Strangest of all, he didn't care anymore if the Qing government tried to behead him. If he survived, he would do what he could for the Chinese people. If he died, he would become a martyr for the cause.

A librarian at the British Museum told him that Karl Marx had written *Das Kapital* within those very walls. Each day Sun would arrive and a stuffy old librarian, Mr. Grant, would have a small stack of books for him to peruse. The fellow glided about silently on felt-soled shoes and had a knack for anticipating his needs. Once they'd even shared a meal at the tavern across the street. He introduced Sun to classical authors such as Aristotle, John Locke, Friedrich Engels, and Adam Smith. Sun Yat-sen studied for months, almost feverishly, but Grant always had more for him to learn.

When he wasn't studying, Sun visited Mr. K'ing. He was aware of the man's shortcomings and his dangerous reputation, but the desire for revolution dwelt in K'ing's heart as keenly as Sun's. Within a month he became a member of the Heaven and Earth Society, dedicated to destroying the Qing government. Sun realized that he was disappointing his old friends, Dr. Cantlie and Dr. Manson. He had a degree in medicine which had been hard-won. He could practice anywhere, open a clinic, or work in a hospital. But why help one poor soul at a time when he could help millions?

A month passed. Two. Five. He filled reams of paper with notes. He didn't ask himself which form of government was the best; rather, he thought about which would be best for China. Most of all, China needed to modernize quickly if they were to defend themselves against the West, which was now crowding its borders, or East where the Japanese were threatening Taiwan.

Then came the day that Grant ran out of books, and K'ing told him he was ready. It was a graduation of sorts. By then Sun had gained poise and confidence. He was no great speaker, but he could talk plainly and honestly, knowing that much of China itself was uneducated. The time was approaching when he must make a decision about his future. There were many willing to help him with the answer, but Sun understood that a man must forge his own path, even if it hurt his friends' feelings. It was time to sail to the other side of the world, to that country he had not even visited until a few years before. He would find his band of brothers there, like-minded men. Patriots. Dangerous men in a way, armed with dreams and plans against a government with rifles and gunboats. He had gone mad, he thought, but he couldn't help himself.

Medicine held no interest for him anymore. It had served its purpose and he had evolved. The chrysalis had split open, and he had crawled out. He had even reached the point where a pacifistic doctor might be willing to pull a trigger if it meant a great change would occur. Well, perhaps not pull the trigger himself, but to see it done.

One day he was combing his short hair in the mirror, and he didn't recognize himself. He was a new man, though an untested one. It was likely he would step off the boat in Hong Kong and be seized at once by the authorities. His body would be carrion for wild dogs by the end of the day. There was a chance, however, a slim chance perhaps, that he could be lost in the crowds long enough to find a cell of the triads, the Heaven and Earth Society. Then perhaps he could do some good.

The work was dangerous, but he understood the risks.

"I'm ready," he said one day to K'ing in his office over the gambling den, the Inn of Double Happiness.

"Are you?" the opium seller asked.

"I'm growing older each day," he said. "I can't be a dilettante for the rest of my life, cloistered in the British Library, glutting myself on classic literature. I need to do something, not simply watch. My brothers are out there doing. I want to do."

A week later he booked a passage to Macao aboard a ship from the Blue Funnel Line. The passengers were Indians, Lascars, Japanese, and his Chinese brothers. Two had been sent to protect him. He'd been forced to shave his head. He wore a pair of spectacles with only glass in them. His new Chinese clothing felt strange after a woolen suit, and he dearly missed his natty mustache, but it would be worth the sacrifice. He looked a typical Chinaman, perhaps a trifle intellectual, like those who passed the Imperial Exams. He had met his first revolutionary cell brothers, and understood he would have to earn their trust, to prove his worth. Naïve visionaries were plentiful, but people were needed to do the work, even if it involved picking rice in a paddy by the Pearl River. When they quit for the day, the clandestine work would begin.

It wouldn't be easy. If he knew how difficult it would be,

perhaps he would have quit that very day and returned to Honolulu, working as a much-needed doctor among the sugarcane fields. It would not be easy, but it would be worthwhile. Let the revolution begin.

AUTHOR'S NOTE

Relevant Timeline for Sun Yat-sen

1893 Having graduated from the College of Medicine for Chinese in Hong Kong, Sun opened a dispensary in Canton, which soon became a base for revolutionary activity.

1894 Sun sent a proposal to the Qing government calling for reform, which angered officials. A call was sent out for his arrest and execution. He fled to his native Honolulu, where he formed a revolutionary group there among the Chinese.

1896 Sun Yat-sen traveled to London to meet his former tutor and friend, Dr. James Cantlie, unaware that his movements had been tracked across America by the Chinese government. While in England, he was kidnapped by Chinese officials and illegally imprisoned. He was released after a public protest, after newspaper articles brought his plight to national attention.

1897 After a few months of study at the British Museum

learning European and Asian politics and history, he returned to the East and opened revolutionary centers in Japan and Taipei.

1899 Sun Yat-sen established the *Chinese Daily*, a newspaper in Hong Kong, favorable to the revolution. Several triads, secret societies, Masonic organizations, and local groups organized into revolutionary cells, appointing Sun as their leader.

1900 The Boxer Rebellion occurred. European compounds were attacked, and there were battles all over China between the Qing armies and disgruntled peasants. Sun attempted his first insurrection in Canton, but it failed quickly.

1903 Sun made another failed attempt at a rebellion and was forced to flee to Japan.

1905 Sun Yat-sen visited London again, hoping to attract interest and support for the Chinese people's cause.

1906 A coup attempt in Jiang Province was quickly routed.

1907 A revolt in Canton lasted six days. Another in Huizhou failed after ten, and a third failed in Guangxi. A fourth revolt ended when the revolutionaries ran out of ammunition and were captured.

1908 Coups were attempted and failed in Guangxi, Yuman, and Anching.

1909 Sun returned to London for more support and funding.

1910 Sun Yat-sen established a newspaper in San Francisco's Chinatown.

1911 After ten failed attempts at revolutions, the Wuchang Uprising erupted, leading to a successful coup against the Qing government. After nearly three hundred years, the native Chinese people were free from Manchu oppression. A provisional government was formed with Sun elected as the acting president.

ACKNOWLEDGMENTS

I'd like to thank my incredible wife, Julia, who will stop the novel she's writing to deadline, in order to edit mine. She'll debate every word, and has declared herself Barker's champion, so I had better not make him do anything she finds out of character, or I'll hear from her. One couldn't find a better partner, or a more staunch defender of the English language. Quite literally, this book could not have been completed without her.

ABOUT THE AUTHOR

Justin Greiman

Will Thomas is the author of the award-winning, critically acclaimed Barker & Llewelyn series of Victorian crime novels, including *Some Danger Involved*, *Heart of the Nile,* and, most recently, *Season of Death. Heart of the Nile* won the Shamus Award for Best Private Eye Hardback in 2024.